
★ ———————

The two shadows jumped and dashed across the street.

I followed, still yelling.

Suddenly there was a roar of thunder and I dived for the ground, trying to make myself as inconspicuous as possible. A large-caliber bullet splatted into the earth much too close for comfort.

Good grief, I could be killed!

I scrabbled across the lawn to crouch in the sheltering bulk of my van, then dashed farther down the street to huddle behind Louis and Rita Spaulding's ornamental wishing well.

A car, started too quickly and gunned too high, shot out of my driveway. A shadow detached itself from the underside of my van and began running toward the car, which slowed only slightly.

I flung myself at the running man, tearing across the yard to intersect him. I grabbed him, getting a handful of thick hair.

One of the car's doors flew open and an apparently disembodied hand motioned to my almost-captured shadow.

Another explosion, this time echoed by the metallic clang of a bullet hitting the car, decided him.

I never saw nor felt any impact, but
feel myself pass throug
swallowed me while the

D1311008

JANIS PATTERSON

BEADED TO DEATH

W✦RLDWIDE®

TORONTO • NEW YORK • LONDON
AMSTERDAM • PARIS • SYDNEY • HAMBURG
STOCKHOLM • ATHENS • TOKYO • MILAN
MADRID • WARSAW • BUDAPEST • AUCKLAND

Recycling programs
for this product may
not exist in your area.

BEADED TO DEATH

A Worldwide Mystery/February 2014

First published by Carina Press

ISBN-13: 978-0-373-26885-6

Copyright © 2012 by J.S.M. Patterson

Printed in U.S.A.

This book is lovingly dedicated to
Ruth Rohman Patterson, the best mother-in-law
and the dearest friend one could ever hope to have
and CAPT Hiram M. Patterson, USN/Ret.,
the most wonderful man in the world

ONE

COMING HOME WAS finally a joy. I still loved doing the rounds of art fairs and craft shows and even a few state fairs, but now—at last—I was finding a pleasure in returning home, even for a short time. When Jim died I didn't know if I would ever enjoy coming home again, a home without him, even a home where he had never lived. But the wheel of time turns, lives change, hurts become bearable and I was looking forward to a few days of sleeping in my own bed, even if I did have a lot of work to do. This had been a demanding tour, there was another just as demanding coming up soon and I was close to exhaustion.

Our little townhouse development was quiet. It usually was this early in the afternoon. I parked in the driveway, as always. The townhouse garage simply wasn't big enough for my enormous Ford van even when it wasn't stuffed full of junk, mainly the boxes of my married life that I hadn't touched since my move from the spacious suburbs. Maybe this time I'd clean all that out, get rid of what I didn't need, finally dispose of the majority of Jim's stuff.

Maybe not.

Grabbing my purse and overnight bag, I locked the van. Everything else could wait until tomorrow morning. It was disturbing that the older I got the more I put things off, as if they didn't matter as much anymore.

Well, some things didn't.

There was a strange smell. I stopped putting the key in the door and sniffed. Nothing really pleasant, but not terrible either. Had one of the neighbors' pets staked out my minuscule front yard as a toilet? I didn't see any obvious evidence, but that didn't prove anything. Odd—usually people in our little cul-de-sac were very punctilious about such things.

I finished putting the key in the lock and turned it, gasping as a thicker clot of smell washed over me, borne on a wave of uncomfortably cold air. This time it was much more unpleasant. My mind raced as I closed the door and punched in the alarm turn-off code. The smell was in the house. Had some rodent managed to get in? How? Had it died in here? And why was it so cold? When I was on the road during the summer I kept the air conditioner at eighty degrees and my electricity bill was still astronomical.

Something had indeed gotten in here, but it was much bigger than a rodent.

Lying in the middle of my hand-woven Indian rug from Mexico was the dark and crumpled body of a man.

A very dead man.

"MRS. *RUIZ?*"

The man's voice sounded skeptical. It was a tone to which I had become accustomed. My late husband Jim had been definitely of Spanish origin, but his ancestors had come from Northern Spain, where the people more nearly resembled those of Europe, not of Mexico. In Dallas one expected more Mexican features.

"Mrs. Lilias Ruiz?"

As for me, I had apparently bypassed a thousand years of mingled European-American heritage and chosen my

genetic patterning straight from long-dead Viking for-
bears. I had dark blue eyes and blond hair cut blunt at
my chin, as often by me as not. In the last few years,
though, strands of silver had begun to creep in. I was
also taller than most men I knew and even sitting down
knew I had at least three inches on this man. I might
not be quite as slender as when I married, but I was still
proportionate to my height. Jim always claimed he liked
my curves, saying what they did for blue jeans should
be illegal. Or at the very least, immoral.

"Yes," I answered. I was tired of explaining and still
too shocked to be polite.

"I'm Detective Webber."

"Your men are in there." I gestured carelessly over
my shoulder. After calling the police, I'd fled to the front
stoop, unable to stay in the same room with that dreadful
thing that had once been a man. The area was not large.
The shrubs poked and stuck at me, but I didn't care. I
would have crawled inside them if I could. I still might.

"I know. Can you tell me what happened?"

The detective was not a shining example of what a
policeman should be. About fifteen pounds over what
could legitimately be called pudgy, he bulged in several
directions, bulges exaggerated by his ill-cut and too-
small suit. His collar was open and his tie hung loosely
like a noose. If one were charitable one could excuse that
in deference to the heat that hung like a damp woolen
blanket even though the calendar said it was almost fall.
There was no way to be charitable about the rolls of
beefy neck that erupted through the collar.

What the heck. No one's perfect.

"I've told everyone," I replied, weary to the bone.
"First the patrolmen, then the doctor, then someone else
in a suit…" A better-fitting suit, I could have said but

didn't. Somehow frivolity in any form didn't seem to fit the situation.

There was a dead man in my living room.

A dead man!

"Well, can you tell me?"

I'd seen this on television. They knew what had happened, or so they thought. They just kept you telling it in hopes that you would make a slip and incriminate yourself, thus saving them a lot of work, to say nothing of wrapping up the case in forty-seven minutes flat.

"All right. I came home and opened the door and there was this awful smell. I thought some sort of varmint had gotten inside and died. Then I turned off the alarm and saw…and saw…" I gulped. No matter how cool I tried to be, there was no way to be nonchalant about a dead man in the living room.

"Did you recognize him?"

For a moment the distorted, blackened face flashed in front of me as if it were a hologram. "Are you kidding? His own mother wouldn't recognize him."

Another wave of mixed feelings—disorientation, disgust, horror—hit me. Whoever that body was, he'd had a mother and a father, maybe a wife and children and cousins…

And it wasn't David. I knew that, even though I hadn't seen my son in over a year. I knew there was no way that…that *thing* in there could be David, and for that I was grateful, whatever problems there were between us.

Detective Webber might not be too sharp in the looks department, but he was quick. I wasn't aware of having moved or even breathed any differently, but he was on it like a duck on a June bug.

"What did you just think of? Do you know him?"

"No. I was just thinking about his family."

"Do you know them?" he asked pointedly.

"No. How could I if I don't know him?"

"How do you know he had a family?"

It was a reasonable question, but it irritated me and aroused my temper. I was tired from the tour. Coming home to find a dead man in my living room was bad enough and being grilled as if I were a criminal was just too much. I said so too.

"You're not being grilled, Mrs. Ruiz. We're just trying to get at the truth."

Jim always said that I should count to ten before saying something unwise. I made it to five before stating with poisonous precision, "I've told you the truth. I don't know who he is. I guessed he had a family because everyone has to have a family somewhere sometime, unless you believe people spring into the world fully grown like Athena. I felt sorry for them because I know how I would feel if my son were killed."

"Does your son live with you?"

Great. I had told them about having a child, and now I would probably have to explain about David.

"No."

"Where does he live?" the detective asked, pencil poised.

I took a deep breath. "I don't know where he lives. We're...estranged, I guess the word is."

"That's tough. Why?"

The nerve of him!

"Nothing to do with this."

"Does he have a key and your alarm code?"

"Yes." On occasion I had regretted giving them to him, but could not bring myself to ask for them back or change them.

The detective was relentless. "Who else has access to your house?"

"'Scuse us."

Detective Webber pulled me to my feet and out of the way while two men rolled a stretcher out of the house and down the walk to the waiting van. I tried not to think of what was inside that long, lumpy dark bag.

A tall, trim young woman in a gray jumpsuit followed the stretcher. She looked terrifyingly competent.

"TOD appears to be about two to three days ago," she said briskly. "Don't have an idea about COD yet. Doesn't appear to have been shot. Might have been strangled, but can't tell for sure. I'll let you know as soon as I have anything definite."

"Thanks," Detective Webber said to her retreating back.

Another gray jumpsuit, this time with a man inside, walked past carrying the hand-woven Indian rug from Mexico.

"Evidence," Detective Webber said. "We'll give you a receipt for it so you can get it back—"

"Don't," I replied more sharply than intended. "I don't ever want to see it again." Even after cleaning it would always have that dead body lying on it, and I didn't want to live with that.

"Have to give you a receipt for it anyway. Now, where were you this last week?"

"I've been out of town for almost a month," I said, furious that he should even ask. My home had been violated, entered without permission and a dead man left there like so much garbage. *I am a victim*, I thought indignantly.

"Long time to be out of town."

"It's my busy season. In the last three weeks I've done

three weekend craft shows and four trunk shows during the week. I've been in Atlanta, Birmingham, New Orleans and a whole lot of towns in between."

"I suppose you can document that?"

"Lilias!"

The detective had no idea of how lucky he was that Annie Monroe, our Homeowners Association president and my best friend, chose that moment to pull to a screeching stop in front of the house and fling herself across the lawn. I was about to lose my temper with him, and although it didn't happen often, that was a fearsome thing from which sensible people fled.

I grabbed Annie and clung to her as tightly as she did to me.

"Lilias, I was so afraid," she squealed. "I saw all the police cars from the corner. Are you all right? What's happened?"

"I just got home and there was a dead man in my living room." Even as I said it, it didn't sound real.

"A what?" Annie shouted.

"And you are, ma'am?" Detective Webber stepped closer and there was an edge in his voice. He almost seemed to loom, if a man so short could loom.

"Angela Monroe, and *you* are...?" Annie asked imperiously, looking up at the detective without releasing me. It's hard for a woman as tiny as she to be imperious, but Annie had honed it to a fine and imposing art—in spite of the fact that she has coppery curls and a round face with more than a passing resemblance to Little Orphan Annie. It was a circumstance that caused her no end of grief.

Poor detective. He didn't seem to be getting the kind of awe and respect he wanted from anybody.

"Detective Brian Webber, DPD. How do you know Mrs. Ruiz?"

Annie's eyes narrowed. "She's my best friend."

"Do you live around here?"

"Across the street. Lilias, you say there's a dead body in your house? It's not…" A wave of horror washed over her face.

I shook my head. "It's not David."

"Thank the Good Lord for that."

"Miss Monroe, have you seen anything suspicious around this house lately?"

"It's Ms. Monroe, and no. I came over a couple of days ago—three? four? I don't remember exactly—and checked the place like I always do when Lilias is on a long tour, and I can assure you there was nothing wrong there then."

"So you have a key and the alarm code?" the detective asked, giving me a sharp look as if he suspected me of hiding things from him.

"Of course."

"And you locked up securely and set the alarm?"

Annie's glare should have been answer enough, but she said, "Of course. Lilias, you look dreadful. Come over to my place and you can take a nap…"

I shook my head. The idea sounded tantalizing, but I didn't think I'd ever be able to sleep again. "No, I've got to clean…" I made a feeble gesture toward the open door of my house. Bleach and cleanser and hot water would probably make the house clean again physically, but I didn't know if I could ever cleanse the image of that dead man from my mind.

"Sorry, Mrs. Ruiz," the detective said mechanically. "The place is a crime scene. You can't go in or take anything out."

JANIS PATTERSON   15

"But that's my house," I shrieked. "My purse and my overnight bag are in there. My medicines…"

"Here." A man in uniform held out my purse and overnight bag to the detective. I reached for them automatically, but Detective Webber took them, his expression making it obvious I was in the wrong for trying to reclaim my things.

"They were on the chair right by the front door."

"I always put them there when I come in and turn off the alarm," I said, then shut my mouth. It wasn't any of their business that even after all this time I was terrified of touching the wrong buttons on the alarm keypad and inevitably bringing down the police—and for all I knew the National Guard and the Marines too—with their guns drawn. Irrational, I know, but most fears are not basically rational.

"I looked through them. Nothing remarkable, just the usual junk women carry," the uniformed officer said. "Don't see any reason we can't give them back to her."

Nothing remarkable? Just my life…

"Just a few more questions—"

"Give me a dollar," Annie demanded, punching my arm. I goggled as if she'd lost her mind. She proved it by repeating the demand, so sharply that both policemen stared at her.

I dug in my jeans pocket and handed her a crumpled dollar bill, which she waved ostentatiously beneath the detective's nose before folding it and putting it in her bra.

"That is what you call a retainer, gentlemen," she said with relish. "Mrs. Ruiz is now officially my client and I'm instructing her not to say a word more until we have had a chance to confer. For the time being all your communications will have to come through me."

Detective Webber's scornful expression took in An-

nie's petite size, her youth, her air of fragile helpless-
ness. "So you're a lawyer, huh?"

Annie smiled. It was not a friendly smile. In fact, it
was frightening. "Yes. I am A. R. Monroe, a partner in
Corgill, Watson and Monroe. I assume you have heard
of us?"

The detective's face went blank. Of course he had.
Everybody in Dallas, if not in Texas, had heard of the
most controversial legal firm in the city. Specializing in
criminal law, CW&M had the reputation of being piranhas and had pulled off a few cases even Perry Mason
couldn't have won.

Detective Webber had been poking half-heartedly
through the scruffy black nylon tote that was my overnight bag. The thought of his hands, a strange man's
hands, on my intimate garments, of a man I had never
even spoken to an hour before not only ordering me
away from my own home but touching and deciding if
I could keep my own necessary possessions, drove me
close to hysteria. For one blinding moment I wanted to
rip him apart.

I must be mellowing in my old age, for instead I burst
into tears.

"I DIDN'T TELL him all the truth," Annie confessed. We
were sitting in her distressingly industrial-décor living
room, sipping her excellent coffee while watching the
anthill of activity across the street that was my house.

My face was puffy and tense from the unfamiliar
bout of weeping, but I was once more in control and
greatly embarrassed. It is always our earliest training
that is the strongest. My mother had always said one did
not indulge in fits of emotion, especially not in public.

"You didn't? You mean you knew...?"

"About the dead man? No, of course not. I would have called the police immediately if he had been there when I came in. I am an officer of the court, you know," she admonished and I dutifully apologized.

"No, it's just that I didn't think anything about it until a little while ago," Annie went on, her face contorted with thought. "I saw something, I think."

"You think? You mean you don't know if you saw something or not?"

"It was about three nights ago, maybe four. I wasn't sleeping well. We'd just wound up the Thornberry trial. You know what I'm like when I'm on a big case. I'd been working almost around the clock and not eating at all well, and that night my stomach was letting me know about it."

I made the appropriate sounds of sympathy, knowing what a complicated case that had been and how hard Annie always worked. "You won, of course?"

"Of course. Anyway, it was the middle of the night, two or three probably, and I was getting up to go to the bathroom again, and I heard slamming doors and voices. Well, you know that's not usual around here, so I peeked out the window."

"Well?"

She shrugged and drained her coffee. "The street was empty, other than that tacky RV the Palacinos keep parking on the street. We're going to have to send them another warning about what's acceptable in the neighborhood."

"Annie, what did you see?"

"Nothing, really, nothing that would stand up in court. I thought I saw a shadow going around the side of your house, through that patch of ground cover under the living room window, but I couldn't be sure even then. I also thought I saw a flash of light through the front windows, but it was windy as heck that night and all the trees were flopping around… Could have been just moonlight reflecting off the glass."

"Or it could have been that man getting killed in my house."

"I don't like to think about it, but it could have been." She shrugged uncomfortably. "Like I said, I really didn't see anything. I even flashed my flashlight around, but it wasn't any good. If I had known…" She laughed and shrugged again. "Those really are the saddest words in the English language, aren't they? If I had known… I'm no better than my own idiot witnesses who can't remember what they saw."

My cup rattled in the saucer. "Who was he, Annie? Who was that man, and why was he killed in my house?"

TWO

We hadn't seen the last of Detective Webber. About half an hour later he came to question us again, this time accompanied by his partner, whom he briefly introduced as Detective Costigan. A thin, dry black man, Detective Costigan didn't say much. Maybe the words were dried up inside him. There was a fearsome intelligence in his eyes, though, and for some reason that scared me.

Annie offered them coffee, which they declined, and somehow that scared me more.

"Answer their questions," Annie said, "but don't volunteer any information. And stop instantly when I tell you to."

Obviously the two policemen didn't like that, but they sat down and stared at me like they were two owls in a tree. The silence stretched and thickened.

"When can I go back in my house?" I asked, as much to break the tension as anything.

They ignored me, of course.

"Is there anyone else with a key to your house besides your son and Miss Monroe here?" Detective Webber asked. He emphasized the word "Miss," which, as he had most likely intended, raised Annie's annoyance rating a notch or two. She had probably had "Ms." on her birth announcement.

"No. My Aunt Vada had both the alarm code and a

key, but she passed away a few months ago, and her son returned the key to me."

"His name and address?"

I told them. Of course Mike could have made a copy, but I didn't see why. We had never been particularly close and had grown further apart during his neglect of his mother in her last days. Besides, he lived in some god-forsaken part of the Idaho wilderness and had had to be shamed into coming to her funeral.

"What about service people?"

"When something needs repair I let it wait until I'm home," I said. "Or if it's an emergency, Annie takes care of it for me."

Detective Webber almost sneered. "So the big attorney stays home to see about your plumbing or whatever?"

"Actually," Annie said in a soft voice that made the words sound like ice cubes dropping into a glass one by one, "I give—and get back—the key to my assistant, who stays there and attends to things. He's been with the firm longer than I have, and is considered an officer of the court too. Would you like his name?"

"Later," he almost growled. "Now, was anything out of place in the house when you went in, Mrs. Ruiz? Anything unusual?"

"Unusual?" I all but shouted. "There was a dead body on my rug! A dead man I didn't even know."

"Besides that."

He had to be kidding. "I didn't see anything but that. You may be used to corpses all over the place, Detective, but I'm not. I took one look at him and ran outside."

"After you called us."

"No. I called you from the front yard on my cell phone. I didn't touch anything in the house."

"And you didn't see anything out of place?"

"I told you I didn't see anything," I snapped, then stopped, struck by a horrid thought. "Out of place? Is my house all right? Did they trash it? Destroy anything? Oh, I've got to get over there…"

The detective didn't touch me, but a motion of his hand was as unyielding as handcuffs. "Later, Mrs. Ruiz. It's still a crime scene. We'll tell you when you can go back in."

"Was there damage to the house?" Annie the attorney asked.

"No, and that's the funny thing. From what we could tell, nothing had been touched, at least not roughly. It had been searched, though, and pretty thoroughly from what we can tell. Still, it looks like you could just walk in and start living."

"Except for a strange dead man on the living room rug," I said tartly. "Do you know who he was yet?"

"We're working on an ID." Detective Webber looked icily at me. Obviously he thought he was the one who should ask all the questions. "Are you sure you don't know him, Mrs. Ruiz?"

"Positive." People I knew didn't get themselves murdered. That was something that always happened to someone else.

"And you didn't notice anything unusual about the house, Mrs. Ruiz?"

"I noticed the smell when I got close to the door. I thought perhaps one of the neighbors had let their pets use my front yard…" How I wished it had been only that.

"Where do you set your thermostat when you're away?"

"Eighty or eighty-five, usually. As much as electricity costs these days…" I stopped short. "Of course. It was freezing in there when I opened the door. What had the air conditioning been set on?"

"Fifty. As low as it would go."

I gulped. My electricity bill would be enormous.

"And it had to have been going that way for some time to get the whole house that cold."

I gulped again, seeing most of this tour's profits going to the power company. "You did reset it, didn't you?"

"We will when we're through."

"And when will that be?" Annie asked in full attorney mode. "That is costing Mrs. Ruiz money."

"We'll be through when we're through," Detective Webber said and there was a glint of steel beneath the flab. "I assume you don't keep your house at fifty."

"I've never set a thermostat at fifty in my life, and I don't see why... Oh. To slow decomposition and throw off the time of death."

Annie glared at me and Detective Costigan leaned forward. "Now how do you know that?"

"Oh, for heaven's sake, Detective, I watch TV. Just about every cop show in recent years has used that hoary old device at least once."

"Don't volunteer information, Lilias," Annie murmured. She was frowning.

"Information is what I want," I said more sharply than I normally would. "How long will it be before I can get in my house?"

"A couple of days at least," Detective Webber said in a dismissive tone. "Now..."

That was not what I wanted to hear.

"No, now you wait a minute! I have a show in two weeks in Amarillo, and I'm almost out of stock. I have to make at least a couple of dozen necklaces and bracelets for that, and there's a wedding in two weeks and I'm not finished with the bride's headpiece… My supplies are in there, and I need them."

"What do you do, Mrs. Ruiz?" asked Detective Costigan. It was the first sign of real interest he had shown.

I knew what they were doing. Every pair of cops on TV had done it a dozen times a season. I was perfectly willing to play good cop, bad cop with them if it meant I could get into my supply room.

"I'm a bead artist," I said. "During the season I travel to art fairs and craft shows and places like that selling my wares. Mostly it's fairly cheap jewelry, but I do sell a few good pieces each venue. I specialize in beaded flowers, and once in a while I'll sell a bouquet. I also do specialty items, for bridal parties and such."

"And you make enough doing that to live here?" He might be being the good cop, but Detective Costigan wasn't good enough of an actor to keep the skepticism out of his voice. Our little townhouse development was on the older side, but it was off Preston Road and just north of the pricey Park Cities areas. Needless to say, it wasn't cheap.

"My client will be happy to disclose her financial records when you produce a warrant," Annie said crisply. "Is there anything else?"

The expression in Detective Webber's eyes was almost equally split between dislike and admiration. "Only Mrs. Ruiz's whereabouts during the last week or so."

Annie had anticipated that and grilled me mercilessly. She produced a couple of pages of paper covered in her sprawling hand. "Here is a list of the venues where Mrs. Ruiz has appeared in the last two weeks, along with names and contact numbers of organizers and people who saw her there. We can also produce motel and gas receipts if demanded."

I could barely repress a shiver. It had taken me several years to build a good enough reputation to enjoy the top tier of the circuit and ensure the best booth locations. What would happen to all that time and work when it got around that I was involved in a murder?

Detective Costigan took the papers, folded them and stuck them in his inner jacket pocket, all without comment or expression.

"We'll get back with you, Mrs. Ruiz. Where will you be staying?"

I hadn't thought of that. Locked out of my own house? It was startling, especially since it was through no fault of my own. On the other hand, I wasn't sure I could ever sleep in that house again. For the rest of my life I'd look and see that dead body lying on my living room rug.

"She will be here," Annie said decisively. "Until she can get back into her own house."

"Annie, I couldn't..."

"It won't be long," she said, but she was talking to the detectives, not to me.

ANNIE KNEW MY weaknesses. After a sumptuous take-out meal from my favorite Chinese restaurant, a bottle of decent wine and a couple of hours of mindless TV—no cop shows, though—I was more than ready to be tucked up into the tiny guest room over her garage. I just wasn't ready to sleep.

Though Annie's townhouse's exterior incongruously (for Annie) resembled a tidy New England cottage and mine a nightmare of Tudor affectations, the floorplans were almost identical. Living room, dining room, bath, kitchen and patio downstairs. Master bedroom suite, bath and two small bedrooms upstairs. The smallest bedroom and upstairs bath were over the garage. Annie kept hers as a proper guest room, ready at a moment's notice for any of the hordes of her relatives who were always descending on her. Mine was a storage and workroom where I kept all my beads and supplies. It was probably the neatest room in my house.

The master bedroom and master bath were normally in the back of the house, overlooking the minuscule gardens, with the second, middle-sized bedroom in front. In my house it was still that way. I used the small front bedroom for a sort of den where I would sit and watch TV. Usually I did more work in there than in my titular workroom. There was a hide-a-bed couch for my infrequent (read almost non-existent) guests, but I don't remember the last time it was used.

Annie, of course, had changed hers, punching into the master bath from the front bedroom and making it part of the master suite. She slept in the smaller room and used the back, larger room that used to be a bedroom for a home office. She said she liked to sit at her desk and look out at the flowers. Of course, she could afford a gardener. My back yard was nothing to look at. I had gone for greenery that thrived on neglect. Anything else I tried to grow inevitably died and usually with incredible speed.

Jim had said I had the kiss of death for the floral kingdom.

Jim.

His name and image had sneaked unbidden into my consciousness. It must be because I was so tired. I usually made conscious efforts not to think of him. His going had made too big of a hole in my life and it still hurt too much.

It had been three years and eight months since Jim had collapsed and died of a heart attack while trying to

sell a customer a better grade of tires. He'd been so proud
of his ability to sell, prouder than he was of being the
manager of the three highest producing tire and battery
stores in the entire national chain. He probably would
have been pleased to have gone out in harness.

I didn't see why he had had to have gone out at all, at
least not then. He hadn't even reached sixty.

There was no way I was going to sleep tonight, no
matter how tired my body was. I could wake Annie and
ask her for the sleeping pill she had offered, but I hate
those things. They always made me feel like wet wool
in the morning.

I rolled over and started counting the roses on the
wallpaper. In contrast to the stark industrial chic of the
rest of the house, this room was a riot of chintz and
painted china and organdy curtains. Annie had never
volunteered why this room was so different and I had
never asked. I was far from fussy about décor, but even
so I was grateful I didn't have to stay here long. One
could get diabetes from prolonged exposure to the ter-
minal cuteness.

A sound, metallic and alien to the silence of our little
neighborhood. I sat up and listened.

Normally this was the quietest of streets. Once a
drunken driver had tried to evade a pursuing police car
by turning off of Preston, not realizing that the street was
a circle feeding back on itself. He had taken out three
brick mailboxes before completely losing control of his
car and being caught. Occasionally a neighbor came in
late or left on some nocturnal errand, or a dinner party
broke up at an unseemly hour, but it was close to two
in the morning and I had never heard a noise like this.

Looking out the window did not make me feel better. My big white van had been moved from my drive-

way—which was a part of the crime scene, according to Detective Costigan—and parked in Annie's. There were two shadows that in the light would probably be men on the right side of the van, long sticks in their hands.

The side double doors opened with a protesting screech. The side double doors that had been securely locked.

Not sticks—crowbars!

Those so-and-sos were breaking into my van.

I don't know how I got down the stairs or out the front door, I just remember running across the front lawn in my bare feet, screaming and waving my arms wildly. Behind me Annie's alarm set up a screech that dwarfed mine.

The two shadows jumped and dashed across the street. Across the street, I noticed, toward my house.

I followed, still yelling.

Lights were popping on up and down the street, including one in my house. That made me madder than ever.

Suddenly there was a roar of thunder and I dived for the ground, trying to make myself as inconspicuous as possible. I knew what was happening and it was terrifying. A large-caliber bullet splatted into the earth much too close for comfort.

Good grief, I could be killed!

The winter before, a certain element had decided that our little development was as good as a shopping mall and for several weeks had simply helped themselves to anything they wanted. The police had probably tried their best, but it wasn't good enough and the miscreants stayed free. Most of the homeowners on the block had bought guns and the robbery spree had ended abruptly when Danny Arthur, an accountant who lived in a stone-

fronted house around the curve, had killed two of the
robbers when they started to slap his wife around. The
Homeowners Association had given him a plaque and
Annie had handled all his legal work for free.

I already had a gun, of course. When concealed carry
permits had first become legal in Texas, Jim had insisted that we each get one. I still kept mine current,
even though I never carried the thing and hadn't been to
a range since before Jim's death except for my requali-
fication class. During the robbery scare Annie was one
of the many who had bought a gun, but she never found
the time to get a license.

Nor, to a number of people's unease, had she learned
how to use the gun properly. An enormous .44 Magnum
pistol with a barrel almost as long as a fishing pole, it
was a ludicrous weapon for such a petite person, but
that didn't stop Annie. Now she had opened her window, pushed out the screen and was letting loose with
her cannon.

At least that might bring the police faster than the
endless screeching of her alarm.

I scrabbled across the lawn to crouch in the sheltering bulk of my van, then dashed further down the street
to huddle behind the stone solidity of Louis and Rita
Spaulding's ornamental wishing well. While Annie was
blasting away with her infant Howitzer I wished myself
back on the road, say maybe in Colorado.

A car, started too quickly and gunned too high, shot
out of my driveway.

Blam! Another shot and a tree in Mrs. DeVoto's yard
suddenly dropped a branch. It would have been some
mighty fancy shooting if Annie had been aiming there
instead of at the car.

A shadow detached itself from the underside of my

van and began running toward the car, which slowed only slightly.

Once aroused, my temper has always been a flaw. Leaving the shelter of the wishing well, I flung myself at the running man, tearing across the yard to intersect him. He didn't like that I grabbed him and pushed me away as yet another explosion from Annie's gun rattled the windows. I grabbed again, this time getting a handful of thick hair. He shrieked like a woman, especially as I was using all my weight trying to pull him down by it.

One of the car's doors flew open and an apparently disembodied hand motioned to my almost-captured shadow. I pulled harder on his hair in the other direction, still trying to down him, and with my other hand scrabbled for a grip.

Another explosion, this time echoed by the metallic clang of a bullet hitting the car, decided him.

I never saw nor felt any impact, but suddenly I could feel myself pass through the ground itself. The darkness swallowed me while the stars laughed above.

THREE

I PICKED UP a bead and with exaggerated precision slid it onto the wire. It was easier now that I didn't see two of each of them.

At my elbow there was a cup of delicious dark roast coffee—with real heavy cream, purchased that morning by a repentant Annie, who was prone to moan, "I thought I had killed you," at regular intervals. Dear as she was, it had been almost a relief when she had dressed and gone to court.

I had all the creature comforts. A DVD of the newest blockbuster movie played on the TV. The "Flower" bead box from my truck was beside my other elbow. My head didn't hurt that much any more—thanks to whatever they'd given me at the emergency room—though my face felt swollen enough to masquerade as an overstuffed pillow. I had been punched, the doctor had told me cheerily, by an expert and was going to have a very bruised and swollen jaw.

Even with all that, though, I was hardly paying attention to what my fingers were doing; twice I had had to strip several minutes' worth of work because of mixed-up colors. Normally working on the beaded flowers was my greatest relaxation. Today I could hardly bother and had started doing it primarily to keep Annie from asking how I was feeling every thirty seconds. That, and to keep from screaming.

My mind was across the street, at my house. The rest of me wasn't. The police had finished with Annie's bedroom before I left the emergency room and, after being informed that I had no intentions of being put to bed, Annie placed me in there with every creature comfort at hand.

My house was still very much a crime scene. There was even more yellow tape—this time enclosing the front and back yards, and probably everything else. People in jumpsuits had been going in and out since my mid-morning return from the hospital, carrying cases that I hoped did not contain any of my belongings. Before she left for a quick trip downtown, Annie had said Detectives Webber and Costigan were in there, too, but I hadn't seen them.

I hadn't seen anything. It was my house, it was now mid-afternoon and I still hadn't seen anything. How *dare* they tell me to stay out of what essentially was my life?

Enough was enough.

Patience had never been my strong point, and I had little sympathy with puffed-up demagogues, be they police detectives or no. I stood, glad that my head didn't swim like it had earlier, then walked carefully downstairs, out the door and across the street, right past the yellow tape into my living room.

What had once been my living room.

Now it was a disaster.

I gasped and stumbled, feeling as if I had been punched again.

Nothing was where it had been. Pillows were tossed off the couch, slashed open and eviscerated, and the couch frame itself upended. Chairs were turned over. Even the muslin on the underside of the furniture had been ripped. Scraps of fabric and pillow stuffing lay around like an obscene snow.

Pictures and photographs had been snatched off the walls. The wooden floor sparkled with shards where glass had shattered. When I had bought the townhouse my one frivolous expense had been to remove every bit of the tacky wall-to-wall carpeting and have wooden laminate floors put in all the rooms. A small part of my mind wondered if the destruction would have been less had it occurred on the carpet.

Probably not. Even the shades had been taken off the lamps and one or two of the bulbous lamp bases deliberately shattered. The contents of the entry closet, my "junk" closet, were dumped on the floor and tossed about as if they had been stirred.

There were holes in the Sheetrock in every room. Two or three of the stair treads had been pried up.

I could see into the dining room and a portion of the kitchen, where every cabinet was gaping open and my dishes and glasses scattered about in pieces on the floor where they had fallen. Even my table linens had been dumped out of the buffet and tossed into an untidy pile.

"Ma'am," a very young uniformed policeman said, "you have to leave. This is a crime scene." He was trying very hard not to stare at my spreading bruises as he reached to escort me out.

"This is my home," I screamed, tears spouting like geysers. I probably would have hit him—and been arrested for it, no doubt—had Detective Webber not appeared from the wreck of the dining room and shaken his head. The young policeman vanished as the detective took my arm.

"You shouldn't be here, Mrs. Ruiz," he said, not even blinking at the damage to my face. Of course, the officers last night would have told him. Either that or he was a cold-hearted son of a sea cook who didn't care.

"This is all your fault," I shouted, ungently knocking his hand from my arm. "It wasn't like this yesterday. If you'd let me stay here last night, this wouldn't have happened!"

"You could have been killed too."

"I have a gun. I could have shot them."

"Like your friend Miss Monroe?" He gave a nasty little chuckle. "You'd have been more likely to kill yourself."

I turned on him with a cold stare honed through many years of teaching and controlling unruly adolescents. It was a fearsome enough glare even when it didn't come from a face that resembled a Halloween mask. "I have handled guns all my life, Detective. I have a Concealed Handgun License and am rated expert in both automatics and revolvers. I'll compete with you or anyone you name any time."

He looked skeptical, but said nothing.

"Is the whole house like this?" I asked, my blood running gelid with fear.

"Pretty much. You might as well come see."

I wasn't sure I wanted to, but it had to be done. I let Detective Webber lead me through the ruins of my living room and dining room, then up the stairs, treading carefully on the steps that had been pulled up.

The upstairs was not quite as bad. Either that or I had become inured to seeing my home as a disaster scene.

My clothes had been tossed on the floor and holes punched in the Sheetrock of the closet walls. The dresser drawers were pulled out and upended onto the floor. The bed had been stripped and the mattress pulled off the springs. Both bathrooms had been ransacked and the medicine chests ripped from the walls.

In my den all the furniture had been tossed, and my collection of DVDs and video tapes strewn around. Even the enormous book case had been emptied, the books scattered like wind-blown petals, and the case itself pulled away from the wall. My winter clothes had been yanked from the closet and dumped.

The workroom was almost unrecognizable. The beads I had been so careful to categorize and separate had been poured from the boxes willy-nilly into a pile on the floor. Not a box or bag remained unviolated. Drawers of thread and wire and findings had been yanked and tossed. It would take months to get this mess straight again, and no matter how hard I worked this place would never be the same.

What made me weep, though, was the senseless destruction. Delicate Victorian chip beads of amethyst glass had been crushed to powder by a careless foot. Antique Venetian glass was slivered. Literally pounds of tiny seed beads in every color had been dumped from half-pound bags into a cascading pile. Old African trade beads were cracked and broken from impact against the wooden floor. Not even the strings of pre-war Czechoslovakian art beads, carefully preserved in cotton-lined boxes, had survived intact. They and their modern Austrian cousins sparkled through the destruction like tears.

"This is your fault," I whispered in a deliberately menacing tone. "If I had been here I could have prevented this. I hold you personally responsible, and I'm going to have Annie sue you and the department and anybody else I can think of."

Detective Webber's pudgy expression did not change, but a thin dew of sweat appeared on his upper lip. Good.

I wanted to scare him. I wanted to hurt him. I wanted to hurt everyone. I especially wanted to hurt those who had done this to my home.

"Now Mrs. Ruiz…"

"Don't you dare 'now Mrs. Ruiz' me. You said your-self—in front of witnesses, I might add—that the house was basically untouched. It's your fault the house was empty and those…those hooligans got in and did this. I'll bet you didn't even set the alarm."

He looked away. "We didn't have your code."

"You could have asked."

"Would you have given it to us? Besides, the place was marked as a crime scene."

"And a fat lot of good that did," Annie said, stalking into the room and ignoring the young policeman who trailed behind her. Wearily Detective Webber signaled and the policeman disappeared gratefully downstairs.

"I want to sue him, Annie, him and the whole drat-ted police department!"

"You can't do that, Mrs. Ruiz…there's a law…"

Annie glared. "There is also such a thing as justice, which my client deserves. Perhaps we can't sue and win, but we can certainly raise one heck of a stink both for you and for City Hall."

At that moment Annie could probably have done just about anything. Yesterday she had looked very profes-sional in a good "office dress." Today she was down-right intimidating in her dressed-to-kill power suit, a thousand-dollar number that looked more like a million. Her hair was elegantly styled and she wore comparable shoes and jewelry. She was even carrying a designer at-taché case. On seeing her attired for war like that, pros-ecuting attorneys had been known to go pale, which is exactly what Detective Webber did. A reaction, I might add, that was entirely understandable, as the cost of her outfit probably would have made at least two payments on my house.

"A crime scene—"

"Is garlanded with pretty yellow tape," Annie interrupted, her voice dripping sweet sarcasm. "And all that yellow tape does is keep the honest people out. Did you post a guard?"

"Are you kidding? With our overtime and manpower shortages…"

"I'll take that as a no. Lilias, are you all right? You shouldn't be seeing this."

"Why not? I'll have to clean it up. As soon as they deign to give my house back to me." I shot a poisonous glance at the detective, who was beginning to look as if he were wishing himself anywhere but here.

"This is a crime scene," the detective stated flatly, obviously thinking that settled everything.

"A crime scene for which you are responsible." My stomach knotted in sudden fear. "Did they get into the garage?"

"I don't think so…"

Annie and I exchanged exasperated glances and headed for the kitchen, the detective trailing in our wake.

"Ladies, this isn't right… At a crime scene?"

"We wouldn't have to do this if you had done your job and kept my house safe," I snapped as I went down the ravaged stairs as quickly as I could.

"Did you ever think of becoming a lawyer, Lilias?" Annie asked and the detective sighed heavily.

By now I should have become accustomed to seeing my belongings smashed and scattered, but the full view of the kitchen almost undid me. The collection of salt and pepper shakers my grandmother had left me—cheap stuff, valuable only in sentiment—had been swept from the shelves in the hutch, as had the good china from the cabinets below and the everyday stuff from the upper shelves. Utensils lay at random among the debris, as did the plastic containers everyone kept for leftovers, grocery store bags and dishtowels. Even the calendar had been ripped from the wall.

Suddenly I couldn't breathe. I wanted to scream, to cry, to curse, but my throat swelled until all I could do was whisper, "Why?"

"That's what we need to find out, Mrs. Ruiz."

"The garage…" I managed to say. "Jim's things…"

"Who's Jim?" Detective Webber asked, grabbing at his notebook.

"Her late husband."

"Oh?" His expression reminded me of a little terrier dog Jim and I had owned in the early part of our marriage. Patches had looked just the same when he found something to worry.

The door to the back yard was open, wrenched off its hinges and hanging at a perilous angle. Ironically, the window was not even cracked. The door to the garage was a plain hollow core one, unobtrusively set next to the broom closet—which had also been ransacked—but it was closed. There was a fair-sized hole in it, about the size a fist or a foot would make, which meant the intruders had been interrupted, probably by Annie's fusillade.

I turned the knob, which worked sweetly under my fingers, and the door swung outward.

"It wasn't locked?" Detective Webber looked stunned.

I switched on the light and heaved a sigh of relief. The boxes and bags that contained all the relics of my darling Jim were still there, neatly stacked and covered with only a faint gray sprinkling of dust.

"They're all right," I said through a sob and sagged against the doorjamb, suddenly almost too weak to stand. "They're all right."

"Lilias, come back to my house. You don't need to be here right now."

"All right."

"Just a few questions—"

Annie shot him a look that could have etched glass. "You can come too, if you have to. Just don't harass my client. Come on, Lilias. You'll feel better away from this."

Annie was wrong. I didn't feel any better when we were out of the wreck that had been my home. I felt as if I had just witnessed a death. Annie shepherded me into her living room, ostentatiously ignoring the fact that Detective Webber was following us, and refused to let either of us say a word until she had fortified us with coffee and cookies.

"I'll bet you didn't eat any lunch, did you, Lilias?"

I shook my head. The cookies were surprisingly good, but until then the thought of food hadn't entered my head.

"Now about this Jim…"

Just like Patches. Once he fixed his sights on something, Detective Webber didn't let go. It was an endearing trait in a terrier. Not so much so in a person. In a few succinct sentences I told him about Jim, his ancestry, his faith, his life, his death.

"And he had no criminal contacts, no shady deals…?"

It took an effort, but I suppressed the urge to smash the coffeepot over his head. "No. None. Jim Ruiz was the most honest, straightforward man I've ever known."

"Now we haven't been able to locate your son, David Ruiz…"

Apparently I was to be spared nothing this horrible

day. "You might look under the name of David Reese. Sometimes my son finds our name to be a drawback," I said with painful dignity.

Detective Webber had the good taste to keep his mouth shut.

"Have you made any progress in identifying the body?"

"No, Miss Monroe."

"I prefer Ms.," Annie said icily.

"Ms. Monroe," the detective dutifully repeated.

"Do you have a cause of death?"

He started to say something, then sighed. "If I don't tell you now, you'll get a court order, right?"

"Right." Annie's smile would have scared small children. "You know the law, Detective."

"Okay. He was stabbed. Long, thin blade, slid up under the breastbone, ruptured the heart, death almost instantaneous."

"And almost no blood," I murmured without thinking, garnering a blistering look from Annie. "It's a very popular method on TV cop shows."

"TV has a lot to answer for," the detective said through his teeth.

"I'll bet they wore gloves, too, and that the only prints you find are mine."

He nodded miserably.

"Any information on his identity?"

"Not yet, Miss Monroe. We're running him through all the alphabet agencies now."

"Fingerprints?"

"Still working on it."

"Time of death?"

"Still vague. Could be as long as four days, with the AC cranked down like it was."

I shuddered, thinking of what my electricity bill would be.

Neither Annie nor the detective noticed; they were too busy looking daggers at each other. They resembled nothing so much as a cobra and a mongoose, except these two were theoretically on the same side. Theoretically.

"And we're still no closer to why," I said. "Why my house? Why didn't the alarm go off? Who could go in and out like that?"

"Someone who has the code," the detective said, patently stating the obvious.

"Are you accusing my son?" My expression hardened so fast my bruised and swollen skin screamed painfully.

"I'm not accusing anyone. Not now. I'm just stating a fact."

He was right about that.

"It could be someone at the alarm company," I said somewhat thoughtfully. "Wouldn't they know the code?"

"You're with Beazler Home Security, right? They don't keep those kind of records. You set your own code and the alarm responds to it, but the company has no record of the code."

"Don't they have some sort of override code in case of emergency?" I was starting to feel desperate.

"Yes, but only a code of their own to shut off the alarm after the house has been entered and a signal sent to the police. They can't turn it off and on like you can, at least not with your code."

"You're getting very close to inferring my client had something to do with this, Detective." Annie's voice had become as sharp as the slivers of glass beads in my workroom.

The detective's gaze locked with Annie's and once again we were back to cobra and mongoose.

"I'm just stating the facts, Miss Monroe. *Ms*. Monroe."

"Can't they tell when the alarm was activated and shut down?" I asked quickly before Annie could start making caustic comments about Jack Webb and *Dragnet*.

He didn't have to say he couldn't tell us. An ongoing investigation and all that stuff. I would have buried my head in my hands and wept, but my face was too sore and I didn't have the energy to cry.

"I'm going to have to call Renee and drop out of the Amarillo show. There's no way I can get enough stock together in time to make the trip worthwhile, especially now that my supplies are…are…" I ended with a gulping sob.

"The show isn't for two weeks, is it?" Annie asked. "What about the stuff in the van? Don't you have enough there?"

I shook my head. "There's a lot of stuff in the van, but not what I need."

"Then what about your regular suppliers?" Annie asked with a tenderness that would have shocked her courtroom opponents. "If you have the stuff overnighted it should be here by day after tomorrow at the latest. If it's a matter of money…"

I shook my head again. Borrowing was bad business, and borrowing from a friend was the fastest way to kill a friendship. Annie had been dear to offer, but it wasn't necessary. Almost all of Jim's insurance money was safely tucked away in various accounts, a circumstance David would be more than happy to change in his never-ending pursuit of the elusive "big deal" that would set him up for life. It had been my refusal to underwrite some of his wilder pie-in-the-sky schemes that had driven a wedge between us.

"No. I'm all right. I'm just so tired I—"

I never got the rest of the sentence out and later couldn't remember what I was going to say. There was the roar of a motorcycle racing at high speed, punctuated with the shattering of Annie's front window.

Whatever else he was, Detective Webber was quick. He was on his feet and running even as the cloud of glass shards still hung in the air, but it was too late. By the time he reached the window the motorcycle was gone, out of the development and lost in the continual swirl of traffic that was Preston Road.

Annie swore, using words of the type my mother had said no lady should ever know.

"Look," I breathed, oozing blood from half a dozen small cuts that didn't even register. All I could see was a small, square object lying just inside the window. What now? A bomb?

"What the...?" Annie shouted, followed by another string of extremely imaginative invective.

"Don't touch it!" Detective Webber ordered in a voice he had not used before and, this time at least, Annie obeyed, stopping in mid-motion.

Snapping on a pair of gloves from his pocket, Detective Webber crouched by the object and examined it carefully before touching.

The thing wasn't a bomb or some sophisticated device, but instead was just about as simple as anything could be. A rock, a squat, squarish rock like those used to edge flowerbeds, covered in a piece of paper held with a rubber band. Moving with exaggerated caution the detective removed the paper, then looked up at me with a calculating expression.

"Well?" Annie asked, once again in her commanding courtroom mode. "What is it?"

Wordlessly Detective Webber turned the paper

around. The message was short and to the point, scrawled in what looked like black felt-tip pen.

YOU HAVE SOMETHING OF OURS. WE WANT IT BACK OR ELSE.

FOUR

"BUT I DON'T know what it is," I said for approximately the millionth time. "I don't know what they're talking about. I don't know who they are. I don't know people like them."

"If you don't know them, how do you know what they're like?" Detective Webber asked in a mild tone.

"I don't know anyone who kills a man or trashes a perfect stranger's house or throws rocks through windows," I said testily. "I don't know what they want."

"But…"

"Stop harassing my client," Annie said, still in her courtroom mode. She strode into the kitchen like a miniature, better-dressed Genghis Khan, a frown on her face. Annie hates having anything happen to her clients, but an attack on her or her possessions is something else. I could almost feel pity for whoever did this if she got her hands on him.

If I didn't get my hands on him first.

"I wasn't—"

"You'd better not." Annie took a last glimpse into the living room where Don Garnett was nailing some plywood over the shattered remains of the window. A retired builder and perhaps the richest man in our little development, he had come immediately at Annie's call, which was amazing. His wife Bettina blushed for shame every time he used his hands for manual labor. It wasn't, she was reputed to have said, classy.

As if using the word "classy" was.

"If we could find what they wanted, we might have an idea of who these creeps are," I said, slowly stirring my coffee. It was almost twenty-four hours since I had driven up, looking forward to a short break from the road. Since then I had found a dead body, been punched in the jaw, had my house vandalized and been uncomfortably close to an imploding picture window.

I had even survived Annie's marksmanship.

All in all, it had been an eventful time, and I was just beginning to feel my brain work again.

"And you have no idea?"

"None." I looked the policeman straight in the eye. "No idea at all."

"Well, you're not the type to hang with criminals," Annie said, pouring herself another cup of coffee, then almost as an afterthought pushing the pot toward Detective Costigan. He'd joined us almost immediately after the window incident, though he had yet to say anything beyond a murmured word or two of private conversation with his partner. His cup was empty, but he didn't fill it, instead just passing the pot on to Detective Webber, who dutifully topped off his cup even though it was barely touched.

"So how did you get it, whatever it is?"

"If she got it," Annie snapped.

"If she got it," the detective agreed with a nod. "But we have to begin somewhere. Have you acquired anything new lately?"

"Just a shipment of beads right before I left on tour," I answered. "I've been dealing with that supplier for over two years. And I bought some things from Martha Sullivan when she sold out."

"This Martha Sullivan—who's she?" Detective Webber had his notebook open before he stopped talking.

"A jewelry vendor on the circuit."

"She's a… What did you say? A bead artist like you?" asked Detective Costigan. I almost jumped, because it was so easy to forget the man even had a voice.

"A…" I paused. Even in charity there was no way I could call Martha a bead artist. "Not really. She made some bead strings and bracelets, like I do, but that was about it. She never tried anything…" I almost said beautiful, but stopped. "Experimental."

"So she sold you her stuff?" Detective Webber asked, his pencil poised and all but quivering.

"Me and several other vendors."

"She's giving up the business?"

"So she said. I just know that she sold everything she had with her."

"You had a lot of stuff at your house, Mrs. Ruiz. Did she too?"

"I have no idea. I don't even know if she and Calvin—he's her husband—even have a house, or where. And no, I didn't ask her. I wasn't really impressed with what she sold me."

"But you bought it."

I shrugged. "It was cheap. There were a few good things in the lot. And I was thinking about doing some experimenting."

I didn't tell him what a sucker I was, giving more money—however small the amount—than I should have for basically a bunch of junk, most of which I didn't really want. It was just because Martha had been so desperate, reducing the price again and again until it was just flat rude to refuse.

"And…?"

"Detective—" Annie said in a warning tone.

"No, Annie, wait a minute. There was something funny about it. I thought Martha and Calvin would never leave the circuit, though they have to be in their sixties at least, maybe even their seventies. They have that huge RV they travel in and I don't think they've missed an event in years. They're a legend on the circuit."

"Maybe they just got tired."

"I don't know, Detective. It was awfully sudden. They've got space at every show for the rest of the season booked and paid for. Calvin bragged about it a couple of months ago."

"He a jewelry vendor too?"

"No, he handles junk, only he calls them antiques. Never know what he's going to have from one show to another. I bought a plate from him a couple of years ago. His prices are high, I think."

"Where is this stuff you bought from Martha?"

"Out in the van, but crooks like this couldn't be interested in that. It's cheap stuff. Ugly, too. I just can't imagine Martha getting rid of her supplies unless she's going to start selling something else. Heaven knows she wasn't selling much jewelry. I didn't hear anything about Calvin selling out his stock, so maybe she's changing lines. Or maybe one of them has a health problem."

"Why don't we take a look at what you bought?" Detective Costigan said as he stood. Obviously there was no stopping him. "Unless you want a warrant, Counselor?"

"I don't object," I said, standing up. "We can go right now. I have nothing to hide."

Annie was about to burst from holding back a spate

of lawyer-words, but she couldn't argue with me. She swallowed heavily once, and then again—some of those words must have been awfully big ones—and finally smiled, the way a cat smiles when it asks a mouse to play.

"I've been meaning to suggest since your van has to be fixed from the break-in, because it wasn't secured—" she added pointedly to the detectives, "—that we put the stuff from your van into my garage. I'm sure these detectives would be delighted to do that little thing for us. Won't you, gentlemen?"

When Annie talked like a sweet Southern belle and managed to sound like a piranha while she was doing so, an entire corps of Army Rangers would have agreed to whatever she suggested. It had to be magic. I'd never known anyone else who could get things done quite like she could.

I didn't think it was quite kosher to order homicide detectives around like moving men, but it worked. They obediently carried every box, chest, suitcase and plastic bag from the van into Annie's spacious garage. Well, actually her garage was the same size as mine, but held only a pegboard hung with a few basic tools, two folded-up aluminum lawn chairs and a small, sporty BMW. There was more than enough room for my junk.

Annie moved to close the overhead door, but Detective Webber shook his head.

"No, leave it up. If somebody's watching, they probably already know we've moved this stuff in here, so let's let them see there's nothing here."

When you're on the road, packing and unpacking, knowing that you're the only one who's going to see how it's done, you tend to get very sloppy. At least I do. Now it was with embarrassment that I watched the two detectives go through every box, chest, suitcase and plastic bag, and I vowed most fervently to be more organized in the future.

Whatever mess there was, though, both detectives were thoroughly businesslike, poking through bags, boxes and drawers of beads without spilling a single one, sifting through bags of various-colored stringing threads, cheap single-strand necklaces, scissors, cutters and clamps, all without changing their expression. Until, that is, they came to the old hatbox filled with crumpled white fabric.

"Please…" I said involuntarily. "Be careful with that."

Detective Webber's interest focused like a terrier's at a rathole, making him look more like Patches than ever, but he gently folded back the tattered square of old sheeting. With an odd expression on his face he lifted out the cluster of white and crystal beads almost reverently.

"What is it?" asked Detective Costigan. He too was staring.

"It's a bride's crown. I have to have it ready soon, since the wedding's in less than two weeks," I said miserably, realizing afresh how much needed to be done. The crown was supposed to be a luxuriant wreath of three tiers of white bead roses with leaves made of crystal. The wreath would sit on the bride's head like a laurel wreath, while the veil fell down the bride's back. So far I was about halfway done, with one and a half circlets completed. The bride had wanted a bouquet to match, but when her father heard how much it would cost he'd put his foot down. I had been almost relieved about that, knowing how much work such a project would take.

"Lilias, that's gorgeous," Annie exclaimed. "It would almost be worth getting married just to wear that. Almost," she added.

There could be no higher praise. Annie loved high

fashion and had exquisite taste, but she intensely disliked frou-frou and "girly" stuff. I, on the other hand, loved it, but was so tall and robust (Jim's word) that it looked ridiculous on me.

"And you made this?" Detective Webber turned the crown this way and that, but gently, as if he were holding some priceless artifact.

"Made and designed. I just hope I can get it finished in time so I can get paid. I'm going to need the money."

"Between insurance and what we'll get as a settlement from the city you'll be all right," Annie said with supreme confidence. She ignored a sudden glare from Detective Webber. "Besides, Don is going to give you a rock-bottom price."

"Don? I—"

"I talked to him. He's agreed to fix up your house and make it better than it was to begin with. Besides, it will do him some good to have some real work. He's spending most of his golfing time at the nineteenth hole, I hear. Bettina just loves it. She calls it social networking."

Great. Now I had a drunk set to fix my house with no idea of what he was going to charge.

"Thank you, Annie, but I think I'd rather see to it myself—"

"That's what I told him," she said with the air of someone talking to a rather slow first-grader, "but he really wants to do it. Not even Bettina could make a fuss about him helping out a neighbor who's been through what you've been through."

Even knowing Bettina Garnett only slightly, I had severe doubts about that.

Annie went on without pause. "Don said for you to get as many bids as you like and he'd beat the lowest of them by at least ten percent. And guarantee you the best work available."

My eyebrows rose. So did everyone else's.

"Ten percent? That's a great deal," said Detective Webber. "My mom had some work done last year and it cost her an arm and a leg."

"It's still going to cost an arm and a leg," I said uneasily. "Minus ten percent." What would that be, exactly? A couple of fingers and toes?

"For heaven's sake, Lilias, stop being such a worrywart. Things are going to work out fine."

"I thought they were fine," I said in a slightly tarter tone than planned. "Then I came home. And I still don't know why this is happening."

Almost reluctantly Detective Webber put the wreath back, carefully tucking the fabric around it, then handed the box to me. "Best keep that safe."

"Thank you."

He pulled a largish cardboard box toward him and slit the thick packing tape with his pocket knife before folding out the flaps.

"That's one of Martha's boxes."

Even the men could see the difference in quality. The packages of beads they took out were bigger, coarser, less elegant looking. There were lots of them, though, neatly sorted into zip-shut plastic bags. Oh, why had I ever bought them? They weren't my style at all.

There was, though, a fair amount of what I called ex-hippie necklaces and bracelets—simple single or double strands of brightly colored beads with a cheap clasp—that sold for a couple of bucks. For some reason these sold well at most events, especially the outdoor ones. Thanks to Martha I would at least have some stock for Amarillo.

If I got to Amarillo.

The second box was bigger, and it was worse. These beads were mostly wooden and large, the kind we had put into macramé when I was younger. Some looked like cut dowels and some like seeds or dried berries. None had been drilled, which meant they were far from ready for stringing. This lot would definitely go.

Some had already been strung, though. Detective Costigan pulled out a great tangled lump of colored wooden beads on what looked to be heavy-grade fishing line, all snarled up into a pillow-sized mess that rivaled the Gordian Knot. The beads were different sizes and colors and strung in random order. Groups of roughly similar size were separated by tiny, irregularly shaped spacers of some sort of pot metal.

The thing was also absolutely filthy.

"Good grief," Annie said, taking a fastidious step backward. "Lilias, what is that thing and what on earth prompted you to buy it?"

"It's a curtain," I said, stepping back from the dust cloud that surrounded it. "And I didn't buy it. At least, I didn't mean to. That was Martha's backdrop. She hung it behind her, against their tent wall."

Both detectives had stood rather quickly, dumping the mess on the floor and swatting the dust from their suits.

Detective Webber said, "Probably to keep the customers away."

"I didn't know she put that in there. I surely didn't want it."

"Well, if it's going to stay in here the first thing to do is wash it," Annie said in a voice that left no room for discussion. "Lilias, take it out to the garden and run the hose over it."

"Why? Seems like it would be kinder just to toss it,"

Detective Webber said and I halfway agreed with him. Still, even under the grime some of the beads were fairly nice for their type, too good for automatic consignment to the trash can. Once the curtain was dismantled maybe I could sell or donate the beads that didn't appeal to me.

I touched the unappealing lump with a cautious toe, raising a small cloud of dust, and coughed. Dust sometimes has that effect on me.

"And you paid money for this?"

My feelings matched the incredulity in Annie's voice. "I didn't know I was. I didn't pay very much for the lot and I didn't know Martha had included this. She was so insistent… She said she wanted out of the business and she'd never do it unless she got rid of everything. She did have a few good things, at least I thought she did."

Detective Costigan reached for the last sealed box and the smallest of the three. "This hers, too?"

"Yes."

"They're all liquor cartons," Annie said, her mouth twisting.

"I knew Calvin liked his whiskey. Never saw him really drunk, though." *Or maybe*, I thought wryly, *I never saw him really sober.*

"Good sturdy boxes. You can get them free at liquor stores," Detective Webber said, stabbing determinedly at a thick layer of masking tape. Once again he reminded me of Patches. If his hair had only been blond and shaggy…

The tape gave way beneath the detective's dogged assault—I almost giggled at the analogy—and the box opened.

"This is what I bought," I said, and picked up a plastic bag of multi-colored flower beads. Beneath that was a smaller assortment of teardrops in jewel colors, and beneath that were some rhinestones and some opaque hexagonal glass and even some flat, hand-painted spinners. There were more beads, too, a couple of big mixed-up assortments that looked mostly of a pedestrian sort, but who knew? I hadn't looked very hard at some of the bags, especially the ones that were assorted. Maybe there were other treasures to be found there.

Under the bags were a couple of hand tools—wire snips and needlenose pliers mostly—and a clutch of various-sized hemostats. There were a few rolls of jeweler's wire and, as I had suspected, several weights of fishing line, sometimes called the poor man's bead cord. There were less than a half-dozen cards of real stringing thread and some of them even had the built-in needles cut off.

"Now these are respectable," Annie said, putting down a baggie of the small flower beads, acting for all the world as if she knew what she was talking about.

"You do beadwork too, Counselor?" Detective Webber asked in a carefully neutral voice.

Ignoring him, Annie picked up the bag of hand-painted spinners. "Not your usual thing, Lilias, but you can probably do something with this bunch."

"This lady do a little surgery on the side?" Detective Webber—whom I was now really thinking of as Patches—held up one of the hemostats, which was a thin-nosed locking clamp that had a handle with finger loops like those of scissors. Originally designed to shut off blood veins during an operation, the handy little gadgets had proved to be almost invaluable to crafters.

"Extra fingers," I said. "If you need to hold something in place while you're doing something else…"

Light dawned and he grinned. "Sneaky."

Detective Costigan glanced at his watch, then made a signal to Patches, who was instantly all business.

"I don't know about you," Detective Costigan said in his rusty voice, "but I sure don't see anything here that's worth killing for."

"There's very little that's above carrying to the dump," Annie said, but she put the spinners down very carefully, for which I was glad. They were glass, I had decided, and probably pre-WWII, maybe even closer to WWI.

"Can you see any connection between this and the body in my house?" I could almost speak normally when talking about it now. "Or with the vandalism?"

Both policemen shook their heads.

"Nope."

"Nothing so far."

"Which reminds me, gentlemen…" Annie switched into her lawyer voice. "We need to talk."

I didn't want to listen to her law talk. I didn't want to hear anything except that everything was solved, I and my possessions were safe and that my house was ready to move back into. That, or it had all been some fantastic fever-dream that had never really happened.

Yeah. Fat chance of that happening.

"I'm going to hose this down," I said to no one in particular and grabbed the snarl of beads.

It was heavier—and dustier—than I had anticipated. I had to get a better grip and the rising dust almost choked me.

"Here—let me," Detective Webber said, moving forward, but I waved him away.

"No, you'll get your suit all filthy." Not that anything much could save that suit, but it could be worse. A little. "You all go talk your law talk. I'll take this."

The look of disappointment Patches gave me was eloquent. I ignored it. If he wanted to talk to me, he could

just do it with Annie present. I got a better grip on the
mass of beads and held my breath as I dragged it into
the back yard, a little gray cloud of dust following me.
Following? I was wearing half of it. Great smears covered my hands and shirt and jeans.

Well, I couldn't get any dirtier. Besides, it was pleasant here on the grass in Annie's flower-filled garden,
and I didn't want to go in and hear more about the last
twenty-odd hours. There were things that would have
to be dealt with, but right now one more word would
send me back into tears. Dragging up one of the heavy
wooden lawn chairs, I began to pick at the tangled
strands, telling myself that the beads would come clean
more easily if there were only a single layer.

If I had envisioned a long-lasting mindless task, it
was a disappointment. The curtain was not so much
knotted as coiled and with very little picking came un-
done, spreading out over the grass. The afternoon sun
put golden lances of light through the sheltering oak
trees, but not even it could make the strings of beads
pretty. About six feet long and four feet wide, with
strings of beads falling every three or four inches, the
curtain looked as if it had been strung by a blind drunk
in a bead factory.

There were great clumps of colored beads, sometimes
two or three identical ones in a row, then a handspan
of plain unpainted wood ones resembling nothing so
much as sliced and drilled dowels. Here and there were
small metal spacer beads scattered randomly, and they
were ugly.

I looked closer, my eyes drawn by a small sparkle.
There…in the middle. What I had thought was wood
now looked like amber. Amber? Not excessively valu-

able, but worth a heck of a lot more than ugly wood, especially a chunk the size of a peach seed.

I grabbed the hose and began to spray, then knelt to look. If it wasn't amber, it was a pretty good imitation. And if that one in the corner wasn't a chunk of matrix amethyst I'd be surprised. Most of the wooden-looking ones were just that, unfortunately, and a few of the biggest ones were unabashedly plastic, but there were a few goodies in the mix, including more amber.

"Got the window boarded up. Replacement should be here tomorrow."

In spite of myself I jumped, then—somewhat embarrassed—turned around with a smile that I didn't really feel.

Don Garnett was a good-looking man; medium height, wiry, gray hair cut in a military style. According to the neighborhood gossip it had been a number of years since he left the Navy, but with his trim figure and erect posture it might have been last week.

"Hello, Don." I shut off the hose. "Annie's in the garage."

"I know, talking to those policemen. That's why I'm out here. Sorry to hear about all your troubles."

"Thank you. I just don't know why…" I took a deep breath and forced down the emotion rising in my throat. "Annie told me about your offer to fix my house. That's very kind of you, but—"

Don grinned and it gave his somewhat austere face a sparkle of personality. "Annie told me about it too. Good idea, I think. Do me good to get back to something practical." He thumped his tight midsection with a fist so hard I could hear the thud. "Help me get rid of this damned middle-aged spread."

There was nothing I could say. He didn't look as if

he had an ounce of fat over his entire body. Even my cellulite was jealous.

He glanced toward the curtain. "What you got here? Looks…"

To my horror he suddenly turned pale, then gasped as he stumbled and grabbed at the same midsection he had just punched before slumping to the wet grass in a compact heap.

FIVE

HE WOULDN'T LET us call an ambulance. By the time I had screamed and everyone had rushed into the yard, Don was sitting up on the grass, looking very embarrassed and reassuring everyone that he was perfectly all right.

"Just a touch of asthma," he said, leaping to his feet with the ease of a healthy young springbok. "Doesn't happen often, but for a second or two I can't get my breath. More frightening than dangerous."

Great. Now the man who was going to fix my house was not only a semi-retired drunk, he was a pass-out asthmatic too. I barely restrained myself from shivering. What was going on? Had I driven into some sort of weird alternate universe yesterday?

"I didn't know you were asthmatic," Annie said. "How awful for you."

"I never tell anyone. If people find out you have a little problem first thing you know they expect you to start falling off ladders and foaming at the mouth."

As that was an approximation of what I had been thinking, I looked away.

"So let's not mention it to Bettina—you know how she is. She'll just make a big fuss over me."

It was hard to imagine Bettina Garnett making a big fuss about anything that did not concern herself, her social status or her charge accounts, but one never really knew about a marriage unless one was in it. Under her culture-vulture exterior she might worship Don.

Sure.

"Of course we won't tell her, Don." Annie was properly sympathetic.

His offer of an ambulance spurned, Detective Webber directed his attention to the curtain. The spots of sun had moved, and in their golden glow some more interesting beads were literally coming to light.

"Hey, this thing's cleaning up pretty nice."

Don looked down his nose. "Pretty isn't the term I'd use. Didn't think that sort of thing was your style, Lilias."

"It was part of a bulk buy from a dealer going out of business," I said. "There are some beads on there I kind of like." Half an hour ago I would have jumped at the chance to get rid of the thing, but now my curiosity was aroused. If this quick spray with a hose had revealed amber and amethyst and—I suspected—a couple of other semi-precious stones, what would a thorough cleaning do?

"When do you want to start fixing your house?" he asked with a smile.

"As soon as possible," I said fervently.

"Mrs. Ruiz's house is still a crime scene," Detective Costigan said and I swear this time I wasn't the only one who jumped a little. It was so easy to forget that he was even there. Could the man make himself invisible?

"Of course... Well, Lilias, when you're ready to start talking about what you want and we can get into the house, call me. Annie, I've covered the window and called in a rush order for the replacement. They're making it tonight and it should be in by this time tomorrow."

"Thanks, Don," Annie said to his retreating back.

"Wow," Detective Webber breathed. "Twenty-four hours? Must be nice to have contacts. Last time I broke a window it took three days."

"Are you in the habit of breaking windows, Detective Webber?" Annie asked in a dry tone.

"Only when necessary, *Miss* Monroe."

With just a sketchy good-bye, the policemen left almost immediately, evading both Annie's questions and her orders, leaving her in an odd mood. I took the hose and sprayed the curtain again. It would really take a handwashing to get all the grime off, but enough was removed to see that there was a lot more than just wood and plastic here.

"Well," she asked, watching me spray and pick and rub, "what are you going to do with that ugly thing? Trash it?" she added hopefully.

"Not until I look at it more carefully. There are some good beads in there. See? That's amber. And that's amethyst. And I think that might be rose quartz."

Annie made a non-committal sound in the back of her throat, then announced she was going up to her office to work.

That was fine with me. I'd had just about enough of people, even Annie, as dear as she was. I needed to do some thinking, something I had done much too little of in the last tumultuous twenty-four hours. Jim had always said I went after things with too much emotion and not enough intellect.

First of all, why was this happening? And to me? I'd never had any dealings with the criminal world. Never even knew a criminal—except for my own son. Oh, David had never been convicted of anything, but I knew that he had been involved in more than one shady deal. Neither Jim nor I had ever had anything more on our record than a traffic ticket. Jim had been the most honest, straightforward man I'd ever known and I had done my best to lead a decent life. How had we given birth to someone who was not only a con man and a scoundrel, but was proud of the fact?

Wishing melancholy thoughts could be handled so easily, I turned off the hose and started hauling the bead curtain onto the patio. Getting saturated wasn't going to help the wooden beads. Even if I didn't like them they were worth something.

The afternoon was a rarity for a Dallas summer. The temperature was not too hot and there was a pleasant breeze. Usually at this time of year sitting outside was like sitting on a griddle, but here in the shade it was almost perfect. Much too nice to leave behind by going inside.

Ten minutes later I was working, really working instead of playing with making odd flowers. The bead curtain was draped over a bench to dry, my hands were carefully washed and the table covered with a thick towel on which reposed the bridal headdress. I had even indulged in a real—not diet—Dr Pepper over ice, an addiction which had to be carefully regulated.

Luckily the design was a relatively simple one. Create two or three leaves out of crystal beads. Set them aside. Create the petals of the rose out of white seed beads, the big ones singly, some of the smaller ones in multiples. Finally wire the whole construct together, then attach it to the crown base. On a good afternoon I could make one complete rose with leaves before my fingers got tired.

Today my fingers seemed to work of their own accord. My mind was elsewhere.

What on earth was happening?

Who was the dead man?

What had he been doing in my house?

Why had he been killed?

Why had he been killed in my house?

Who killed him?

How had *they* gotten in—and out—without triggering the alarm?

And why? Why?

Why my house?

Why me?

There was only one answer that even began to make sense, and it was very ugly.

How can any mother acknowledge that not only is her son a criminal at heart, but that he could involve her in something so dangerous? This was something infinitely more than his youthful forging of his father's name to a credit card application or petty thievery.

I shivered, but it had nothing to do with the temperature even though the sun had now completely left the garden in a pool of deep shadow. Looking down, I saw I had made two complete roses and nine large crystal leaves, and each of them was perfect. My fingertips also ached like fury. Fine gauge silver wire might look fragile, but taming it to your requirements takes strength and pressure. The Dr Pepper was gone, but some ice remained in the glass and I held it against my throbbing fingers.

I couldn't think of a single answer to my questions.

My cell phone rang and with fingers stiff and clumsy from the ice I pulled it from my pocket. I didn't even get the chance to say hello.

"What the hell did you mean telling the cops to call me?"

"Hello, David," I said.

"I've got a big deal going here! I just hope to hell it's

not blown out of the water by the cops showing up to ask me about a damned dead body!"

David was speaking in exclamation points again. He usually did and even more so when he was upset. He was upset now. Well, so was I.

"I'm doing well, thank you. Annie's taken me in, since the house is not only off limits, it's been vandalized."

"Why'd she do that? God knows you've got enough money to stay at the Adolphus for as long as you like." Even through his rage the bitterness still shone in his voice. He had never forgiven Jim and me for not taking him along when we spent a weekend in the ultra-fancy hotel in downtown Dallas for our twenty-fifth anniversary. David never forgot what he perceived as a slight.

"I didn't send the police after you, David. They asked who had a key to the house and knew the alarm code. I couldn't lie."

"Why couldn't you? I didn't have anything to do with it."

"David, a man has been murdered. In my house."

"I didn't do it." He drew deeply on his eternal cigarette and blew the smoke into the telephone mic. Probably he was wishing it was my face, because he knew how much I hated cigarette smoke. "And I didn't have anything to do with it, and it's going to take a lot of explaining to my contacts what the police want with me. This deal is going to solidify in two weeks for certain, and it's going to be easy street from then on. I can't afford any risks."

I sighed. Whatever deal David was involved in was always going to come together for certain in two weeks. It had been the longest two weeks in history.

"I hope it comes through for you, David," I said wearily.

"Oh, it will. With just a little bit more solid financing…"

"Which you want me to supply."

"It's a sure deal, Mom. In two weeks you'll have all your money back three or four times over."

"No, David."

"No. You've got to keep it hidden away earning diddily squat in interest. If you really wanted things to go right for me, you'd have turned loose some of Dad's money years ago. Then I could have gotten somewhere, but no, you have to sit on it and count your pennies…" His voice got harder, uglier.

How could he have kept his anger alive for so many years?

This was where I always told him that his dad and I had not been rich people and that our savings had been to take care of us in our old age. After the first time I didn't remind him of his legacy from his father. It had been small—a few thousand—but because of it he blamed me for his failure. His first deal had fallen through, he said, because he hadn't inherited enough money to make it work, and nothing had succeeded ever since because who wanted to work with a failure? I would always end up promising to think about underwriting whatever he was working on at the moment, which meant I had to put up with several calls of escalating temperament wondering where the money was. The deal always fell through because I was too slow.

Not any longer! We love our children, but there comes a time when they aren't children any more, and parents should stop being a punching bag.

"I'm sorry the police bothered you, David, but there was nothing I could do about it. I hope your deal comes through this time."

"This one will, I know," he said quickly, a hint of confusion in his voice. I wasn't following the time-honored script. "With just a little more financing…"

"I don't want to talk to you any more, David. Not right now."

I snapped the cell phone shut. It only made a small click, but it felt as if someone had clamped something hard and cold and ugly around my heart. I didn't doubt he would call again after a while, and be as loving and charming as could be believed. At least he would as long as I held the purse strings. Without them… I didn't know. We always want to believe the best of our children, but I wouldn't bet on it.

"Bravo," Annie said. Her high heels clicked against the fieldstone as she walked across the patio. "I've been waiting for you to do that."

"It's not something to celebrate."

Annie's expression showed she thought it was, but she kept her voice low, almost a whisper, and I realized why when Detective Webber followed her out onto the patio. "I know it hurt you, but he's got to grow up sometime and realize that his big deals are all pie in the sky."

The death of dreams could be just as devastating as the death of a loved one. Sometimes there were problems that just had no solution. I couldn't change David, never could, so I just had to live with what was, whatever it cost in emotional pain.

"Let's drop the subject, shall we?" I whispered back, then smiled up at Patches. "Hello, Detective Webber."

He sat down across from me. Annie took the place between us, picking up a beaded leaf and scrutinizing it. "I wasn't eavesdropping, Lilias. Detective Webber wanted to talk to you. This is simply beautiful, you know. Imagine a crystal vase full of these with crystal roses."

"They're real pretty," the detective said.

"What did you want to see me about, Detective? Can I get back into my house?"

"Soon," Annie said, and this time she sounded positive. "They've discovered the identity of the corpse."

I sat forward, mouth agape. "They have? Who was he?"

Patches looked annoyed. Apparently he preferred to make such announcements himself. "His name was Patrick Goodman, ironically enough, since he seems to have been everything except a good man."

"Well, who was Patrick Goodman, and what was he doing in my house?" I demanded, having run through my mental computer for any mention of a Patrick Goodman and coming up dry. Of course, over the years I had taught a number of children and could remember only a few names, but as I hadn't taught for years that was only to be expected.

"A cheap hood," Patches said. "A sneak thief, low-level drug runner, cheap muscle. A real sterling example of what not to do with your life. He'd been in and out of police hands ever since he was big enough to filch candy from a store counter. Nothing ever too bad, but lots and lots of little stuff."

"Good heavens. What was he doing in my house?" I repeated.

Detective Webber glared at Annie as she opened her mouth to answer. She closed it. "It appears they might have been using your house for a storage and exchange point," he said with some reluctance. "You were gone most of the time, high fence around the back yard… A perfect set-up."

"An exchange point?" The bottom seemed to drop out of my stomach.

"And a storage place. Apparently they'd put stuff in

your garage. It's full of boxes anyway. No one would notice a few extra, probably not even you when you came home."

Late summer in Dallas is very warm, even on milder days in a pleasantly shaded back yard. There was no reason for me to suddenly start shivering so violently my shoulders heaved and my teeth chattered. No reason except that in my absence—and maybe even in my presence—my home had been used as a place for hooligans to store God only knew what, maybe even have meetings. Had they sat in my chairs? Eaten my food? Used my bathroom? Gone through my intimate things? Slept in my bed?

It took every ounce of will I possessed not to throw up right there on my brand-new crystal leaves.

"How did they get in?" I formed every word out of pure determination and forced them one by one out of my mouth. "The alarm…"

"We're curious about that, too. What do you know about it?"

"Nothing, I turn it on and turn it off and pay the bills. What were they keeping in my house?"

The detective shrugged beefy shoulders. "Dunno. Stolen stuff? Drugs? What do you think, Mrs. Ruiz?"

Annie frowned at him, but he paid no attention. "Detective…"

I didn't pay any attention to her either. I could feel the heat rising in my battered face. "Why are you asking me? I don't know anything about stolen stuff. I don't know anything about drugs."

"But they were in your house."

"Not with my permission. I didn't know anything about it."

"What about your son?" He was pushing harder now. His eyes had the same determined glint the first Patches had had when he was closing in on some small rodent, but now I didn't find the comparison funny at all.

"He just called me. He was very upset because he thought I'd said he had done it. I didn't, you know that."

"Do you think he did it?"

"No," I said, but—God forgive me—my voice lacked conviction. When he wanted something, David was capable of almost anything. Theft? Drugs? Murder? I didn't know. "He's not even in Dallas."

"Tacoma's not that long a plane trip away."

So David was in Washington State? The last time I'd known his location he'd been in Scottsdale. How sad that I didn't even know where he was.

"He could have come here and gone back a dozen times in the time that body lay in the house," Detective Webber went on. "And there's your cousin, whom we haven't been able to locate yet. Seems he doesn't like the authorities."

I was beginning to feel very much in sympathy with Mike, and said so.

He ignored me. "So that leaves Miss Monroe here."

I had expected an explosion, a flood of multi-syllabic lawyer-talk cresting a wave of righteous wrath, but Annie shocked me by laughing. "You're reaching, Detective, and doing it badly. You don't have one solid piece of evidence against anyone, do you? And it's still Ms. Monroe."

Once he had his teeth into a bone nothing could have made Patches turn it loose. Detective Webber was running a close second. "It makes sense... A widow woman, reduced income, living in a ritzy area like this… Letting drug dealers rent her house while she's gone would be an easy way to pick up some extra cash on the side."

I spluttered with fury while Annie laughed again. "You're ridiculous, Detective. Lilias can account for every penny of her money, and you won't find anything out of place. But you've already looked, haven't you?"

At least he had the good manners to look abashed. "Of course."

"And what did you find?"

"Nothing. No irregular expenses. Though you ought to get rid of that gas-guzzling van. You're paying out a heck of a lot of money for fuel."

He was right about that. "The van was my husband's," I said slowly, surprised that there was still pain. "He had always wanted one. We bought it less than a year before he died. I'll never get rid of it."

"And as soon as you release it as a crime scene," Annie said pointedly, "we'll have it repaired so Lilias can go on driving it."

"You can have it repaired right away." The detective sounded weary.

"No fingerprints?"

"No."

"Of course not," I said. "Those men wore gloves. I saw them. I could have told you that."

But of course the police wouldn't have believed me. I was probably the best suspect they had.

"When can I get back into my house? I have to get it fixed and cleaned… I have obligations. I'm booked for two more months of shows all over the country."

Detective Webber stood and stepped back as if preparing for flight. "Soon."

"How soon, Detective?" Annie's voice held an edge. "Surely you don't regard my client as a suspect any longer."

"Everyone's a suspect, Ms. Monroe. Everyone. And, Mrs. Ruiz, don't plan on leaving town for a while, huh?"

SIX

LEAVE TOWN? I didn't even leave Annie's house, practically didn't leave my little bedroom. Filled with a wild mix of emotions—half shame at being suspected as part of this unsavory whatever it was and half anger for the same reason—I didn't dare do anything but bead. I made white bead roses and crystal leaves until my fingers bled, then I piled on the Band-Aids and kept on working, finishing the bride's headpiece in just about half the time I had allotted for it.

I was only glad that Mrs. Parkhurst hadn't called me to check on the headpiece's progress. Emily, the bride, was okay, a meek little thing who was kind and helpful and eager to please. I guess she'd had to become that way, because her mother was a sharp-edged mother-of-the-bride-zilla who would send battle-hardened war veterans howling for backup. Still, every run of luck has to end, and mine ended on the third evening with the ringing of my cell phone.

"So you aren't in jail yet."

I didn't have to ask who it was. Mrs. Parkhurst—Mrs. Ronald Parkhurst the third, as she constantly reminded people—had a nasal, determinedly cultured voice that was unmistakable.

"No."

"Well, thank heavens for that," she said without sounding grateful at all. "It's humiliating enough to know that my daughter's tiara is being made by a criminal without having to go to the jail to fetch it."

"I'm not going to jail, Mrs. Parkhurst."

"But you've been running a drug house. The TV said so."

"Then the TV is wrong. I'm an innocent victim."

"Oh, the jails are all full of innocent people. I certainly hope you don't intend to charge me full price for the tiara."

I blinked. "I most certainly do. Why wouldn't I?"

"Because you won't be needing as much money in jail, and I'm doing you such a favor in accepting it. Not everyone would permit their daughter to wear something made by a drug dealer, you know, especially when the wedding is going to be one of the foremost social events of the year."

Mrs. Parkhurst was overly fond of announcing her social status. It had ceased to be amusing long ago and had never been impressive.

"Mrs. Parkhurst, we have a contract, and I'm going to hold you to it."

She protested a little more, then flatly refused to come even to Annie's house to pick the headpiece up. She didn't, she said haughtily, feel safe coming to "that kind" of neighborhood. We made arrangements to meet the next day at a very public coffee shop on Central Expressway.

"You're not going," Annie said that evening when I repeated the conversation to her. By then I had forced myself to laugh at it. Just a little, but still laughter. "There's no way you're going to meet that creature face to face."

"But I have to. I want to give her the dratted crown and be able to forget about it. I also need the money."

Annie gave a small smile, the kind of smile that

made sensible people run for cover. "Oh, you'll get your money. Give me the monster madam's telephone number, then wrap that thing up ready to deliver."

"I can't let you—"

Annie's smile widened. "Oh, yes you can. I've seen how hard you've worked on that and I'm not going to let you be cheated out of a penny. You know she's going to try."

I nodded. That had been a foregone conclusion. Mrs. Parkhurst was the kind of person who would never pay a cent she could possibly weasel out of. "Bless you, Annie. Whatever you do, put it on my bill. I know I'm going to owe you a lot."

"Don't think about that now." Annie waved an airy hand. "I'm going to enjoy this."

And she did too. I listened—at her instruction—as she called Mrs. Parkhurst, identified herself as my attorney, then proceeded to go to town with threats of lawsuits and arcane legal actions if one malign word was whispered about me, if my bridal business (which was sparse to nonexistent so far) suffered one whit of diminution from anything which could be even remotely traced back to Mrs. P., if I suffered pretty much anything about anything. After a few obligatory squawks Mrs. Parkhurst caved and was almost craven.

"She's a bully," Annie said triumphantly after she hung up the phone while Mrs. P. was still babbling. "Bullies give in easily. I hate bullies."

"But you told her she'd have to come down to your office to get the headpiece," I said, half delighted, half appalled. "Your office is all the way downtown, and she just lives on the other side of Central."

"I know. It'll be good for her." Inspecting the crown,

Annie frowned. "You know, you don't charge enough for your work. This is exquisite."

"If I charged what it's worth," I said dryly, "no one would be able to afford it."

Annie shrugged. "At least tomorrow you'll have some walking-around cash. I'll make sure she pays you every penny you contracted for. What's for supper?"

To repay Annie for her hospitality in even a very small way, I had taken to preparing our dinner. If I did have a real talent it was cooking, one that had been sadly neglected in my later years. Cooking for Jim had been wonderful. Cooking for one is ridiculous.

"Meat loaf and mashed potatoes and sliced tomatoes. And I made some pepper cheese biscuits."

"We've got to get you back in your house," Annie said with mock seriousness. "I won't be able to get into any of my clothes."

When Annie decreed something should happen, that something happened. It really did seem like magic. We'd barely finished dinner when the doorbell rang.

"Sorry to interrupt your dinner…"

"Nonsense, Detective Webber," Annie said. "We're done. How can we help you?"

There was a tension in the air as we settled in the living room. The new window had been installed and the evening light poured in, softening the industrial tenor of the room. Looking more like Patches than ever, Detective Webber sniffed the air.

"Smells like meat loaf."

"It was, and it was delicious." Annie was brusque. "Do you have any news?"

I wished I hadn't eaten so much. My stomach roiled. Had he come to arrest me? Would I be taken down and booked and thrown in jail? What if I couldn't afford to make bail? What if I were denied bail? What if I were sent to trial? What if they found me guilty?

My hands started to shake.

The detective sniffed the air again, then apparently gave up on being offered a plate. "Have you had any more thoughts about what these people want from you, Mrs. Ruiz?"

I shook my head. "I don't know. I don't have anything like that."

"Like what?"

Annie was not in a hospitable mood. "That's enough, Detective."

"Like something criminals would want. They've seen everything I own and broken most of it," I snapped, then shut my mouth tightly. There was no need of going on a tirade again.

"Thanks to you," Annie added relentlessly.

He sighed. "We're releasing your house tomorrow morning, Mrs. Ruiz. You can start doing whatever you want to it."

I sighed and for the first time in days felt I could breathe without having to work at it. Maybe it was a cliché, but it really did feel as if a great weight had been lifted from me.

"It's about time," Annie said. "I take it you've solved the case."

He nodded. I thought he looked disappointed. Had he wanted me to be guilty?

"Yes. Sort of."

His expression was sheepish and embarrassed, I decided, not disappointed.

"So tell us," I demanded. "What happened? What do they think I have? Who did this? Who's been using my house?"

"Not just yours. We've found four other storage houses so far."

"Four?" Even Annie was astonished. She was skilled at keeping a poker face, but this time her eyes grew so round she could have been the model for Little Orphan Annie.

"And there's probably more. This thing keeps snow-balling."

"And all alarmed and monitored by Beazler Home Security, I'll bet."

"What makes you say that, Mrs. Ruiz?" This police-man might look like a hick sheriff in a bad movie, but he was quick. His eyes were on me like lasers.

"For heaven's sake, Patc—Detective Webber, don't you ever watch television? What else do these houses have in common?"

"Nothing." He shrugged and smiled, which made him look startlingly boyish.

"So how did you solve it?" Annie asked.

"Pure old-fashioned detective work. We traced Pat Goodman's acquaintances. We looked at his jobs."

"But he couldn't have worked for Beazler Home Se-curity," I blurted. "I made sure they were bonded. You said he had a record, and they couldn't hire anyone who couldn't pass a security check."

"Television again?"

"Common sense. Who's going to trust their house to a company that hires former criminals?"

He nodded. "Smart lady," he said to Annie, jerking a thumb at me. "Anyway, you're right. He never worked for Beazler. But he had a boyfriend who did. Boyfriend was squeaky clean—church member, neighborhood volun-teer, the whole nine yards. He worked the inside. Found houses that were alarmed for weeks at a time with no entry or exit on a regular basis…voy-la! Instant storage house. Even had a pattern worked out—who was gone when."

I felt a rush of reluctant admiration for the squeaky-clean crook who could devise such a scheme.

Annie was made of sterner stuff. "So how did he know the alarm codes? Each homeowner sets his own and they aren't on file at the company, or they shouldn't be."

"You're right." Patches grinned and I resisted the sudden urge to toss him a treat. "The company doesn't know them, but the company computer does. How else could it tell if the code was right when the door was opened?"

"And a good hacker could get into the computer, especially when he worked there," I said. "Was the boyfriend involved with the drug ring?"

"He says no, that he just gave Goodman the information, but we're working on it."

"Did he kill Goodman?"

"No." Patches sounded disappointed. "Has a rock-solid alibi. The entire week that Goodman could have been killed he was out of town at some comic book collectors' convention in San Francisco. There's dozens of witnesses."

"Could Goodman have been killed earlier, and his body frozen? That could really set the time of death back," I murmured. "Did the M.E. check for cellular anomalies?"

Detective Webber stared at me, as did Annie. "Did you ever think you might be watching too much television, Mrs. Ruiz?" he asked. "Anyway, the M.E. said there was nothing unusual about the body. The low AC couldn't have affected decomp for more than twenty-four hours, and the boyfriend was gone several days on either side of the death window."

"So who killed Goodman?" asked Annie.

"Don't know, so far. Boyfriend swears it was a mechanic from the drug supplier. We're looking into it."

"So you haven't really solved the case at all."

Detective Webber's expression hardened to match Annie's. "No, not in the sense that we're ready to issue an arrest warrant, Miss Monroe, but we're pretty sure now that Mrs. Ruiz had nothing to do with any of it."

"And I'm glad of it," I said hastily.

"We told you that in the beginning," Annie said simultaneously in an icy tone.

Their gazes locked in a glare so palpable it could almost be broken with a hammer.

"So," I forged bravely on, "does this mean I can leave town?"

"As long as you let us know where you're going."

"I'll call you every day," I promised. "I'll even email you if you want."

Detective Webber's hard and almost frightening expression softened into a smile. "You email?"

"Of course. Your men went all over my laptop, so I assume they read my emails too. Doubtless they were bored silly."

The policeman chuckled. "I dunno—those crafter's loops can sometimes get really interesting."

Although I subscribed to several because rarely—very rarely—there was something useful about beading, I found few things more stultifying than a bunch of housewives going on-line to chatter about a tidbit of history regarding some ugly quilt pattern or a new source for vintage fabrics. I laughed, really laughed, for probably the first time since opening my front door onto that horror.

Patches laughed too. Annie frowned.

"So why was Goodman killed?"

"According to the boyfriend, he was getting angry with his boss—"

"Who is?"

"We dunno. Somebody fairly new to the business, we're guessing, because there's not much of a trail. Nobody's ratted on him yet, which means he's very good or very ruthless. Take your pick."

"Any unexplained bodies? Besides the one in Lilias's house, I mean."

Patches shrugged. "Always lots of bodies. There's a couple we think might be connected."

"Is there any chance they might come after me?" I asked in a small voice that was totally unlike my own.

"They already have, Mrs. Ruiz. They didn't trash your house and throw a rock through Miss Monroe's window just for fun. You have something of theirs and they seem to want it pretty badly."

"But I don't. I've thought and thought, and I can't think of a single thing."

"What about the boxes in the garage? Could something be in there?"

"I packed those boxes when my husband died. That was almost four years ago. They haven't been opened or even touched since I moved here. By anyone."

"Do you have any idea why this Goodman was killed in Lilias's house?" Annie asked. "And why the body simply left there?"

"First part is the easiest to answer. It's a lot harder to move and dispose of a dead body than TV would have us believe. Leaving it was probably the easiest thing to do." Patches shrugged. "As for why, it could have been a falling out between dealers. Or a warning."

"So they intended me to find the body," I said slowly, a sickish taste in my mouth. "That's cruel."

The detective shrugged again. "So was killing him."

"I'm going to leave," I said suddenly. "I'm going to move, sell the house…"

"And go where?" Annie asked. "Besides, in this real estate market, you'll lose money. It'll be easier once the house is fixed up again. Think how nice it will be to buy new furniture."

Most of what was destroyed had been new. The stuff Jim and I had used had never been of the best quality, as most of it was hand-me-downs given to us when we married. We were always going to get some good stuff, but after buying the big house out in Garland there was never enough money to get more than one or two pieces, then Jim died. I hadn't thought most of our stuff worth moving when I bought the townhouse. Instead I'd just gone to one of those places that sells entire rooms, thinking it would be easier, but the results had been bland and not excessively pleasing.

Annie jumped up. "Which reminds me, I need to call your insurance agent so he can get a claim going."

"I can do that—"

"He'll do it faster for me," Annie said with a wicked little smile. It was true, too. "Is there anything else, Detective?"

"Nope." Patches stood and held out his paw—his hand. "I'll be around, though, and don't hesitate to call me if you remember anything or if anything happens. My private number's on this." He gave each of us a card.

After he was gone, Annie looked at me. "Are you attracted to him?"

I goggled. "Are you crazy? Of course not. I'm almost old enough to be his mother."

"That doesn't mean anything these days. You do have a pet name for him, don't you?"

"I was afraid you'd catch that." My cheeks flared. "It's not really a pet name…"

Annie urged, using her most persuasive courtroom technique, and of course I caved, telling her about the little terrier we had called Patches.

As I explained her eyes grew round and she looked at me with barely contained amusement. "Patches? It's perfect. Fits him to the life."

"Please don't tell him. It's not very flattering being compared to a dog."

Annie dissolved into laughter. "But Patches sounds like he was such a lovely dog."

THERE WAS NO laughter the next day. As I'd predicted, Annie had the insurance adjuster out almost at dawn, and before morning coffee he had written me an enormous check, much larger than the one I had anticipated. Annie's magic again, I suspected, or—more likely—she had something on him.

"Of course not." She appeared scandalized when I said so. "I am an officer of the court, and blackmailing people is illegal. I just urge them to do what's right."

"Yeah. I wonder how long it would have been if I'd called them."

"You just let people walk over you, Lilias. You're much too nice. Take control. Give orders. Say what you want and don't take no for an answer. You'd be amazed at the results."

"Humph. Easy for you to say."

What came next wasn't easy. There had been a uniformed officer there almost as early as we were, and he had removed the useless yellow crime-scene tape. With Annie and the insurance man beside me, walking through the house had been bearable. The insurance man was gone now, though, and Annie was trying to hide her impatience to get to work. In a minute or two I'd be left alone to clean up the wreckage of my life, to throw away that which I had loved which was now irreparably shattered. I'm not a very strong woman, and I was not looking forward to it.

"I wish I could stay here and help you with this." Annie sounded apologetic. "But I can't. There's a big case brewing and I have—"

"Of course you don't have to stay." I plastered on a smile that hopefully did not look as fake as it felt and gave her a quick hug. "You've already done so much. I don't know what I would have done without you. You go on to work. I'll be all right."

She gave me a long look. "Yes, I think you will." Surprisingly, because she was not a kissy person, Annie pecked me on the cheek, then ran, leaving me to my fate.

I had survived Jim's death.

I had survived many terrible moments with my only child, and had, to all intents and purposes, lost him long ago. If I'd ever really had him, that is.

Compared to those monumental wounds, this shouldn't be too bad.

It was bad, of course, but not as much as I had feared. I did the workroom first, sweeping all the scattered beads together and putting them into a clean popcorn tin from the attic. Sorting them would be a monumental pain, but it could be a mindless chore saved for a frosty winter's evening while watching TV. In the meantime, I had ordered new supplies of the staples I would need which should be arriving in a day or two. After the drawers were replaced, the tools and stringing thread put away and the floor swept, the room looked as if someday it might be normal again.

Don arrived shortly before noon, bristling with plans and budgets. He could put the house back the way it was before in just a couple of days, and for a great deal less than I'd expected. Annie had said I might make a profit from this, and it was beginning to look like she was right.

"And you have no idea of who did this?" He sounded half-fascinated, half-frightened. I guess most people would sound the same, thinking there but for the grace of God…

We were sitting cross-legged on the workroom floor—the only floor I trusted, since I had cleaned it myself. "None. All I know is what the police tell me."

"Wow. That must have been really scary for you."

"It was. For a day or so I thought I was going to move and sell out, but that would be foolish."

"Yeah, I don't know where you'd find a setup as sweet as this. After I'm finished with it, it'll be home again."

"Thanks, Don. Can you put a pergola in the back yard, over the patio? With a fan?" That had been a vague dream since I'd first moved in. It would be a lovely place to sit on spring and fall evenings.

He smiled, softening the military set of his face. "You bet. We can do anything you want, make everything right for you. In fact, I'm going to give you some advice. Go through the house and pick out what you want to save. Put it in the garage. I'll get you some boxes. Then I'll get in a cleaning crew and have the whole house cleared out in one fell swoop. Any big stuff you want to keep, just put a tag on it. It'll save you a lot of time."

And a lot of heartache, he didn't say, or maybe didn't even think, but it was true. Putting something in a trash bag was so final. It would be easier if it all just went away.

"I'll do that. I had been wondering what to do with everything. Thank you."

"All part of the service," he said, and then winked. I had known Don Garnett since I had moved in three years ago, but that single, unflirtatious wink opened up a whole new facet of his personality, turning him from a rather reserved, uninteresting man into someone I would like to know better. "Oh, hey—did you ever decide what to do with that bead curtain? I've got a buddy who owns a bar who could use it."

I shook my head. "Just stuck it in a box. I still want to examine it carefully before deciding. I know there are some good beads in there I think I'd like to use. If I do sell it, though, I'll call you first."

He grimaced as he stood up. "Fair enough. I'm going to go start rounding up supplies and a crew. Say we start day after tomorrow morning?"

Day after tomorrow morning. I could salvage what was left of my life by then.

"Sure. Why not?" I allowed him to pull me to my feet. Floors were lower and harder to sit on these days, to say nothing of getting up.

Things, I thought, *are starting to look up.*

And the gods laughed.

SEVEN

THE TEXAS STATE Pride Craft Festival in Amarillo was one of the biggest in the Southwest, and capitalized heavily on Amarillo's image of a wild west Texas town. There were more things Texana displayed than probably existed in the rest of the state—metal cutouts of Lone Stars and cowboy silhouettes and howling coyotes, enough varieties of hot sauce to fill a lake and beaded vests into infinity. You could hardly go a step without bumping into a man wearing a Stetson the size of a patio umbrella or a pair of lethally pointy-toed cowboy boots or, most likely, both.

Whatever their age or size, the women seemed to favor jeans so tight and low it was questionable why they bothered, skimpy tops that revealed more than they concealed and a mind-blowing display of ornate tattoos on places I didn't think you could tattoo, including the smalls of their backs.

"They call them 'tramp stamps'," sniffed Florene Halliday, a self-styled "quilt artist" who had the booth next to me. Over the years we'd done a fair number of the same shows and, although I didn't know her well, Florene seemed okay, if a trifle obsessed. Her booth overflowed with anything and everything that could be quilted, from bedcoverings to bookmarks. "I think that's right fitting, don't you?"

I made some wordlessly neutral reply, which she seemed to take as agreement.

The year before the fair had been held in the spacious South Exhibit Hall of the Amarillo Convention Center, and I missed it. This year we were in a gigantic building which appeared to have started life as a WWII airplane hangar. It was graceless, uncomfortable and permeated with the pungent aroma of the refinery that sat not far from its northern edge. Such considerations aside, Florene and I were in a prime location, on the center aisle close to the entrance. Even though it was just the first day I had almost made my expenses just on the ex-hippie jewelry (a great deal of it Martha's) and a couple of what I called Lover's Roses—a single long-stem beaded red rose.

At this show I was trying out a new design, a beaded bluebonnet. If the Texas state flower didn't sell here, it wouldn't sell anywhere. The spiky, multi-bloom flower did bring in a lot of interest. Almost everyone who passed my booth was fascinated, so much so that the poor specimen was close to being mangled. Unfortunately, the piece was very intricate and to make my price point on time and materials the price had to be so high it was out of most people's reach. For now, at least, the bluebonnet was simply a showpiece. To my surprise I did sell a small flowerpot bouquet of beaded daisies that had been around so long I feared I might have to plant it.

I had also sold some single, loose beads—the kind that might come in good someday but never really seem to. I always kept them in a big old Mason jar on the table, as much for atmosphere as anything. Lots of people were asking for loose beads this time, some rather forcefully. I had explained repeatedly that I was an artist, not a wholesaler.

Apparently they took their beading seriously up here in Amarillo.

"Never would have seen anything like that in my growing-up years," Florene grumbled, looking after a woman as lavishly tattooed as she was scantily clad. "What do their parents mean letting them trash themselves out like that?"

Considering that most of the women I had seen so "trashed out" had been on the shady side of thirty, I couldn't even come up with an appropriate wordless grunt.

"Big crowd this year. Lots of customers." Her thin face brightened as one paused to inspect a table of small items. "Be back..." she whispered and hustled over, extolling the craftsmanship in her hand-quilted Bible cover.

At least a thousand years old and thin as a buggy whip, Florene was spry as a child and as inquisitive as one too. She must have set up her booth the night before, for as I unpacked my wares that morning she examined everything, and I mean *examined*, even so far as to point out two cracked beads in the stem of a Lover's Rose.

It could be worse. I could be next to Henrietta and Vernon Alquist, a precious pair in their fifties who made wooden signs that were either house numbers, owners' names or fairly vulgar sayings. To make it worse, Henrietta had a shrill laugh that could etch glass, and it seemed she was always laughing. Between the high whine of the routing machine they used to make their signs ("Any saying cut while you wait") and Henrietta's laugh, being next to them was a test of nerves. When Henrietta really got going, it was a test being two aisles over from them.

It seemed for the moment traffic had thinned, so I relaxed and reached for my working tray. I had thought long and hard about what to do to thank Annie for all her help. My insistence that she bill me for the hours spent on my behalf met with thorough refusal, so that left only my art. Her house was too stark for most of my work, but there was always a way around that.

"Now that's right purty," Florene said, stuffing a handful of bills into her jeans pocket. Quality hand-quilted Bible covers apparently commanded a respectable price. "Sorta bleak, ain't it though? Think it'll sell?"

I looked at the long rose in my hand. Bleak wasn't the word I would have chosen, but the flower was indeed stark. "It's a special order. The customer likes plain things."

She picked up one of the finished roses from the flat box and inspected it carefully. Under the high-power convention center lighting the crystal beads appeared almost electrified.

Except for being larger and longer stemmed, the design was identical to the Lover's Rose, but for Annie I had used only crystal seed beads. The stem and leaves were of plain round beads strung on a plastic-coated florists' wire which gave the finished product a greenish cast. The bloom was made of barely faceted crystal beads only a tiny bit larger than the ones on the stem. On the bloom I had used a fine gauge of clear plastic-coated silver wire, which made the petals both clear and almost luminescent. On three of the petals I had added one larger, more sharply faceted crystal to make a faux dewdrop. Even I had to admit the finished product was spectacular. Now if I could only get a dozen finished and buy a tall, slim crystal vase in these two weeks on the road before I went home… I didn't want Annie to have to wait.

"I think the real-colored ones are prettier. Nothing better looking on God's earth than a red rose. But these're right interesting. Right interesting." She laid the rose back with the care of a craftsman who respected another's work. "I'm going over to the food court. Want me to bring you something?"

"No thanks, I brought my lunch."

"Won't be but a minute. Watch my booth, will you? Don't want to let a sucker get away." With a smile and a wink she was gone.

Having someone keep an eye on a booth was essential. Sometimes customers did get away, not wanting to stay around for a few minutes until the vendor returned, but a much more palpable threat was theft. A well organized group of two or three could hit a booth, strip it all but bare and vanish in less than a minute.

"Hey, are you the bead lady?"

He was tall, painfully thin, spotty, badly dressed and not over eighteen or nineteen—hardly the kind of person one associates with beads. However, a customer is a customer, so I smiled.

"I am a bead artist, yes. I usually sell just the finished product, but I do have a few loose beads. What kind are you looking for?"

"Some of that. On the end." He gestured toward the back of the booth.

All right, I will admit I sometimes indulge in quirky behavior. During the time I'd spent at Annie's I had gone over Martha's hanging bead curtain, washing each bead by hand, and in doing so had discovered a treasure trove. There were not only a fair amount of tumbled semi-precious stones and amber, but some beautiful old hollow-cast metal beads that had to be at least a hundred years old. Yes, there were also some hideous plastic ones and the clunky wooden styles of the '70s, but—once cleaned—the curtain did hold some interesting if not downright valuable specimens. It was a strong statement about Martha's taste—or lack of it—that she had put together such a weird combination in so aggressively irregular a design. Before long I would take it apart, hopefully before someone thought that odd mixture was my doing, but for the moment I had hung it at the back of my booth. Cleaned, it was almost spectacular in a weird kind of way.

Leaning over the table, the customer was pointing vigorously to the chunky wooden beads that hung in a plain string on one side of the curtain, the ugly old macramé kind that looked like cut dowels. I took a step backward. He was pointing so vigorously that his unwashed body odor was overwhelmingly repellent.

It seemed like there had been a bag of those ugly things, but I wouldn't swear to where they were now. Had I thrown them away? Had I left them in Annie's garage or brought them with me? The days after I had found that dead body in my house were slightly fuzzy, and the few days before I left had been a non-stop endurance test of cleaning out the wreckage from the vandals, getting some product made to bring with me, and deciding on what I wanted Don to do to repair the house. Needless to say, Don's estimate of a quick clean-out had been pure fantasy. I had still been finding things I wanted to salvage—whether broken or not—the afternoon before I left.

I simply couldn't remember what I had done with that bag.

"I'm sorry," I said. "I don't have any of that kind."

His expression hardened. "I've got money. I want a bead!"

"I don't really carry beads, per se," I went on in the

most soothing voice I could muster. The way he kept
clenching and unclenching his fists was unnerving me.
"I just have those in the jar. I'm a bead artist, you see,
and sell…"

"I want one of those beads, you stupid old bitch," he
roared, pounding his fists on the table. "I want some
now."

"This scum bothering you, ma'am?"

Never again will I make any comments about men in
pointy-toed boots and hats the size of patio umbrellas.
Two of them materialized from the crowd and stood on
either side of the suddenly silent young man.

"Yes, he's being very disruptive."

"I just wanna buy a bead," he whimpered. "Nothing
wrong with that. Just a bead."

"You're disturbing people," the first white knight
said.

"The lady says she doesn't sell beads," the second
white knight said, a man considerably younger than the
first.

"Now you'd better get out of here and stop bothering
people," the older man said with menace, "or we'll get
security over here and see what they'll think."

The smelly young man was shrinking almost visibly.
"I just wanted to get a bead," he mumbled before melt-
ing off into the crowd. "Didn't do anything wrong…
Just wanted a bead."

"Are you all right, ma'am?" the first white knight
asked.

He appeared old enough to be the second man's father, but there was no resemblance between them. Both
were slender, but the older man was not only a head
taller but strong-featured, with a face that might have
been hacked out of some hard wood. The younger was

rounder, softer, almost fresh out of the egg. Still there
was some sort of connection, I could feel it. It was obvious in their stance, in the small glances that had flicked
between them. Friends? Co-workers? A gay couple?
(*What a waste*, I thought involuntarily.)

It was none of my concern. Although surely I could
have solved the problem on my own, their appearance
had saved me from a potentially unpleasant incident,
and I thanked them profusely.

"Our pleasure, ma'am," the older man replied. "We're
just sorry you had to go through that. Hope it doesn't
turn you off Amarillo."

As I had never really been turned *on* to Amarillo the
idea had never entered my mind. I answered politely that
I was enjoying my stay—and I was, for the most part.
The sales were good.

"It's the drugs." The older man seemed inclined to be
chatty even as the younger grew restive, looking around
as if anxious to be gone. "These stupid kids get high,
then they get irrational. They see something and they
have to have it."

Drugs? Of course. It had been several years, since
before Jim's death, that I had quit teaching, and there
hadn't been much of a problem in the middle school
grades then, but it wasn't unknown. Yes, that unfortunate young man had all the earmarks.

"Tragic," I said. "How can they be so stupid as to ruin
their lives like that?"

The older man picked up one of the Lover's Roses and
examined it. "This is real pretty. You make it?"

I nodded. "I call them Lover's Roses. They're quite
popular."

"Lotta work here." He glanced at the price tag and

though his eyelids flickered at the amount his expression didn't change. "Sell many?"

"Enough."

The younger man had drifted over to Florene's booth, where—a Styrofoam food box still in her hand—she was backing him into a corner while extolling the virtues of hand-quilted storage cases, which she had for all sizes of pistols.

"Isn't it kind of dangerous, a pretty lady like you traveling around alone to all these shows? That kid isn't the only one out there on drugs, you know."

Until then I had thought—arrogantly, perhaps—that this exceedingly handsome man was working up to come on to me. That had happened more than I'd expected, as apparently some men found a woman on her own alluring, no matter her age or appearance. Something about his so-artfully thrown away question, however, set my nerves jangling. There is no better way to develop a built-in lie detector than to teach middle school kids, and having taught them for the better part of a generation, I was a master at the art.

What was going on? Was he selling protection? That was a new and very nasty wrinkle in the traveling art fair business. Spiritually the descendent of Al Capone's protection racket—i.e., pay us not to hurt you—it had been revamped by a bunch of nasty young entrepreneurs around the country who preyed on lone vendors, primarily women.

"And where is safe?" I asked, struggling and failing to achieve a light tone. Not even home was safe any more. When I did return after this trip, I wondered how much it would cost me emotionally to open my door and walk inside.

Craggy-face grinned, and the effect was electrifying.

Apparently he could turn the charm on and off, which made him an exceedingly dangerous man.

"Well, you just be sure you take care of yourself," he said, reaching for his wallet. "And I'll take this rose, too."

Of course he had a lady friend somewhere. A man with his looks would. It was ridiculous, this tiny frisson of disappointment I felt. Was I so starved for male companionship that a simple rescue and a few bantering words could touch me?

I think not. I smiled, put the rose in a sack and handed him his change, then watched as he extricated his somewhat stunned younger friend from Florene's determined salesmanship and both of them vanished into the crowd.

It was getting closer to closing time and the crowd, in the mistaken belief that vendors would charge less at the end of a day than at the beginning, picked up their buying. I was almost sold out of ex-hippie necklaces and bracelets, which meant that I would have to pass on Annie's roses tonight and instead work on replenishing stock. That was okay, I supposed. I was tired and making those simple bits of jewelry could be done almost on autopilot. Personally, I never could see why people didn't make their own, as it was such an easy and basically unskilled task—but I was glad they didn't. These simple bits of adornment constituted a fair portion of my income.

I was packing my wares and my projects back into their respective boxes when Florene bounced into my booth, seemingly as energetic as she had been that morning.

"Where you going to eat tonight, Lilias?" she asked, flipping some tired sheets over her tables. I wondered why she hadn't quilted some table covers.

"In my room. I've got to work, so I'll just have a sandwich." Actually, I didn't know what I was going to do about eating. The prospect of another sandwich was not at all enticing. I did know that I didn't want to spend an entire meal listening to quilting stories, and though she was something of a bore Florene was a good old soul whom I didn't want to offend.

"Go-getter, ain't you?" She looked at me curiously. "You pack up everything every night?"

"Yes. Old habit. Some people aren't as honest as they might be, and beads are so terribly portable."

I had already finished boxing everything, and was folding away the tablecloths. The only thing of mine left in the booth was my chair, a simple folding metal model from the hardware store, so old and battered that it wasn't worth the trouble of hauling back and forth to the van.

Then there was the curtain. In the beginning I would have been content to leave it there, with the sneaking hope that someone would carry the ugly thing off, but now that I knew how valuable some of the beads were, my conscience pricked me. With a sigh I lifted the thing down from the metal rod on which it hung and wrapped it in a tablecloth. If carefully done, it wouldn't need much unsnarling in the morning. It added a lot of weight to my rolling cart, but somehow I felt better. Amber had gone up a lot lately, and those beads alone were worth the aggravation.

"Yeah, can't trust anybody any more. Would you believe I had someone try to walk out wearing a quilted skirt in Sweetwater? Had the nerve to say she had worn it in. Sexy little thing she was, too—almost had security convinced she was telling the truth." She picked up her purse and cackled with bitter laughter. "No one wants to believe an ugly old woman when a young pretty one's telling them something else."

"What did you do? Surely she didn't get away with it."

"Accourse not. Told 'em I could prove the skirt was mine. Made her take it off and there was my label in the waistband, big as life. She said she'd bought it from me last year, then told the security I was a senile old bat."

Now we were walking down the nearly deserted aisles toward the vendor's entrance, my loaded rolling cart hissing over the concrete floor. There were a few vendors still open, desperately trying to make just one more sale. Like everyone else I could always use one more sale, but instead made it a point never to be the last one out. Jim had made me promise that when I first started doing local Dallas shows.

"So how did you prove she hadn't?"

"Second price tag, pinned under my label." Florene grinned with pride, showing a startling display of obviously store-bought teeth. "My clothes are expensive. People are constantly switching the tags that hang on the outside, or they fall off or get lost or whatever, but the official price tag is always pinned under the label." She laughed uproariously as we walked out into the parking lot and the chilly wind that was the signature of an Amarillo night, summer or winter. "I even date them. I might be a senile old bat, but I'm a helluva smart one."

I laughed with her. I'd known who Florene was since starting on the circuit, enough to say howdy to if we met, at least, but never as a person. I was starting to like her.

"Does it never stop blowing here?" I asked.

She shook her head. "If so I've never seen it. In the winter they say the only thing between here and the North Pole is a broken-down barb-wire fence somewhere in Kansas."

I laughed again and maneuvered my cart around a pothole roughly the size of a bathtub. Apparently asphalted a generation or so ago and ignored ever since, the parking lot looked like a minefield.

"Well, here's my old bus," she said, stopping by an old VW van so time-worn and decrepit it was a wonder it still ran.

Did people, I wondered, *and their vehicles start to resemble each other after long association, the way owners did with dogs?*

"Where're you?" Florene asked, her hooded old eyes scanning the lot like a hawk's. The parking lot lights hadn't come on yet, but there was still a fair amount of light in the sky. I gestured two rows over. Usually I tried to park closer to the door—both for security and ease in loading and unloading, but a number of people had gotten here earlier than I this morning. That was something I'd have to do better, as tomorrow was the last day of the show. "Want me to walk you over there, seeing as you've got all that stuff?"

I shook my head. Her offer was kindly meant, I'm sure, but I couldn't picture wizened old Florene being anything but a liability if anything should happen. "Thanks, but it's still light, and it's only a few steps. I'll see you in the morning."

Pride, says the Bible, goeth before a fall. Well, I wasn't feeling particularly proud that day. In fact, I wasn't feeling anything but tired and hungry. I didn't want to make ex-hippie necklaces that night either, but I had no choice. A quick trip through a drive-thru for some deliciously greasy fast food and...

Strong hands caught me from behind and threw me to the uneven ground, where I lay stunned, unable to move in spite of the boulder-sized pebbles that were digging

into my back. When you're as tall as I am there's a long
way to fall, and the impact knocked the breath from me.
For a moment I didn't know if I would be able to breathe
again or not. Time seemed, if not to stop, at least to dis-
tort, slowing and warping as if it were a giant balloon.

With the dispassionate perversity of inanimate ob-
jects, the high mercury vapor parking lot lights chose
that moment to snap on, bathing everything in a sickly
orangish glare and blinding me even as I gasped for
breath. I was conscious of a hideous wailing that sounded
as if all the banshees of Irish legend had formed a heavy
metal chorus. Around me there was movement as two
pairs of feet thundered away into the low shadows between the parked vehicles.

In all my days as a craft vendor I had never been
attacked. I didn't like it.

"You okay, honey?"

Florene was stronger than she looked. Her wiry little
arms pulled me up off the ground almost without effort.

"What was that?" It was an idiotic thing to say, but
the first that came to mind. I almost looked around for
the banshees.

Florene laughed. "Got me a screamer. Handy little
thing—pepper spray on one end, screamer on the other."

With some effort I focused on the flashlight-sized
object in her hand. Somewhat embarrassed, I realized
how much more effective it had been than the pistol so
carefully secreted under the van's seat. I was going to
have to get me one of those.

"Reckon he was after your day's take," she said, looking at the tumbled mess of boxes. "Hope he didn't get it."

I shook my head. "In my pocket."

Florene looked at my tight jeans and cackled. "No
man'd get it there, leastaways, no decent one."

There were other voices, footsteps, as the departing vendors converged from all parts of the parking lot, wanting to know what was going on. Florene explained that I had been the victim of a snatch-and-grab artist, probably after my day's take. There was an outpouring of concern and sympathy, followed by a general grumble of fear and discontent. *There isn't anyplace safe any more*, some said. *Security isn't tight enough*, grumbled others.

Eventually the security man arrived, bore with fortitude the contentions of the crowd and gratefully vanished after being reassured that I wasn't hurt. Two male vendors picked up my scattered boxes and tossed them into the van with no more effort than I would a tissue box. Then, as if suddenly conscious that their wares were unguarded in other parts of the lot, the little group of vendors vanished, leaving Florene and me alone.

"You sure you're okay, Lilias? Not seeing double or anything?"

I laughed, albeit a little shakily. "I didn't hit my head, Florene. They just pushed me over."

"They? You are seeing double. There was just one of them, honey, that was all I saw."

She was wrong, though I didn't argue the point. There had been two men, but with the lights flaring in my eyes I could see very little detail. There had been a younger one, lither and faster, and he had been followed by a taller one. Both had been dressed in black and, judging from the way they ran, wearing athletic shoes. It was a standard trick used on television shows since the days of black and white—one thug to keep watch, one to do the actual snatching and when both ran it would confuse anyone trying to help.

One thing was for sure, though. I recognized the last

one without any problem, even though the last time I'd
seen his craggy, rough-hewn face he had been wearing pointy boots and a hat the size of a patio umbrella.

EIGHT

THAT NIGHT I set the alarm on the van—an accessory added at the urgings of my insurance agent and never used until now.

I also stuck my trusty automatic in my waistband when I unloaded my few things at the hotel. It was a violation of my concealed handgun license, which stated that all firearms had to be completely concealed when carried, but at this particular moment I didn't care. The motel parking lot was well lit but empty and I wasn't taking any chances. As Jim had always said, it was better to be tried by twelve jurors instead of carried by six pallbearers. Tonight I was in full agreement.

The High Country Motel was just like all others of its kind—come down in the world from its beginnings as a semi-luxury chain motel, a little shabby, a little out of date, but still clean and respectable. And safe, I hoped, but as I said, I wasn't taking any chances.

I ate my drive-thru burger and fries, which tasted just like every other drive-thru burger and fries in the world, while watching something mindless on TV without really being aware of what it was. Later, full and slightly sleepy, I made myself start making more necklaces.

And I thought.

Luckily the necklace making was simple. Loop the thread through a jump ring and knot it, then just barely flick it with a lighter to seal the threads. String on as many beads as I wanted, in whatever design I felt like. Tonight I was Martha, simply sliding beads onto the thread with no thought to design or color or anything. When the string was long enough, knot the thread through the jump ring attached to the catch—usually a cheap spring ring or lobster claw of poor quality steel— and with another flick of a lighter, there was a necklace. A cheap necklace to be sure, but still something pretty for just a couple of dollars and a great money maker for me. Comparing these to my beaded flowers, the necklaces brought in several hundred percent more when figured on a materials-cost and time-expended basis.

I still preferred the flowers.

I had been a professional bead artist and craft vendor for almost six years, and on the road for more than two since Jim had passed away. In all that time no one had ever attempted to rob me. Of course, there had been a shoplift or two from the booth, but those were just an unfortunate given in a vendor's life. I'd certainly never been assaulted. Of course, before the last couple of weeks, I'd never found a dead body in my house, never had my van broken into and never been socked in the jaw, either.

Coincidence, as far as I'm concerned, is just a word in the dictionary.

It was barely past nine, not too late to make a call. Wouldn't matter if it were. I dug out my cell phone.

"Hello?" Annie's voice was soft and, for Annie, remarkably feminine.

"Did I wake you?"

"Lilias? No, of course not. I was just having a glass of wine out here in the back yard. Do you think I should put in a hot tub?"

My eyebrows rose. A hot tub? Annie the workaholic? "When would you use it?"

She sighed. "I guess you're right. But it would be nice." She sighed again, and I would have laid odds that by the time I returned Annie would have the Cadillac of hot tubs installed in her yard. "How's the show going?"

"I was assaulted tonight."

There was a gasp over the phone and I swear I could hear the crackle of electric energy as Annie switched into powerhouse attorney mode. She scrabbled for a pad and pen, both never far from her reach, and began shooting questions at me so quickly it was all I could do to keep up.

"So you didn't report it," she said at last.

"Just to security. No use in calling the police. I'll talk to Renee tomorrow. She should give the lone vendors escorts from the building to their cars."

Annie sniffed. "From what I've seen of most private security, that would be stacking the deck in favor of the crooks. And you say you recognized one of them?"

"I *think* I recognized one of them. Tall, craggy cowboy." I paused and tried to think. Had I actually seen the man who had come to my booth running away into the darkness, or just someone who resembled him? There had been lots of tall men around today with roughhewn faces and rangy bodies. "I'm not sure. That's almost a stereotype up here, you know."

"I wish you'd come home. Don's making wonderful progress with your house."

I gaped. I'd only left Dallas two days before. "So soon?"

"Must be lots of men looking for work right now, because he got in a huge crew right after you left. After they got all the mess out there apparently isn't that much to do structurally. He says some Sheetrock and a couple of new doors and some paint are all you need. Oh," she added in a voice that was much too casual, "we thought he could add a couple of little extra touches here and there."

"Touches? What kind of touches?"

"Oh, just a few things he and I thought you might like." Annie giggled. "Don't worry—it's not going to cost you any more. Not much, at least."

The thought made me go cold. Annie was not a giggler. What would I be going home to? And how much would it cost me? "Annie, what have you done?"

"Nothing you wouldn't have done yourself. I wish I hadn't mentioned it, because now you'll be wondering instead of being careful. Nothing to worry about, I promise. Do you have your gun and your CHL?"

I patted the smooth steel of the 9 mm Beretta semiautomatic that had been Jim's, now nestled against my thigh. "Yes, and I always have my CHL behind my driver's license, whether I'm carrying or not."

"Are concealed weapons allowed in the building?"

"I don't know, and quite frankly, I don't care."

"That's dangerous, Lilias, to say nothing of being potentially illegal. Local laws—"

"I don't care." I chuckled. "I have a very good lawyer."

My very good lawyer made an indecipherable sound deep in her throat.

"Have they found out who killed the man in my house? Goodman, or whatever his name was?" Strange. Even without closing my eyes I could see it all, him lying all dark and stiff on the hand-woven Mexican rug, right next to my coffee table. I had never known him, and I would never be able to forget him.

"They say, according to word they're getting on the street, that it was done by a professional from out west somewhere."

A professional killer in my house? That was almost as bad as a dead body. I gulped as my deliciously greasy fast food dinner turned to a lump of stone in my stomach.

"But who hired him? How did he get into my house?"

"Who hired him is the bazillion-dollar question. As for knowing your alarm code, presumably the person who hired him gave it to him. They're thinking it was some sort of prearranged meeting. Patches says a career thug like Goodman wouldn't come to a deserted meeting place alone unless he knew and trusted whoever he was supposed to be meeting."

"So he might have gone there expecting to meet—" I stopped short, gasping. "*Patches?* You mean Detective Webber?"

Annie giggled again, alarming me no end. "The same."

"What are you up to, Annie? You don't call him Patches to his face, do you?"

"Of course I do. It fits him perfectly."

"And of course you told him where it came from. Oh God, you didn't did you?"

"He thought it was funny—especially when I told him what a lovely dog Patches was."

"You never met him," I snapped, mortified to the core of my being. I'd probably be arrested when I got home. "You didn't even know he existed until a few days ago."

"Don't be silly," Annie said with a soft laugh. "Patches—the dog—had to be nice, because I can't picture you having a bad dog."

"I'll never be able to face Detective Webber again."

"Oh, he's looking forward to it. Told me he hopes you bring him a nice bunch of Milk-Bones," Annie said, then dissolved into laughter.

"He didn't."

Now Annie was chortling so hard it was difficult to understand her. "He did, but then he told me to tell you that he was nicely trained and he promised never to make a mess on your front lawn."

I groaned. Surely somewhere there was a law against making fun, however gentle, of a policeman.

There was a soft knock at my door, one so timorous that had I been asleep or even watching a noisy movie, it would have been hard to hear. Instantly I was alert and so tense that my muscles hurt.

"Hold on," I whispered urgently into the phone. "There's someone at my door."

Annie's laughter died instantly. I put the phone on the nightstand and, picking up the Beretta, eased off the bed. Ignoring the spill of beads and thread across the coverlet, I flicked off the safety so it was ready to fire. There was a round in the chamber, which is not recommended, but I didn't want to have to waste time cocking the thing.

By the time I reached the door there was another knock, a louder one this time. Like most motel doors, it was a fairly flimsy affair, with an electronic deadbolt and a chain nightlatch, both designed to keep out honest people. One good kick could probably send the whole door crashing in.

My hand started to sweat against the plastic gun grip.

"Who is it?" I asked, trying to will my voice not to shake.

"It's Florene," replied that distinctive voice. "Just wanted to make sure you're okay after your shaking up earlier."

"I'm fine, thank you."

"Did you get some dinner?"

"Yes, thank you." It took a great deal of concentration to keep my voice steady.

"Want some company for a while? Sometimes people get nervous after something like that."

"No, thank you," I said, then told a deliberate lie. "I'm just getting ready for bed. I'll see you in the morning."

"Okay," she said. "Tomorrow."

Sagging against the doorjamb, I listened intently, but could hear no sound of her departure. Of course, the halls were carpeted and she had been wearing sneakers earlier, so she could have been able to do a kick-line routine down the hall without making enough sound to be heard.

One of the nastiest side effects of fear is that you start to distrust everyone. Was Florene really just an eccentric vendor of quilted everythings, or something more sinister? Had she been just a good-hearted old woman coming to check on a colleague, or had she had some other, darker motive? Had the parking lot attack been a set-up designed to bring her close to me?

And *why?*

I was snapped back to the present by a tinny squawking coming from my cell phone. Oh, Lord, I had forgotten all about Annie! I picked up the phone and almost had to shout to make her hear me. When I did she seemed remarkably unrelieved to know that I was well and safe.

"What on earth did you do? I couldn't hear a thing—I thought I was going to have to call the Amarillo police to come rescue you," she snapped, cranky with what I hoped was relief. "Who was at the door?"

"It was the woman who rescued me tonight," I said, regarding the puddles of beads over the bed with dismay. Like in all hotel rooms, the spread was a dark and busy pattern, heavily quilted. A lot of the beads simply seemed to disappear into the design. I'd never find them all. "Florene. I don't remember her last name. Oh, yes I do—Holliday, or Halliday, or something like that."

"Ah, yes, the crazy quilter." The scritch of Annie's pen over the paper came through the phone with a clarity that would have pleased the company no end. "You didn't open the door to her, did you?"

"Of course not."

"What did she want?"

"To check up on me. Make sure I'm all right."

"Or make sure you're there." Annie was being her cynical best. "Maybe you should change rooms. Or even motels."

Somehow it was distressing to find that Annie had a mind as suspicious as mine.

"It's too late and I'm too tired to pack up." *And*, I was too ashamed to add, *too scared to go out into the night.*

"Maybe in the morning you should come home. There's something hinky about all this."

"Tomorrow is the big day. I can't afford to lose the sales."

"I'm serious, Lilias."

"So am I."

Annie almost said something, then snorted. "Never could convince you of anything practical. Where are you going from there?"

"Tulsa. The Chestnut Plaza Art Fair. Set up and early opening on Thursday, runs through Sunday. I'll be at the Sky Hills Motel. Then I'll head for Branson and the Mountain Days Festival."

"I still think you should come home until this whole thing is solved."

For a moment the idea of having someplace to go and hide sounded good, except that it would be a long time before that invaded, violated townhouse on that deceptively quiet cul-de-sac felt like home again. If it ever did.

"And when will that be? I can't spend the rest of my life hiding. I have to earn a living."

Annie's sigh was clearly audible. "Why doesn't that surprise me? You know if it's a matter of money, I'll make you a loan."

"Yes, and you're a darling to offer, but one should never borrow money from friends. Besides, we don't know when this is going to be resolved, or if it even will be," I said with a fine display of false courage. "You might have to adopt me."

Annie sighed again. "Sometimes you're so damn logical you seem like a lawyer. Be careful, will you?"

"I have every intention of it."

"Maybe you should start driving right after the show. Confuse them. And call me tomorrow night, no matter what you do."

"Yes, Mother."

She rang off almost instantly, with only the briefest of admonitions to look after myself. I could bet she was going to call Patches and tell him all that had happened.

Methodically I began scooping the spilled beads into the box. It was an automatic chore, which was good because my mind was occupied. There was no avoiding the obvious conclusion. What happened tonight had to be connected somehow with that dead man in my house.

Why had he been killed?

And why in *my* house?

And why had they come back to search so viciously that it destroyed my home? According to Patches, none of the other "storage" houses had been damaged.

Only mine.

Had the dead man really been meant as a warning to me?

Why? What did they think I had?

Okay, I couldn't even speculate about the murder. Weren't crooks and druggies always killing each other for some reason or another? It was possible that it was just the luck of the draw that Patrick Goodman happened to be in my house when he was murdered.

But that still didn't explain away their belief that I had something they thought belonged to them.

What did make it different was the scope of the vandalism. Obviously they—whoever *they* were—had been looking for something. Stairs pried up, holes punched in the walls and all my belongings tossed was more than just random violence. They had to have been looking for something, something specific, and they thought they knew where it was. Then, when they couldn't find it, they threw the note through Annie's front window.

They! It! I snorted. I was getting desperately tired of pronouns. Who were these people and what did they want?

Obviously it had something to do with drugs, and just as obviously they thought I knew not only what it was, but where it was, or there wouldn't have been that attack on me tonight.

Or was I truly becoming paranoid? Everyone on the circuit had heard tales of vendors who'd been jumped and robbed in various parking lots across the country. Maybe it had just been my turn.

Yeah. Like I believed that. Still I made myself analyze the event dispassionately.

It had been a relatively average day. I had made a fair amount, but nothing compared to some of the big ven-

dors. Anyone hanging around the place with an eye to
fast cash could have scoped out several more lucrative
targets than I. Was it because I was an easy hit? Huh?
I'm a big woman, taller than most men. Were I going to
do a quick shove and grab, I'd pick someone little like
Florene instead of a Viking like me. No one could have
known that Florene would carry a nasty combo of air
horn and pepper spray.

Unless they had seen her use it before, which was a
possibility.

But there were other lone women vendors, most of
whom would appear more vulnerable than I.

Why me?

The only thing that made sense was someone in the
drug mess thought I had something.

What?

I didn't know.

I sat on the bed, hardly noticing the bite of an unno-
ticed bead as it dug into my flesh. I knew I could never
get them all.

My mind ran like a hamster on an exercise wheel. It
was a hopelessly outdated comparison, but so very true.
No matter how I came at the problem, I neither learned
nor changed anything.

What was I going to do? I couldn't give up selling.
because as I had told Annie, it was my livelihood. I had
to keep doing it, because who would hire me for a real
job at my age? Despite what David thought, his father
hadn't left enough for me to live and still have something
tucked away for the future. I had no illusions about who
would be paying for my old age, if I were so fortunate as
to live long enough to have one. Jim and I had learned
long ago that to depend on David for anything was folly.

How did you convince someone, especially someone

unknown, of a negative? I couldn't take an ad in the personal columns (did newspapers still even have them?) saying, *Dear Drug Dealers, I don't have anything of yours and don't know what you're talking about.*

I could only wish it were that easy.

But obviously someone thought I did, or they wouldn't have thrown that brick through Annie's window.

Of course, it could be that the note was meant for Annie. As a criminal attorney she dealt with a lot of unsavory types and could have legions of bad guys who wanted to mess with her one way or another. That would be a perfectly logical solution, except I had a hard time accepting that it would just happen the day after I found a dead body in my house. Of course, such a coincidence was possible, but not bloody likely.

I didn't even know who and/or what I was up against.

No, that wasn't quite true. There was the someone who had decided to use my house as a storage facility. The boyfriend at Beazler Home Security, perhaps? He kept saying he was innocent, but so far he seemed to be the lynchpin. Maybe he was really the mastermind.

A mastermind who went to a comic book collector's convention in San Francisco? Again, possible, but…

Obviously the dreamboat in the patio-umbrella hat was a bad guy, and the only one I could really identify. He'd chased away that pathetic kid with the fixation on beads, but then he had jumped me in the parking lot, and I'd bet it wasn't because of my beautiful blue eyes. But how did he fit into the pattern? And what about his friend?

How many other bad guys were out there, watching me, waiting until they could—they thought—come get whatever it was they wanted?

Whatever it was that I didn't have…

NINE

THE POUNDING ON my door sent me flying from bed to an ungraceful—and uncomfortable—position on the floor, the Beretta grasped tightly in my trembling hands.

"Lilias? Gal, you still alive in there?"

I stood up unsteadily. "I'm fine, Florene."

"Good to hear your voice. I've been pounding on your door forever. Didn't see you at breakfast, and wondered if you were okay."

There were great bars of sunlight creeping around the blackout curtains. I groaned inwardly as my watch showed nine-thirty. The show opened at ten, so I should be down at the exhibition hall and set up by now.

"I overslept, I guess."

Even through the door her chuckle was unmistakable. "Thought you might have, after that nastiness yesterday. You okay?"

"I'm fine. Thanks for waking me. I'll see you at the show in a few minutes."

"Don't you want me to wait and drive in with you? I got my screamer handy."

Oh, Lord, what had I sunk to when little old ladies no bigger than a child were offering to protect me?

I made myself smile. "No thanks, Florene. I'll see you there."

She left, but only after reassuring me that if I didn't show up she'd come back for me. She would, too—I just didn't know why. We weren't that good friends. Was she a guardian angel or stalking demon?

Moving like a demon myself, I dressed and packed in record time. I should have been at the hall by nine, no matter how badly I had slept. There had been a pinkish tinge of dawn at the edge of the curtains before I had really fallen asleep. Apparently I'd turned off the alarm without ever waking, all of which was a very rare occurrence. Normally I slept very well and woke early, but what had been normal lately?

Sometimes things did seem to work out for the best, though. I had been thinking about what Annie'd said about leaving early. The show closed at eight, because of the long summer day. Usually afterward a bunch of us vendors would come back to the motel and sit around shooting the breeze, inflating our sales figures and swapping horror stories. In the morning we would all take off for our various destinations—some home, some to other shows. It was a pattern I'd followed every time I'd been in Amarillo and almost everywhere else. Not everyone did every show, but after a while on the art/craft fair circuit you pretty much got to know all the vendors casually.

Everyone would be at the hall, unless they were specifically waiting to spy on me, and why would they? I had the biggest day of selling yet to go. By now everyone would have heard the news of last night's attack, from vendors to management to probably half the population of Amarillo, for all I knew. No one would think it unusual for me to be a bit late.

And I was going to take advantage of that.

I carried all my stuff to the van, which stood like a lonely white elephant in the deserted asphalt parking lot, then went back to the office and checked out.

Whatever it cost me in sales, I was going to be on the
road by four, and not to Tulsa, either. Under normal circumstances I would have gone back home for the time
between shows. These were not normal circumstances
and I had no place to go to in Dallas, not now, maybe
not ever again. So I would go elsewhere. My disappearing should cause some consternation and maybe worry
some people. If so, so be it. I would feel safe, and that
was all that counted.

The word had indeed spread. As I trundled my little rolling cart down the aisle I could feel the waves of
curiosity and pity emanating from almost every booth.
And fear. If it could happen to me, it could happen to
them. Whatever the other vendors felt about me, though,
it didn't affect the customers. I made several sales—two
ex-hippie necklaces and a Lover's Rose—before I was
even set up. The fair was crowded and Florene was so
busy she couldn't give me more than a wave and a smile.

Beyond spreading a cloth over the battered table I
only put out what I intended to sell—a rack of ex-hippie
necklaces, a couple of stands of nicer necklaces and accessories, and a cheap but pretty vase of Lover's Roses.
There wasn't time for any of the decorating I loved to
do. Today the serious shoppers were out and everyone
seemed to be benefiting. Florene was never still and Vernon Alquist's routing machine cut sign after sign. Henrietta's laugh never seemed to stop and it was a toss-up
as to which was more irritating.

Even Bernie and Carole Freeman, the couple across
from me, seemed to be doing good business. I knew
them only slightly, but it seemed that at every venue they
had some different product. This time it was microfiber
cloths that, if you believed their sales patter, could clean
glass and carpets and absorb every smidgen of red wine

from white pants. I wouldn't be surprised to hear them claim they could remove paint and heal cuts.

A little after one the crowd thinned as the early bargain hunters went home and the late bargain hunters hadn't started to swarm yet. Most vendors were glad of the semi-lull, as it gave them a chance to re-stock and grab a bite of lunch. I was hungry, but I was going to have to live with it. In the rush to leave the hotel I had neglected to make a sandwich from the supplies in the big ice chest. I'd even neglected to replenish the ice. Food would just have to wait until I was on the road and could eat yet another drive-thru burger and fries. No way was I going to pay the $8 the food concession charged for a tiny little malnourished burger.

"Lilias?"

I had been expecting her. "Hello, Renee."

Renee whatever-her-last-name-was had been running this particular show since its inception at least a dozen years ago. A size-14 bottle blonde poured into size-10 jeans, she wore enormous sparkly rings on every finger. One of the main sources of gossip among the vendors was if they were diamonds or CZs. Considering what she charged for a booth, they could have been diamonds. Even CZs of that size and number were fairly costly.

She shook her exuberantly styled hair. "I just wanted to see with my own eyes that you were all right after last night. You know how stories get exaggerated."

I knew how her insurance rates would go up if a claim were filed for negligence, but I only smiled. This was a good show, one of my best money-makers, and I didn't want to find myself ostracized.

"I'm not hurt. Just a scrape or two. It was more frightening than anything."

She smiled, showing a great number of large teeth too

coffee-stained to be anything but real. "I'm just so glad you weren't hurt. There are a lot of wild stories going around, you know." Her tone was almost accusatory, as if I'd been guilty of spreading them.

"Oh? I haven't heard any. Someone pushed me down, trying to grab my day's take I suppose, and then they were frightened away by Florene's air horn. Of course," I added with malice aforethought, "if Florene hadn't had her air horn, things could have been a lot different. I think there really should be some security in the parking lot, especially around closing time."

Renee blinked as if I had bitten her and I could see my next booth assignment—if I were allowed to return at all—being in the far back by the fire exit.

"Really? We just upgraded the lights."

"The lights weren't on when this happened. They came on as the men were running away."

"Oh. Maybe I should set the timer earlier, then."

"That would help, but a solid security patrol would be better."

She thought about arguing that, but snapped her mouth closed. "Well, we'll just have to see. We've already upped security around here and haven't had a problem until this."

Neatly she implied it was all my fault without the drastic step of making a direct accusation. What was frightening was she might be closer to the truth than she realized.

"It could have happened to anyone," I said easily. "I'm sure you want all your vendors to be safe."

"Of course." Her plastic smile slid into full glory. "I do hope you'll be coming back."

In for a penny, in for a pound. I smiled right back at

her. "Of course, as long as I can get a spot as good as this one."

"We'll have to see what we can do. I just hope there's no bad publicity about this."

"Why would there be?"

We smiled again in perfect understanding and she sashayed off down the aisle. Very few people can be said literally to sashay, but Renee whatever-her-last-name-was had it down to a T.

I sold another two ex-hippie necklaces and a wide beadwork collar that I had thought would never move when Calvin Sullivan walked up to my booth.

"Where are those beads, Lilias?" he asked without any polite preamble. A not-so-faint miasma of liquor floated out on his breath. "Martha changed her mind and wants them back."

My hackles rose of their own volition. While I had always been vaguely neutral about Martha, I'd never liked Calvin. Short, round and oily both in skin and personality, he seemed to carry a perpetual grudge against the world. It was hard to imagine that he and soft, vague Martha were both the Army veterans they claimed to be.

"Huh? She seemed real anxious to get rid of them."

"Well, she's changed her mind." Exasperation began to color his fluty little voice. "I've come to get them back. The deal is off, so you can just hand them over. I'll pay you back, of course. Even give you a little something for your trouble."

"No, Calvin." Perversity is a terrible curse. For days I had regretted the deal, though the cost had been ludicrously low. The amber and semi-precious stones in the curtain alone were worth more than I had paid. But it was more than that. This officious, self-centered little man had always irked me.

His eyes bulged. "What? You can't mean that. It was a mistake."

"The deal is done, Calvin. The beads aren't even here. I put them," I said with spontaneous mendacity, "in a storage unit."

He clenched his fists, then leaned forward across the table, sending a display stand toppling. The smell of liquor was still strong, but now it was underpinned by the stench of an old man in need of a bath. "Well, you have the curtain. You had it hung up yesterday, right here. Where is it?"

At the moment it was wrapped in a tablecloth in a box below the table, but Hell would freeze over before I told this pompous little toad that. I just stared at him.

"It's my curtain. I want it back."

"It's my curtain," I said in level tones. "I bought it from Martha."

"But I tell you it was a mistake." His voice, normally high, was edging toward the stratosphere. "She should never have sold it."

"Why is it so important to you, Calvin? You don't deal in beads."

"I don't have to tell you. I just want those beads back." In spite of the hall's better-than-expected air conditioning, beads of sweat were popping out on his face. It made a most unpleasant aspect.

Now I was getting curious. Why did he want what was at best an undistinguished bunch of craft beads back? There were some nice glass ones in the bags, and the curtain had a few good specimens, but nothing antique or truly rare.

"Sounds like the lady doesn't want to sell them back to you," said a low, slow, drawly voice that sounded horribly familiar. His face was shaded by the same patio umbrella-sized hat, but not even that could soften his expression. It might have been cut from stone.

The beads of moisture on Calvin's face became rivulets. His mouth opened and closed a few times, but no sound came out. At last he squeaked, "They're mine."

"Not if she bought them, they aren't. Why don't you just run along now?"

For a moment it seemed Calvin might stand his ground, but abruptly he snapped his mouth shut, turned on his heel and stalked away, which was a first. Calvin Sullivan's tantrums were legendary on the circuit.

"Annoying little fellow," the cowboy said. "Good customer of yours?"

"Hardly," I said, then almost bit my tongue to keep from saying more. Don't give out information, Annie had said again and again. My opinion of Calvin was none of this man's business. "Hello again. How did your lady like the rose?"

For a half-second his face was completely blank, then he gave a most polished boyish grin. "Thought it was just beautiful. Matter of fact, I think I'll get another one."

I gave him a smile as real as the one he had given me and pulled a beaded rose from the vase. He might be a rat, but there was no reason to turn down a sale.

"Two lady friends? Aren't you extravagant. Or do you just like living dangerously?"

Again he looked disconcerted, but handed over the money. "I hear you had some excitement last night."

I looked him squarely in the face as I made change and handed over one of the generic white paper bags. "It was nothing. Just a cheap thief trying to get my day's take, I guess."

An indefinable emotion flickered in the back of his eyes and was gone. Well, maybe it had. Under the shade of that hat it would be hard to prove he even had eyes. "You'd best take care of yourself. Things can be difficult for a woman alone."

Though the words were uttered in the softest of voices, they carried the unmistakable aura of a threat. I glanced away, suddenly finding it necessary to rearrange the display of bib necklaces.

"Your friend not with you today?"

"My… Oh, no, he had to go in to the office today."

"On a Sunday? What does he do?"

"Insurance."

Another threat? There were many kinds of insurance, and some of them were called protection.

I forced a smile. It probably resembled a death rictus more than a smile, but it was the best I could do. "Well, tell him he needs to get his girlfriend a Lover's Rose too. The show's open until eight tonight."

That was true. The show was open until then. Only I wouldn't be here.

He muttered something polite, then nodded and touched the brim of his hat just like they did in the old Western movies before moseying on. He had barely turned the corner when Florene all but flew into my booth.

"Olly-golly, girl, you got yourself a prime specimen there." She was just about twitching with excitement. "Ain't he just the handsomest thing? Came by yesterday and then again today… Knew when he came by this morning he was smitten with you, Lilias. Hot dawg, a real cowboy. Girl, you've got it made!"

"This morning?" I tried to pick the important things out of the spate of words. "What about this morning?"

In her joy Florene looked almost like an animated apple doll, all smiles and wrinkles. "Why, he came by first thing when I opened up, wantin' to know if you were going to be coming soon. You two make a right pretty couple, you know, both of you so tall and you so fair..."

She babbled on, but I paid no attention. So he'd been looking for me, huh? Did he just want to know if I recognized him from the night before? If so, walking straight up to me in public was a pretty dumb move. What if I had started screaming that he was my attacker?

Right. Who would believe it if I accused a man who looked like a soap star of being a snatch-and-grab thief?

Somehow I felt as if he wanted something more from me, and it had nothing to do with the romantic drivel Florene was still spouting. I had lived long enough to know that he was up to no good. All too often men who traded on their rugged good looks could never be trusted. Jim Ruiz had been the only one who had ever been able to pull that off.

Who was this man? I didn't intend to stay long enough to find out.

I was on the road by three.

After the fastest pack-up session in my entire life and a garbled explanation to Florene, which she would no doubt translate into an elopement with the rough-hewn cowboy, I all but ran out of the building, tossed everything into the van and sped away.

It would be nice to say that I drove a deliberately circuitous route in Amarillo so as to elude any possible followers, but the truth was I flat got lost. At least by the time I did find the highway, it was a reasonable certainty no one was tailing me.

The sad thing was that no one would really have to. For the first time I almost regretted keeping Jim's van. It was handy to have something that held so much, but it was conspicuous. Very few things on the road other than eighteen-wheelers and commercial vehicles were quite so enormous. On the highway it was visible for miles.

To make things worse, half the vendors in Amarillo were going to the Tulsa art fair, and probably half of them knew I was going to be there. Most of us didn't bother to go home in between venues unless it was real close. There was a subculture of traveling artists, and we all knew the motels in every town on the circuit that would give us a break on rates. Finding me would be easy as pie. If anyone was looking, they could save themselves the trouble of tailing me and just be waiting when I got to Tulsa.

At least, they could if I were going to Tulsa. I was tired of feeling like a target. I was going to ground.

The shortest route from Amarillo to Tulsa is to take I-40 East straight across to Oklahoma City, then go northeast on I-44. A couple of hours of fast driving over flat open country and you're there. Instead I went southeast on State Highway 287 to Wichita Falls, then zig-zagged due east through southern Oklahoma on small state roads, passing through towns with musical names like Waurika, Tishomingo and Atoka until I crossed over into Arkansas at DeQueen. The country had changed from the open prairie of the Panhandle and Oklahoma into the fringe hills and woods of the Ouachita Mountains.

Yes, I could have gotten back to Dallas in less time than it took to get here. There was a certain neat logic in returning to the big city, where Annie was across the street and Patches and Detective Costigan were there to protect me, but all I could think of was I didn't want to go home to a house that was in the middle of renovation. A house where a man had been murdered. A house that had been destroyed by someone looking for something, where I could be a sitting duck in what used to be my home.

I had stopped at a large anonymous chain grocery in Atoka and bought supplies—coffee, lunch meat, milk, eggs, a few cans of stuff so I wouldn't starve while in isolation. Normally I would have called Jim's cousin, custodian of the cabin that had been in the Ruiz family for generations, for permission to use it, but I didn't want anyone to know where I was. No one in the family used it much any more. After Jim's death I had been reassured that I was still part of the family and could use it any time. I hadn't been there since Jim and I had gone together half a dozen years or so ago, and the memories of being there, with him, were another battle I would have to fight.

At first it seemed the road to the cabin itself had disappeared. I had to drive past it twice before seeing the ghost of a path beyond the overgrowth. By now it was almost black dark, giving the woods an eerie, menacing appearance. Apparently no one had been here in a very long time. I hoped the cabin still stood, though surely someone in the family would have told me if it had been destroyed. I inched the van slowly through the tangle of creepers and weeds and hopeful saplings and tried not to think of what those protesting plants were doing to the paint job.

The road wasn't much better, though to call it a road was a wild exaggeration. Jim's cousin simply had the path graded every couple of years, but the runoff from the mountain rains quickly gouged and rutted the naked earth. It was well past due for a grading and I kept muttering prayers every time the low-slung van scraped the rocky ground. All I needed was to crack the oil pan or break an axle out here.

The cabin, by contrast, looked neat and well cared for in the glare of my headlights, though it would never be beautiful. Squat and sprawling, made of native wood and stone, it almost appeared to have grown from the ground itself rather than having been constructed by man. Someone had obviously been here recently, I decided, then gulped as I saw a faint glow of light at the windows and a wisp of smoke drift upward from the chimney.

So someone was here. Well, I hadn't called Jim's cousin and this was the result. Surely they had extra bedspace for the night—there was no way I was going to try to go back down that road tonight, no way at all—and if they didn't, well, it wouldn't be the first time I had spent the night in the van.

The door opened before I got all the way across the noisy old wooden porch. The light from inside cast the occupant into silhouette, but didn't hide the fact he was one of the tallest men I had ever seen, topping my own respectable height by more than a foot.

Neither did it hide that he was pointing a very large pistol right at me.

TEN

"Aunt Lilias?"

My heart started to beat again, albeit somewhat errati-
cally. The giant lowered the pistol instantly and stepped
back, gesturing for me to come into the room.

"Don't you know me, Aunt Lilias? I'm Toby."

Toby? The youngest son of Jim's youngest sister, Toby
had been a tall, skinny, gangly kid of thirteen or so the
last time I had seen him, so he had to be at least eighteen
or nineteen now. And he was even taller, still skinny and
gangly, but this time it was as a man, not a boy. A very
tall man. Aside from his height, there was no Ruiz in
Toby. His curly hair, pale complexion and sweet expression were direct copies of his father, a kind if somewhat
forgetful man who managed a TV station somewhere
in Minnesota.

I stepped into the enormous main room, somewhat
disconcerted at how watery my knees still felt. Fear was
such an embarrassing thing at times.

"I didn't know that anyone was expected up here,"
Toby was saying as he closed and locked the door behind me.

"Who were *you* expecting?" I asked in a somewhat
shaky voice, gesturing toward the small cannon in his
hand. It looked to be a long-barreled .44 mag revolver,
suitable for stopping trucks or exploding people.

"No one. Just a precaution. There's a lot of drug traffic up in these hills. Uncle Arthur hid this up here a couple of years ago. Didn't they tell you?"

I shook my head. Drugs here, too, in this remote and leafy Eden? Was there no place safe? Unbidden, a faint memory surfaced. In one of the round-robin what-the-family's-doing letters someone had mentioned that the cabin had been broken into several times. I assumed it had been hunters, or kids looking for a place to party. No one had mentioned drugs.

"I haven't been up here in a long time," I murmured, wanting to make sure I had control of my voice. "I decided to come at the last minute."

"And I scare the life out of you." Toby's tone was merry. "Come over here and sit down by the fire. I'm afraid there's no electricity."

Though it was fairly cool at night here in the mountains it was really too warm for a fire, but I could see why he had built one. The great room was almost stark, but full of shadowy nooks and crannies that seemed somewhat sinister in spite of the half-dozen oil lamps that struggled against the dark. The fire gave the room a feeling of cheeriness. No, not cheeriness exactly, but something close to it.

I sat in the big wooden chair by the fireplace. "You didn't get here early enough to have it turned on?"

Toby looked away. "No, I've been here a couple of days. I—I just didn't want anyone to know I was here. If I asked for the electricity to be turned on, the office would contact Uncle Pete for authorization and he would call my parents. There's no keeping any secrets in this family. You know that."

"You don't... You've run away from home?"

He tried to look abashed, but it didn't work. "Yeah. From college, actually."

The Applegate contingent had been so proud of Toby's winning a complete, all-inclusive scholarship—for basketball, of course. It'd been the talk of the family for months. He'd had his pick of schools and, to his parents' displeasure, had chosen a small, academically rich college in Pennsylvania. From which he'd apparently bolted.

"You mean no one knows you're here?"

"Just you."

"But…" I shook my head. "I want to hear everything, but first of all I've got to have something to eat."

"About all I've got is canned chili…"

"I brought food," I said. "You see, I'm sort of running away too."

It didn't take but a minute or two to bring in the ice chest and my overnight bag. Toby watched me set the alarm on the van with curious eyes, but didn't say anything. Once the front door was securely locked again, I scrounged pots from the kitchen, took a longing glance at the useless electric stove and proceeded to heat up some soup in the fireplace. I put Toby to toasting bread, using the blackened old pieces of wire that had been used for that purpose probably since the cabin was built several generations ago.

Two cans of soup and probably half a loaf of bread later, Toby was at last full. He smiled with repletion and said for the umpteenth time how good it was.

"It's just soup."

"Yeah. It's not chili, and that's good."

"Don't tell me that's all you've been eating."

"No money. Luckily someone left a case of chili here in the cabin." He shrugged. "Besides, I didn't want to go into town where I'd be seen. Someone would be sure to see me and tell someone in the family."

I thought about calling him a silly boy, but he wasn't

a boy any more and, having had some experience of the Ruiz family telegraph, he wasn't being all that silly. "So why did you leave college?"

"The semester was over."

He was being evasive, which reminded me of David. Please God, he wasn't another David. Or maybe it was all boys. I fixed him with my beady-eyed "teacher" glare. "There's more to it than that."

He looked away uncomfortably, then sighed. "I'm not going back."

"Why, Toby?" Visions of reasons danced through my head, each more horrific than the last. Failure. A girl. Criminal activity.

He sighed again. "I hate basketball, and when you have a basketball scholarship, they expect you to eat, breathe, sleep, probably even dream basketball. It's just that I'm so damn tall. I'm not really that good at it, anyway."

Having seen him play as a youngster I wondered at that, but it was his feelings that counted on this subject, not mine. I had received a storm of questions when I'd suddenly quit teaching for reasons I still refused to discuss.

"Anyway, Mom and Dad went all ballistic when I told them I wanted to quit college."

"I can see why. College is pretty much a necessity these days."

"Oh, I want to go to college, but I want to sit out a year and earn some money, so I can go back and study what I want to study. It might take me an extra year, working my way through, but at least I wouldn't be weighed down with all that basketball crap. I mean, everyone looks at me."

"You're kind of hard to miss," I said, trying for a light

note. I was almost dizzy with relief. At least it was nothing seriously illegal. Having raised a child like David gave one a different perspective.

Toby grinned. "Yeah, but you know what I mean. They don't see me, they see the basketball star who's going to win championships… Until we lose, and then I'm about as popular as a terrorist."

"So what do you want to study?"

"Math. Math and physics." His long, thin face lit up. "I love numbers. I know I'm probably not good enough to get into any of the space programs or anything like that, but I could teach. If things got bad enough, I could become an accountant. They work with numbers."

So far as I had ever known, the Ruiz family had pretty much been among the perpetually mathematically challenged. Toby must have gotten something from his father besides his looks.

"So why numbers?"

"There's a…" he hesitated. His hands flopped helplessly in inarticulate frustration, imperiling not only his soup dish but the lamp and perhaps even the side table on which it stood. We both leaped to steady everything. At last he said, more calmly, "…a logic, an elegance about them. The way they interact and are always so predictable… I'm not explaining it very well."

At least he's interested in something normal, I thought. *Interested and willing to work for what he wants.* Chrissy and Hank Applegate should be supporting him and his choices, not fighting him. Of course, they had never had to deal with a son like David.

They didn't know how lucky they were.

"So you're going to hide out until when?"

"I don't know. I came here to think it out."

"How did you get here? I didn't see another car."

He grinned impishly. "I hitched. Got rides as far as DeQueen, then hiked the rest of the way."

"But it's miles."

"Not so far if you go cross-country."

And what if he had run into some of those drug people who had broken into the cabin? Apparently the idea had never occurred to him, or perhaps he was uneasy only at night. My mother-gene, which once turned on never really turns off again, shuddered at what might have been.

"So what about you? What brings you up here?"

I shouldn't have told him. For all his size and seeming maturity, he was still little more than a boy. All the rational arguments made no difference, for suddenly my entire story was spilling out, from the moment I'd noticed the odd smell at my front door until my erratic flight from Amarillo. I told him about everything—the dead body, the note thrown through Annie's window, the way my house had been used, the vandalism, the cowboy, the assault the night before and Florene coming to my rescue.

Toby stared. "Wow. That's as good as the movies."

"Not when you're living it, it's not. So I came here to hide for a while."

"Are you going on to Tulsa from here?"

"I don't know. I need the money, but it seems so stupid to walk into the lion's mouth..."

"Are you sure there's a lion there?" he asked after a moment of thought, his face serious. "Could this cowboy who jumped you just have been a cheap crook out for some quick cash and a quick flirt? He doesn't have to be connected to that man in your house or any of the other stuff."

I thought for a moment. Could I have misread things

so much? Had the business with my house and the dead man so unsettled me I was seeing spooks where there was nothing? My nerves were admittedly raw—whose wouldn't be, after everything that had gone on? Was that totally crazy?

Oddly enough, the idea that I might be going crazy was somehow comforting. I didn't think there was anything to fear from monsters who existed only in my head.

"The brick wasn't in my head," I said, probably confusing Toby no end. "The brick that was thrown through Annie's window. The note said I had something of theirs and they wanted it back."

Toby thought for a moment. "Did the note have your name on it?"

"No, just the message."

"Then what makes you so sure it was for you? Isn't your friend Annie a criminal attorney? It might have been for her."

"I'd thought of that," I said. "And believe me I'd like to believe it, but right after a man is murdered in my house and the place vandalized? That's a big coincidence." Still, it made me feel good that someone else came up with the same idea. That meant it might be true.

He nodded. "Could be, but it's not impossible. Statistically…"

"If you start quoting numbers at me, I'll call your mother myself and turn you in."

"You wouldn't do that," he said with a grin, but there was a momentary flash of fear across his face. "Not when I'm going to be your assistant and traveling companion."

"What?" I squeaked.

"It's the perfect solution. You said you have to go to these shows, but you're afraid to go alone. If I go with you, you won't be alone. I'm strong. I can carry things for you and watch the booth if you want to get out for a few minutes. I can even bring in customers. Pretend I don't know you and tell everyone about the beautiful bead bargains at this booth I found." He grinned from ear to ear. The effect was startlingly impish, if I could imagine an imp almost as tall as a house. "Heck, if you want you can tell people I'm your boy toy. I hear younger men are very popular with older women now."

"Toby!"

"Don't you want to be thought of as a cougar?"

"Toby!"

Smiling, he ignored my startled indignation. "And my folks can't object if I'm spending part of the summer with you. You're my aunt, after all. Uncle Jim would have wanted me to look after you. Besides, I don't know if I can face any more chili."

I couldn't help it. I laughed. After heaven only knew how many meals of it, the boy might never eat chili again.

As for his being my traveling companion—the idea was ridiculous. First of all, I wasn't fully convinced that there was no danger. Who was it who said, 'Just because you're paranoid doesn't mean someone isn't out to get you?' There was no way I could put this sweet, gentle giant at risk if there was even the barest risk to our safety. Besides that, there would be the additional expense of a hotel room for him and feeding him—good grief, filling a bottomless pit would be nothing compared to keeping this boy fed. It just wouldn't work at all, and I said so as gently as possible.

It didn't faze him a bit. "We'll talk more about it in the morning," he said, sounding so much like Jim it tore at my heart. "Right now let's just go to bed. You're probably exhausted. You didn't happen to bring any cinnamon rolls with you, did you?"

I shook my head, not trusting my voice. Cinnamon rolls had been Jim's favorite Sunday morning breakfast. Apparently they were Toby's too, even if tomorrow was Monday.

"Well," Toby sighed, disappointment coloring his voice, "that's okay. When do you need to be in Tulsa?"

"Thursday."

"Not 'til then? That's cool." His face split into a grin. "Tomorrow I'll bring your bead stuff in and you can rest or work or do whatever you want to do until Thursday morning, then we can scoot over to Tulsa. Trip shouldn't take more than a couple of hours."

For all that it was almost exactly what I had planned to do, I felt a certain reluctance. Somehow Toby being here changed everything. He might be just a boy, but he was a very sensible boy, and after three days of company I might not feel so strongly about going out on my own again.

"I'm not sure..."

"Aw, come on, Aunt Lilias. You need to rest. You look awful, all tired and strung out."

"Thanks," I snapped, made more angry by the fact it was true. "One thing we have to do is let your mother know you're all right. She'll be out of her mind with worry."

"Oh, no, she won't. I left her and Dad a voice mail before I left, telling them that I needed to think for a while, so I was going traveling. I told them everything would be fine." He grinned, obviously proud of himself.

"Words guaranteed to strike terror into any parent's heart," I said with heavy irony. "I won't tell her where you are, just that you're with me. Then Thursday morn-

ing I'll put you on a bus for home and you can talk it out
with them face to face."

He looked at me and for a moment I could see what
he would look like in later years, when he'd finished ma-
turing. His voice was slow, but his words were decisive.
"You don't get it, Aunt Lilias, do you? I'm a man now. I
need to make my own decisions, plan my own life. You
and Mom and Dad still see me as a kid. I'm young, yes,
but I'm grown up. I know what I want to do and what it
takes to do it and what risks are involved, and I'm the
one who has to deal with it all. I can't go on letting everyone else make my decisions for me."

My heart broke. David was a dozen years older than
this boy, but of the two Toby was by far the more mature.

"I'm not trying to interfere in your life," I said at last.
"I'm just trying to save your mother and father some
grief. They have to know you're all right."

"Okay. We can call them from Tulsa."

"You're not going to Tulsa. We can call them here
and now."

"Nope. Phone's not on."

I laughed. "I've got my cell."

He laughed right back at me, and it was only a little
superior. "It won't work up here. This place is a dead
zone."

He was right. The little magnifying glass icon circled
the screen endlessly, showing that the phone was search-
ing futilely for service. I muttered and turned the thing
off. Living my life mainly in cities I had forgotten that
there were places where cell phones didn't work.

Once the idea of being isolated from the world had
been wonderful. Jim and I hadn't had the money for a
proper honeymoon, so we had come up here for a week.
Only two people deeply in love could have enjoyed such

primitive conditions for a honeymoon, but we were and we had. We'd come up here many times since, both alone and as part of family gatherings, but none of those trips had been as special as the first.

I had not been here since Jim's death, though the family had been very good about asking me often.

"All right," I said as if it were my choice, "we'll wait until I take you into town for the bus. We'll have to let her know you're coming, anyway."

Toby smiled. "We'll call her from Tulsa."

"You're not going to Tulsa."

ELEVEN

WE ENDED UP leaving for Tulsa on Wednesday.

During those peaceful two days I did get a lot of work done, and some resting too. Sitting on the cabin's big apron porch and working on Annie's roses was just about as close to heaven as one could get in this lifetime. Toby seemed fascinated by the beading process and after a while—mainly to shut him up about all the reasons I should take him with me—I taught him a few of the basics of beaded flowers. After only one or two tries he turned out some very credible simple leaves.

We left early because my stock of food had run out, which meant there would have to be a run to the store in town anyway, and I was thoroughly sick of cooking in the fireplace. I guess I have no pioneer-gene at all.

Loading the van was child's play with Toby to do the heavy lifting and sorting. I should have taken advantage of the time to rearrange and go through and inspect all the junk and boxes that seemed to breed in the back, but just sitting and beading had been so heavenly everything else could just wait. Toby effortlessly moved things that left me gasping and by judicious arrangement made so much more space it was amazing.

Getting the van down that horror of a road was more frightening than getting it up, because in daylight I could see what had been mercifully obscured by darkness. We made it though, and eventually my fingers loosened their death grip on the wheel. By the time we hit the highway I was relaxed and almost resigned to my fate.

Toby was coming with me, of course, at least as far as Tulsa. Buses and planes left Tulsa for Minnesota every day, and as long as Chrissy and Hank knew he was with me, a couple of hours more couldn't matter, could they?

Once we got to the Indian Nation Turnpike I decided to use Toby and let him drive. I thought I was being quite clever—if his hands were on the wheel, he couldn't stop me from calling his parents.

His face fell when he saw me turn on the cell phone. "What are you doing?"

"Calling your parents. They have to know you're all right."

The screen was blinking. My voice mail box was full. It had never been full before. Resolutely I pulled up Chrissy's work number and pushed "call."

The next few minutes were not pleasant. Between tears and anger and demands to speak to Toby *this minute* (which I refused) Chrissy made quite a scene. She had always been the emotional one of the Ruiz clan and today she more than lived up to her reputation. I'd thought Toby was exaggerating about the way his mother would react. He wasn't. Finally I simply shouted Toby was all right and I would call her later when she was less emotional, then hung up.

"Told you," he said in a soft voice.

What I had found amazing was not that she was relieved to hear he was safe. She sort of just accepted that he would be. She was blazingly angry that he was even thinking about giving up the scholarship. She didn't want him to come home, she wanted him to go back to school *this very minute,* presumably to wait around until they opened the doors for fall semester. At that moment I wanted to adopt him.

"I owe you an apology, Toby. Is your dad the same way?"

"Pretty much. They're okay, they just don't like their plans changed."

"Obviously."

I stared at my phone. Twenty-six voice mails. What on earth was going on?

I listened to them all, though after the first two or three it really wasn't necessary. Twenty-five calls, all from Annie, ranging from friendly to businesslike to angry to nearly hysterical. Where was I? Was I all right? Why wasn't I calling in? What had happened? The other call was a blessedly sane one from my dentist's office, reminding me it was time to schedule a yearly cleaning and check-up.

There was a kindly deity overseeing me, I decided, for the receptionist at Annie's office said she was in a conference and would I like to leave a message on her voice mail? I did, apologizing and telling her I was all right and that perhaps I had been a little overwrought in imagining that people were after me. I explained about the Ruiz cabin and how I hadn't realized that cell phones didn't work there because the last time I was there I didn't own a cell phone. I didn't mention Toby because he would be on his way to Minnesota as soon as we got to Tulsa.

"Who's that?" Toby asked after I rang off.

"My best friend Annie. I should have checked in with her before going up to the cabin. It was very rude of me just to disappear like that."

"You were pretty strung out, Aunt Lilias. And like

you said, you didn't know cell phones wouldn't work there. She'll understand."

Annie did not understand. We had barely gone twenty miles before the phone rang. I wasn't even given a chance to say hello.

"Lilias, I could kill you for this. Do you know how frightened I've been? We've had the Tulsa police checking all the hotels and the hospitals for you."

"Annie—"

I couldn't get a word in, edge- or otherwise. Short of hanging up I had no choice but to sit and listen to her. It was the least I could do, because she must have been really scared. I had never heard her so upset.

Finally she slowed for breath and I said quickly, "Annie, I'm really sorry. I had no idea you'd get so hysterical about it, but I don't think—"

"They broke into your house again, Lilias."

My throat seemed to close of its own volition and I could only make strange gurgling noises. Toby looked over and immediately began slowing the van, pulling over to the wide shoulder.

"What's wrong?" he asked. "Are you all right?"

"Who's that?" Annie asked.

"What did they do to my house?" I asked.

None of us sounded normal.

"Who is that?" Annie demanded again.

"I'm fine," I murmured to Toby. "Let's go on."

The van gave a little shudder as it went from the gravel shoulder back onto the smooth highway. I gave a little shudder too. When would this nightmare end? Would I ever be able to live peacefully in that house again, or would I always be in eternal expectation of someone breaking in?

"Lilias, have you picked up a hitchhiker? Don't you

know how dangerous that is?" Annie's voice was becoming shrill.

"He's my nephew. What happened to my house?"

"Your nephew? You're babysitting? Or is it really your nephew?" she asked, adding the last in a completely different tone after a minuscule pause. Annie's mind works in convoluted ways.

"My house, Annie! What did they do to my house?"

She sighed. "Not much. It's all done except for some touchups. At least it was. Sometime Monday night someone broke in. Broke out the dining room window, you know the one in the corner that opens on the back yard?"

I knew. Right under the spreading lavender tree and hidden in deep shadow. Between the tall fence, the house next door and that enormous shrub on steroids, the window was next to invisible. Perfect place for a housebreaker to get in without being seen.

"What did they do?" Visions of walls—fixed, newly painted and as of yet unseen by me—once again holed and destroyed danced before my closed eyes.

"That's the odd part. Nothing. Aside from the smashed window, and a couple of things moved, nothing. No destruction, no damage, nothing. Everything had been searched, of course, and Jim's boxes…"

The wave of relaxation that had hit me vanished and once again I was painfully tense. "Yes? What about Jim's boxes?"

"They were moved. Almost all of them, but none were opened." Annie sounded as confused as I was. "I can't say exactly, because everything in the garage was stirred around, but I don't think any are missing. They were just moved. They were also absolutely grubby. I bet you haven't dusted them since you put them in there."

I was speechless. The few things left in the house

were pretty worthless, monetarily. Whatever valuables I had—my late mother's sterling flatware, my few pieces of decent jewelry—had been moved to Annie's. All my necessary documents—passport, probate papers, deed, etc.—were in the bank. There were some fairly valuable things in Jim's boxes, valuable in the money sense, not just sentimental. A burglar could have found some things more than worth his time if he had cared to look.

If he were an ordinary thief looking for things to sell.

If he weren't... What could he have been looking for?

I had spoken aloud, for Annie said thickly, "I don't know. I couldn't tell where anything was missing. What is going on, Lilias?"

"I don't know," I said and my voice was choked with unshed tears. "I wish I did, but I don't."

"Anyway," Annie went on, sounding more like her brisk self. "Don has replaced the window and cleaned up the mess. We didn't touch Jim's boxes other than to be sure they hadn't been opened, because we didn't know if you had them in any order."

"What about the alarm?"

"It was off. Don hasn't been setting it. We thought... Anyway, we're keeping it set now, and we've changed the code. I'll give you the new one when you get home. When are you coming home, by the way?"

When was I going home? Right now the neat little patio house on a neat little cul-de-sac in one of the better areas of Dallas wasn't home. Home was where you were supposed to be able to tune out the world and all its problems. Home was where you were supposed to feel safe. I didn't know if it ever would be home again.

"I don't know," I said slowly. "I'll let you know." After a few more apologies and platitudes I hung up. Yeah, she could give me the new code when I got back, but I was not only changing codes immediately, I was changing companies. If I stayed, I might even put in a portcullis and a moat stocked with piranhas.

Wisely, Toby was silent as I thought.

What were people looking for in my house? It had not only been searched, it had darn near been destroyed in the process. Surely anything that was to be found would have been found in the first, unbelievably vicious search. What could anyone have thought might have survived that?

Unless whoever did the second search didn't know about the first one.

Two sets of criminals looking for an unknown something in my house? In spite of being totally illogical, the thought was unbelievably depressing.

What could it be? Goodman had been involved in drugs. I didn't know anything about drugs other than what I saw on television, but supposedly small amounts were worth lots of money. The question was, how small? And how much? People were killed for pocket change today, but this seemed more sophisticated.

There couldn't be anything in the house. If the first searchers hadn't found it, Don would have during construction.

But…what if the second searchers didn't know or believe that it had been found?

Whatever *it* was.

I shook my head, tired of the whole puzzle. There didn't seem to be any logic to it. Why my house? Other houses had been used, but they hadn't been vandalized. Just mine. I should have asked Annie if any of the other storage houses had been broken into, but I didn't want to call her back. She was busy. She might not know. Maybe

I didn't want to know. If they hadn't, it meant my house was special, and I didn't know why.

"Your house okay?" Toby asked after a while.

"Just a broken window."

"This is the second break-in, right?"

"I think. It's the third if you count when that man was killed. I know—I think I know—it's the first since the place has been repaired."

"Any idea of what they're looking for?"

I shook my head wearily, then closed my eyes and leaned back against the seat. The bazillion-dollar question: What did everyone want?

"You're hungry," Toby said with finality. "I am too. McAlester is just a few miles away. What about some lunch?"

Perhaps it was auto-suggestion or something, but suddenly I was ravenous. "Sounds like a plan."

Toby wheeled off the highway at the first McAlester exit, then he and the attendant waited patiently as I dug out money to pay the toll. I was going to have to remember that Toby had no money. Any grown man who will eat canned chili at least three times a day for several days is guaranteed to be broke.

We stopped at the first hamburger stand we came to, a ramshackle place called Pop's that had the look of a local cultural icon. The parking lot was full and inside every table was full. I was on the verge of suggesting that we go somewhere else when it happened.

Toby stood at least a head over most people. When everyone else was sitting down the effect magnified. He was very noticeable to say the least. The waitress came up immediately, looking like a god from Olympus had suddenly descended. Magically a table was produced for us and our orders taken with lightning speed.

"Does this always happen to you?" I asked.

He nodded, slurping at his Coke. "Pretty much. It gets embarrassing."

I took a deep drink of my diet version. It had been days since either of us had had any kind of soda, and the bubbles were unexpectedly refreshing. "Handy is what I'd call it. We could have waited half an hour or more."

Toby's eyes sparkled. "I never wait."

"And how do you manage that?"

"I don't like basketball, but I don't mind using it. Everyone just assumes I'm a player and they treat me accordingly." He grinned. "And sometimes I push it just a little. No one is going to make the new draftee for whatever NBA team is closest wait, are they?"

I stared at him with equal parts of amusement, amazement and horror. Even after a lifetime of dealing with David's self-serving schemes my mother-gene was appalled that Toby could be so dishonest. The rest of me was astonished that a member of the steadfast, largely unimaginative and highly respectable Ruiz clan could even have thought of such a ploy. All of me was hard put to keep from laughing at the spectacles he must have created.

"You're terrible."

"I know," he replied without a trace of repentance. His grin grew wider. "But God gave me this body, so I'm just using God's gift."

"God is probably going to smite you royally for it too."

"Probably," he agreed amiably. "But not today, and definitely not before lunch."

Our burger baskets and extra sides of onion rings appeared with amazing speed. After a diet provided by a succession of national chain drive-thrus I had all but forgotten what it was like to eat real homemade food in a little mom-and-pop place. The onion rings alone would have made a decent meal. The burgers were fresh and roughly the same diameter as saucers. The French fries were thickly cut and sprinkled with coarse salt, and there were enough of them on each plate to fill an ice bucket. I plowed manfully through mine, enjoying every bite until the last five or six, when my neck suddenly felt at least a foot long and my jeans several sizes too small.

Toby swiped up some ketchup and chomped on his last French fry. "That was good. Can I have another?"

"Another? You're kidding. How could you possibly eat another basket that big?"

He grinned. "Easy. It's not chili. Or can't we afford it?" he added suddenly, his face crumpling with real distress.

"We can afford it," I said and gestured toward the watchful waitress, who came immediately. When the second order came—with remarkable speed—Toby lit into it with the same gusto as he had the first. I watched in bemused fascination.

This just proved why Toby had to go back home. First of all, it would be moral cowardice if he didn't. Second, and probably most important, I could go broke just feeding him. Comparing him to a bottomless pit had been a profound understatement. Third, I would have to spring for a hotel room for him. He was much too big a boy to be sharing a room with his old auntie, however innocently.

No, once we reached Tulsa Toby would be put on a plane for Minnesota and I would head back to Dallas. To find what? I didn't know and I didn't know if I really wanted to know. In a way this was like the time right after Jim died. My entire world had changed without my

permission or input and I wanted it back the way it had
been even as I knew it was impossible.

I drove the rest of the way into Tulsa, my mind wor-
rying with a thousand things as a replete and somnolent
Toby dozed in a hamburger-induced coma. In spite of
it, though, he had managed to convince me to let him
stay through this show. At least, he had pleaded, until
his parents calmed down a little. I finally gave in, as
much to protect him from his parents' wrath as for my
own selfish reasons. The closer we got to Tulsa the more
apprehensive I became, and the idea of a strong, sturdy
young partner was increasingly appealing.

Toby was sort of awake when we finally reached the
motel where I always stayed. It was a middle-grade chain
inn, but the closest to the park where the Chestnut Plaza
Art Fair was held. Besides that, they gave very nice rates
to the vendors.

Not today, though. The desk clerk was most apologetic, but since I was a day early there was no way
they could accommodate me for tonight, and absolutely
no extra rooms were available for the run of the show.
She was very nice, but very firm that nothing could be
done. At least, she was until Toby walked in, wondering what was taking me so long. By now I should have
been prepared for Toby's effect on people—women especially—but it was still astonishing to see this portly
and unabashedly middle-aged woman melt when Toby
leaned over the desk. He said something about recom-
mending another hotel, though this was where we really
wanted to be, and could she…?

The clerk fluttered and smiled and clicked madly on
the computer, finally saying there were two rooms that
had not been guaranteed, but they weren't together. Was

that all right? Toby assured her it was and waited for me to hand over my credit card, smiling at her all the time.

I was beginning to feel positively incompetent in dealing with people. Simple good manners and logic apparently didn't stand a chance these days. Annie could boss people around like a drill sergeant, while Toby just had to smile—to women, at least. God help all of us if Annie and Toby ever decided to work together. It was frightening to contemplate what their combined talents could do.

Still, thanks to Toby's intervention we had rooms. Mine was on the third floor and Toby's on the second, but at least they were on the same side of the motel and, joyously, that side was away from the freeway. Sometimes you can be satisfied with very small things.

With Toby's help, moving in was very easy. One trip brought up not only my big bag and overnighter, but Toby's backpack and the workbox containing Annie's crystal roses as well. It was barely late afternoon and the prospect of a leisurely evening was enticing.

"What," Toby asked, "about dinner?"

I stared. "Dinner? After the lunch we ate?"

"That was hours ago, Aunt Lilias. Aren't you hungry?"

I felt as if I might possibly be hungry again sometime around Christmas, but it was becoming obvious that feeding Toby was going to be a full-time occupation.

"Let's take a little rest, then we can get something to eat. We have to go to the grocery store for lunch stuff anyway."

"Lunch? Don't these places have food courts?"

"Yes, but I don't have enough money for us to eat there. I always take a sandwich. We'll find something to fill you up," I said with more confidence than I felt.

The air filled with a remote screeching. I hardly paid attention, being used to the random noises of city life, but Toby jumped as if he had been prodded with a sharp stick. He flung himself out of the room and, not even pausing at the elevator, took the outside stairs down two and three at a time. I followed, more slowly.

"What is it?" I shouted.

"The alarm," he shouted over his shoulder. Already he was almost to the parking lot. "Someone's breaking into the van!"

TWELVE

OF COURSE WHOEVER it was had vanished by the time
we reached the parking lot. Thankfully the van was
unharmed and whoever it was hadn't gotten in. I only
wished I had an idea of who it was.

"Probably," Toby said with the uncanny wisdom of
youth, "they just grabbed the handle and tried to open
the door. That's enough to set off the alarm."

I unlocked the driver's door and switched off the in-
cessant shrieking, then relocked the door. "I've only just
started using the alarm," I said slowly. "They probably
weren't expecting it."

This off-freeway side of the motel the parking lot
was close to empty. In an area that could hold probably
a hundred vehicles there were no more than a dozen or
so, widely spaced as if each were staking out its own
territory. Except for one sad-looking compact car they
were all SUVs or pick-ups or vans, though none as enormous as mine, and I could probably guess who most
belonged to.

"Wonder if they broke into any of these other cars?"
Toby looked around as if expecting to see open doors
and shattered glass.

With a terrifying surety the fears that had seemed
so ridiculous in the cabin came back in full bloom. I
would be willing to bet that no other vehicle had been
touched. Only mine.

Why?

Convulsively I hugged my purse, hung over my shoulder and forgotten until now. It contained my cash, my credit cards, my gun—everything I had that was valuable. That I thought was valuable. Surely no simple sneak thief would think anyone would leave their money in a van in a nearly empty parking lot.

No, someone wanted something they thought was in my van. They hadn't found it in my house, so in their minds it had to be in the van.

Whatever *it* was.

"Aunt Lilias? Are you all right?"

I nodded yes, though it was a lie. I was far from all right. My life was being taken out of my hands and I didn't like it.

"Toby, run upstairs and make sure that both our rooms are securely locked." I didn't remember closing the door to mine when the shrieking started, not that anyone would find anything up there. I just didn't want to return to find my work boxes upended and my personal items pawed through. "Then come back down. We're going through this van with a fine tooth comb."

Doubtless Toby would rather have gone in search of dinner, but he went willingly and was back before I could get half the boxes pulled out.

With Toby's enthusiastic if somewhat bewildered help the job went quickly, and I didn't find anything I didn't expect to. The ice chest, containing nothing but a few leftovers and a lot of lukewarm water. Four flat boxes of Lover's Roses. One box of assorted bib necklaces. The plastic sack of ex-hippie necklaces and bracelets I had been working on. One box of assorted earrings, which I had forgotten about and not put out. It went up into the front seat for the moment. Those earrings, showy and

easy to make, had been some of my best sellers. A rack
for the earrings. A black velvet board for the better necklaces. My tool kit. A box of miscellaneous bead flowers,
including my poor battered bluebonnet. Three beaded
floral arrangements, each in a pretty vase complete with
floral foam and moss. The box with the beaded curtain.
A box full of miscellaneous stuff, including the loose
bead jar, some tools and findings, and a bunch of odd
bits and pieces. A messy mass of old sheets I used as
dust covers. The folding metal chair.

And…Martha's boxes of beads. Of course. Annie
and the policemen and I had gone through everything
in the van and the shabby liquor boxes had been shoved
back into the van with everything else. I hadn't thought
of them again.

I poked desultorily through each box. The bags of
beads hadn't changed. Clunky undrilled wood and some
halfway decent glass and some absolutely awful plastic. If Calvin Sullivan showed up again demanding the
beads back I'd just sell them to him for what I'd paid.
Nasty stuff, most of it.

"You know, Aunt Lilias," Toby said, hefting the boxes
back into the van at my direction, "this'd be a lot easier
if you had shelves in here."

"Shelves?"

"Yeah. They could be slanted so things wouldn't fall
off, and have a lip on the edge for extra stability. You
could even tie things down with bungee cords to make
sure they aren't going to move. Like those stretchy nets
they put over the back of pickups."

"But shelves… Who would do something like that?"
Even as I asked, the idea was delightful. I could see how
much simpler it would make things.

"Oh, it wouldn't be any trouble," Toby said with conspicuous innocence. "I can do them for you once we get back to Dallas."

"Once we get back…" I was astonished. Not even David could have been more manipulative. Toby was not the wooly lamb I'd thought.

"We are going back to Dallas after the Branson show, aren't we?" Hoisting with insulting ease two boxes that I could barely move, he looked at me with innocent eyes.

"I am going back to Dallas after the Branson show," I said as sternly as possible. "You are going back to Minnesota on Sunday, if not sooner."

"Oh, Aunt Lilias…" Wise enough not to push it, he turned and put the boxes in their places, but I knew this wasn't the end of it.

And I wasn't really sure I wanted that to be the end of it. He was a good kid and it was surprisingly fun having him around, to say nothing of being a great deal easier. Things I struggled with he lifted with one hand, and there was his gift for getting things done and making people agree with him. He also was good company. It surprised me to realize how lonely I had been until he joined me.

But did I have the right to put him into danger? For all his height he was still hardly more than a boy.

That, I decided like all good reluctant authority figures, could wait for a while. The sun was sinking low. After all the exercise of what I still tried to think of as an inventory, I decided I might be able to enjoy food again sometime before Christmas. Toby, I was sure, was regarding himself on the edge of starvation.

I did stop at the office to report the attempted theft, but when the bored clerk—this time a man who was seemingly immune to either my logic or Toby's personality—found out that the van hadn't been entered he almost immediately lost interest. His attitude implied that we might have made the story up and I left in disgust, a grumbling Toby at my heels.

We found a fixed-price all you can eat buffet not far from the hotel. While it was more than I usually liked to pay for a meal, it was downright cheap when it came to filling Toby up. They lost money on him that night. The food was simple, but ample, and Toby ate until I thought he would surely burst. It was amazing to watch the pleasure and determination with which he demolished several platefuls in a row, though I came close to hating him for his ability to eat so much so happily and seemingly never put on an ounce.

Then we went to the closest supermarket and stocked up—lunch meat, cheese, bread, fruit and ice for me, colas, chips, cookies and jerky for Toby. I drew the line at a four-pound bag of candy bars.

"Chili. Chips. Cookies. Candy," I muttered, steeling myself against the inevitable astronomical total on the cash register. "Does everything you eat begin with *C?*"

"No. There's the jerky…and hamburgers and steaks and ravioli," he answered with due gravity. "If it makes you feel any better, though, I don't like corn."

"It's a wonder you don't have rickets, or scurvy, or some such."

Toby grinned, drawing sighs from several women behind us in line. "But just think how big I would be with a good diet," he said in serious tones and I had to laugh.

The total was as bad as I had feared, but I counted out the money without comment. It was impossible to stay piqued with Toby. He was simply too good-natured. He just gave me that goofy grin, said something off the wall and everything was all right again. Basketball or no, the girls must have gone totally ape over him. I would bet there was a string of if not broken, at least severely bruised feminine hearts in Pennsylvania.

I took advantage of the bright lights and busy parking lot of the supermarket to pack the ice chest. Toby could bring it in to the booth tomorrow and I'd make our sandwiches there. If he thought the action odd, he didn't say anything. When I parked the van as close as possible to the office, though, he did.

"Aunt Lilias, our rooms are on the other side of the hotel."

"I know. I also know that someone tried to break into the van this afternoon and that idiot clerk didn't believe us. It'll be interesting to hear what he says if someone tries it again with the van right next to the office."

Again that grin. "You're a wicked woman, Aunt Lilias."

After Toby had extracted a couple of soft drinks and a large bag of chips from the back—presumably to ward off incipient malnutrition during the night—I set the alarm and locked the van.

Toby insisted on walking me to my room, an attention which I tried to refuse. In fact, I felt I should take him to his.

"And tuck me in and hear my prayers?" he asked, flashing a grin. "I'm not a child, Aunt Lilias."

"And I'm not a feeble old woman," I answered, though in the back of my mind the words *not yet* echoed with a mocking solemnity.

"No, you're a woman who found a dead man in her house, a house that was later broken into and almost destroyed, and whose van was almost broken into this afternoon. Besides, Uncle Jim will come back and haunt me if I don't look after you."

We'd reached my room. He tried rather unsuccessfully to check the room for intrusion without seeming to, but everything was untouched.

It was only after we had exchanged a good-night hug and I had locked the door behind him, I realized he now believed all this was more than just a happenstance string of coincidences.

THE CHESTNUT PLAZA Art Fair was one of the larger venues, with at least a hundred vendors. A number of booths were scattered along dirt paths outside, shielded either by trees or sheet metal canopies or the vendors' own tents, but those of us who had been there before always tried to reserve spaces in the building. I don't know what it'd been before becoming a show barn, but the enormous old tin building possessed a concrete floor, lots of fans and a rudimentary air conditioning system for which we were pathetically grateful.

In spite of that I appeared dressed for cooler temperatures. Over my semi-uniform of faded jeans, T-shirt and sneakers, I wore an oversized old chambray shirt, loose, like a jacket. It had been one of Jim's and I would keep wearing it until it dissolved—though usually not in August. Toby looked at it quizzically, but said nothing. He was learning I seldom did anything without a reason.

After a blessedly uneventful night, we breakfasted at a nearby coffee shop's early bird buffet. I was beginning to bless buffets. In spite of being propitiated by chips and soda the night before, Toby's appetite had sharpened overnight and he did justice to just about every one of the advertised eighty items. When he finally declared himself full, for the moment at least, we left for the show. Although the show didn't open to the public until ten, vendors could come in for set-up at eight-thirty. After the past few days of catch-as-catch-can set-up and tear-down, it was purest luxury to have both time and help in setting up my booth.

This was a larger venue than I had done in a while and though there were a lot of vendors I knew—Florene, for one, and the Alquists—the booth was located in the middle of a bunch of strangers. On one side there was a grizzled old codger selling T-shirts with near-obscene sayings and on the other a young man selling jewelry cleaner. Across the aisle was a display of photos and brochures about some hunting lodge in Missouri. I guess the booth was unmanned, because there never seemed to be anyone in it.

Toby was a gem. He fetched, he carried, he did everything he could to prove that he was indispensable to me.

That's not being fair. He never mentioned Minnesota, or staying with me, or anything. He did work, though. He hung the bead curtain on the divider wall at the back of the booth without standing on anything or even stretching. He helped me spread out the table covers. He arranged the bead floral arrangements and even made sandwiches, so we wouldn't have to worry about them later.

It was his idea to bring in everything from the van. It would, he said, be safer to have everything under our eye instead of having to worry about what was happening outside. There was plenty of room under the table, he said, and the tablecloths went all the way to the ground. Plus, we could cover the extra boxes with tablecloths and use them for extra display space. Besides, he added artlessly, with two of us there would always be someone there to watch the booth.

I was beginning to wonder how I'd ever managed without him, which was probably exactly the reaction he was wanting.

"I think I'll walk around and see what's available," he said after everything was done. "Maybe check out the girls."

"Good luck on finding any," I said. "This is a grown-up's game."

He only laughed at that and strode away down the aisle. Oh, how I wished that Chrissy and Hank knew how lucky they were. At that same age David would have been…

A bunch of ugly memories surfaced. David, not only stealing test questions his only semester in college, but selling them to other students. David, scalping football tickets. David, running a social club that was little more than a cover for swinging couples. David…

Ruthlessly I pushed the memories down. That part of my life was past, and I would not let myself relive it.

Toby hadn't reached the end of the aisle before Florene bounced into my booth, her withered-apple face alight.

"Hot damn, girl, you done caught yourself another 'un, and he's as good looking as that one in Amarillo. Younger, too. You using a new perfume or something?"

"He's my nephew, Florene. He's never been to a show like this…"

Devils danced in her faded eyes and she winked significantly. "If that's what you want to tell people, hon, go right ahead. I'll back you up. Where'd you find him?"

I sighed. Sometimes truth was the most unbelievable alternative. "In Arkansas."

"I allus did love a tall man, and he's just about the tallest I've ever seen. Maybe I should go over to Arkansas and see what I can pick up." She cackled obscenely.

"Where are you set up?"

"Next aisle over, coupla booths down. Not a bad spot.

I'll probably do okay there, but then I don't have a draw like you do. Ain't you hot in that thing?" She gestured toward my overshirt.

Actually I was near boiling, but there was no way I was going to take it off. "I'm fine. It's really very comfortable."

Florene grinned and gave me a knowing wink. "We all get to the age we think it's better to keep our butt covered. You'd best be careful, Lilias. It's hard, having a younger man like that. You'll be beating girls off with a stick." Her last words were jarringly serious.

"Not until they've bought some beads, I won't."

She glanced at her watch. "'Bout time for them to open up. Gotta get back to my place. Come on by if you can and we'll have a chat."

She was gone as the big doors at the far end of the building swung open. As if attached to the same switch, Vernon Alquist's wood router whined into life. It was nearly on the other side of the building and still irritating.

The morning went slowly, as first mornings tend to. I sold two necklaces—a rather complex design of floriform beads and an ex-hippie single strand—and two or three pairs of earrings before I realized rather guiltily I had no idea of where Toby was.

Toby is, I thought with a hollow sternness, *a grown man fully capable of looking after himself at a craft fair.*

A large boy, a dark side of my mind jeered, *whose aunt is involved with dead bodies and burglars.*

"Here," said the large boy, suddenly appearing behind me. I jumped in spite of myself. He appeared not to notice and stuck a piece of warm, sugared crispiness into my mouth. "Try this."

I had been about to light into him for disappearing,

which would have been ridiculous and worthy of Chrissy at her worst, but it's impossible to say anything with a large chunk of freshly fried funnel cake in your mouth. I chewed and swallowed.

"Isn't that great?" he asked.

"Where did you get this?" I was finally able to ask and tried not to spew crumbs.

"At the concession stand. I see what you mean about the prices. They're charging six dollars for this little bitty thing." He sounded outraged, at least as outraged as anyone could with a mouth full of funnel cake.

Even considering that probably at least half the treat was gone, what was left was still bigger than any concession stand funnel cake I'd ever seen.

"How did you get this? You didn't have any money."

"Don't look at me as if I stole it," he said, aggrieved. "Patsy gave it to me. She was testing to make sure the oil was the right temperature."

"Patsy?"

"At the concession stand. She's a nice girl. Likes to barrel race. Has a really fast pinto pony."

I had never known any concessionaire to give away their wares at the beginning of the day, let alone such an outsized specimen. Now I was beginning to understand why Chrissy didn't worry much about Toby being out on his own. Like Annie, he created his own rules and everyone else seemed to obey them.

"Here." He broke off another piece and stuffed it into my mouth. "We don't want to let it get cold. What were you thinking about when I came up? You looked like you had the weight of the world on you."

Weight of the world. That had been one of Jim's favorite phrases and was probably another Ruiz family legacy. I always missed him, but suddenly it was with a deep and stabbing pain. None of this would be happening if he were here with me. I would be safe, and I would be loved…and happy. Oh, how happy I would be!

"Just things…"

Toby was smart enough to recognize an evasion when he saw it. He crunched down on another bite of funnel cake and asked, "How's business?" He didn't spew crumbs, either.

"Not bad. Sold a couple of things." I glanced out at the growing crowd drifting by. Early on the first day there usually weren't many buyers. People generally just scoped out what was available, then came back later to dicker over what had caught their eye. "Lots of lookers."

He gave me the last chunk of funnel cake and dusted his hands on the seat of his jeans. I made a mental note that we both needed to do laundry in the next day or two.

"Can I try and sell?"

"Sure. Everything's priced. Don't take any checks without my approval and I'll handle it if someone wants to use a credit card."

He grinned. "This is going to be fun."

I envied his enthusiasm. While selling my work was generally pleasurable, it had stopped being fun a long time ago. The fun was in creating. Selling was just an inevitable and necessary by-product.

After an hour of watching Toby, I became a firm believer in magic. In that time he sold as much as I had hoped to sell during the entire day. Not just cheap earrings and ex-hippie necklaces, either, though those seemed to fly out of the booth. He sold two large and intricate necklaces, one of the bead flower arrangements—the most expensive one, too—and four Lover's Roses.

After standing by and watching for the first few minutes, I gave up and sat down, workbox across my lap as

I strung more necklaces and bracelets. If he was going to keep selling like that, I was going to have to make a lot more stock quickly.

The magic ended when I stepped up to take care of a charge card transaction. By then Toby had watched me do several and I felt almost certain that he could do them as well as I, but I wasn't quite ready for that. I ran the card through my handy-dandy little cell phone attachment and while waiting for authorization happened to look up.

It was just a glimpse, and I'm sure that Tulsa is full of tall, rangy men with rough-hewn faces and hats the size of patio umbrellas, but still I was certain. There was no mistaking that lean, panther-like stride or misleadingly handsome, Marlboro-man profile.

The man from Amarillo, the man who had attacked me in the parking lot, was here, not ten yards away.

THIRTEEN

SOMEHOW I MANAGED to finish the transaction with a smile, but Toby knew something was wrong.

"What is it, Aunt Lilias? Do you feel all right?"

I should have kept my mouth shut. I should have smiled and said it was nothing more than a gas pain, or a cramp, or some other innocuous thing, but I didn't. I was too scared to think of a convincing lie.

"The man from Amarillo. I just saw him."

Someday I will learn to think before I speak, I hope. His face grim, Toby dashed from the booth and was gone before I could call him back. I had no doubt he would find the man. The building wasn't that big, and up at the cabin I had foolishly given Toby a very good description. Surely there wouldn't be shooting, not in a crowded venue like this.

But what if Toby followed him out into the parking lot, or the open spaces beyond? What about tonight, when it was time to shut down? My stomach knotted painfully.

Toby was going to be on the next plane to Minnesota, and I was going back to Dallas. This afternoon!

"Mrs. Ruiz?"

I glanced up and it felt as if all the blood drained from my body. Once, not long before David was born, I had fainted. This felt much the same.

The man from Amarillo was standing in front of the booth, absurdly large hat and all.

Most important of all, how did he know my name?

I forced a smile that felt more like a death grin and tried to speak lightly. "It's you again. Are you following me?"

Something flickered in his eyes. They were cold eyes, hard eyes that looked as if they would be more comfortable staring into some hostile distance. They were also a brilliant crystalline blue.

"Or do you have another girlfriend up here in Tulsa?" I babbled on, suddenly not wanting to know the answer to my question. "You are a busy fellow. You need another Lover's Rose for her, you know. Can't afford to play favorites among your ladies. And in your case I can give you a bulk discount, if there are more…"

I sounded like an idiot, but his face didn't change.

"We need to talk, Mrs. Ruiz," he said in neutral tones.

"I'm back." Toby strode into the booth and I'd never been more glad to see anyone. Then he draped his arm around my shoulders in a most unnephewlike way and looked straight at the man from Amarillo. "Friend of yours, Lilias?" he asked in a voice that seemed to have dropped almost an octave.

The air was suddenly full of crackling testosterone.

"A customer," I replied bemusedly. "He likes Lover's Roses."

The craggy-faced man didn't say anything. He just stared up at Toby. It was apparent that he was unused to having to look up to anyone. It was also apparent that he didn't like it.

"They're one of our specialties," Toby said, giving me an overt little squeeze that could have cracked rocks. I almost yelped. "How many do you need?"

"None right now," the man replied. He gave me a strange, calculating glance, then before leaving inclined his head and touched his hat again. This time it seemed a parody of a movie cowboy. "Later."

I was intensely annoyed to find that I was shaking. Toby embraced me, this time in a most proper nephew-ish way. He was trembling too.

"Are you okay?" he asked and I nodded.

"You?"

"Fine. That is one scary dude."

"Agreed. Let's get out of here."

"And go where?"

"You to Minnesota, where you'll be safe. I…"

Putting his hands on my shoulders, Toby held me at arm's length. "Believe me, I would rather face that scary dude than my folks right now. And we're all right here. I mean, there're people all around. Besides, we're making money."

His use of the word "we" was not lost on me. Somehow this had become a partnership, and in spite of the way my mother-gene kept nagging, I sort of liked the idea.

I couldn't let it be, though. Toby needed to be out of this.

So did I.

"Can I help you?" he asked an approaching customer before I could formulate a rational argument. In one way, he was correct. Right here, right now, in the middle of all this, we were safe. Not even the hard-eyed man in the big hat would try anything in this crowd.

At least, I hoped not.

The stream of customers was light but steady, as was the flow of cash coming in. Toby was handling it all with ease, so I let him. I sat in the back of the booth and made necklaces. And I thought. Tulsa and Amarillo were not that far apart. It wasn't too big a stretch of the imagination for someone in Amarillo to show up a week later in Tulsa. It was, though, for him to show up at two different arts and crafts fairs. The worst thing was that he knew my name. I wished I hadn't been so cowardly and had talked to him. After all, I was safe in the middle of all these people. I was dying to know what he wanted to talk to me about. Did he think I had something that belonged to him? Did he know what this mysterious something I was supposed to have was?

Was he the one who had killed the man in my house?

Finally things slowed down around lunchtime as the customers went outside to picnic under the trees or drove into Tulsa in search of better air conditioning.

Toby handed over a fistful of cash. "How are we doing?"

"You," I said with emphasis, glancing at the startling number of bills. There might be profit in this trip after all. "You are doing great. Including this, so far this morning we've taken in more than what I hoped to do all day."

Toby smiled, but said nothing other than he was hungry.

"The sandwiches are in the ice chest. And eat some fruit. It's good for you."

He dropped cross-legged to the floor and began to eat, watching intently as I finished off a necklace before getting my own lunch.

"That doesn't look too hard," he said, downing the last bite of sandwich number three.

"It isn't." I bit into my own sandwich, realizing with a start that I was very hungry.

"Would you teach me?"

"You want to learn how to make necklaces? Don't you think it's kind of a…feminine thing to do?" I knew he had made a few leaves up at the cabin, but then there had been nothing else to do at the cabin.

He shrugged. "Yeah, but we're already running low on stock. It'll be better if we both can make them. Besides, if I make the simple stuff, you can work on the high-dollar pieces."

It was simple, it was logical, and it was diabolical. Another day or two of this and I wouldn't have the strength of mind to send him home. If only David had been like him…

"What's wrong, Aunt Lilias? Don't you want to teach me?"

No, I didn't. I wanted to stop sharing with him. I wanted… I wanted…

"I was just thinking how much nicer my life would have been had my son been like you," I said. "David—"

He looked uncomfortable. "Yeah, I know about David. When I was ten I thought he was the best, coolest guy in the world. Then I grew up."

Of course the family knew about David. After all, he had hit them up for "investments," most of them several times, all the while complaining bitterly about how I wouldn't give him any of his father's money, how I wouldn't support his dreams. To think that they didn't talk about him—and me, and what was more painful, Jim—was foolish. I was only glad that my own parents had never known what a scoundrel their only grandson had become. When they died he had barely passed the toddler stage and was still adorable—a phase that didn't last long. By the second grade he was proud of being able to make his little classmates give him their lunch money. I still did and would always love my son. I didn't really like him, though, and that hurt. Always would.

"So," Toby said with a false brightness, "show me how to make one of those."

Of course he caught on before I had finished the first knot. As I've said, making the ex-hippie necklaces was about as simple as beadwork could get, but still it was gratifying to see how quickly he understood the principle. It was more so to see how he became enthralled with the process, so much so that he forgot to eat his fourth sandwich. I took over the counter, dealing with the few customers who drifted past, while he concentrated on stringing beads. Perhaps it was a good thing his parents weren't here to see this.

He'd made three or four before I went back to see his work. Construction-wise, they were indistinguishable from mine, except that instead of being totally random, the beads were strung in patterns. They were prettier than either mine or Martha's, too.

"Wow. You really have a gift for design."

Toby shook his head but didn't look up. "No. It's all math."

"Math?"

"Yeah. Each bead is a unit and you can put them together in patterns. Like this." He held up the one he had just finished tying off. "This is a Fibonacci and reverse."

"A what?"

"A Fibonacci. It's a mathematical series where every unit is the total of the two units before it. See? One. Two. Three. Five. Eight. Thirteen. Then I put in a different bead and started going backward. Thirteen. Eight. Five. Three. Two. One."

I looked at the necklace in awe. It was beautiful. The beads were the same length and roughly the same ovoid shape, but they alternated between blocks of clear with gold flecks and a shiny brown. The dividing center bead was reconstituted amber, pressed into a vaguely flori-form pattern.

"This is not an ex-hippie necklace," I said. "This is a work of art."

"That's how I feel about math and numbers," Toby said, his eyes shining. "You can do anything with math-ematical patterns—send messages, create codes, any-thing. Think about computers. All they do is based on ones and zeroes. For that matter, think about the old Morse code—dots and dashes, which are nothing but ones and zeroes in a different form."

"Here," I said, digging out a handful of money and giving him two twenties. "I'm going to buy this neck-lace for me. It's beautiful."

The boy actually blushed and tried to hand them back. "I can't take this. I mean, they're your beads. I can't sell you your own stuff."

"You can do what I say, for once. Count it as your day's pay. You can't go around with no money in your pocket anyway." I stepped back from the extended bills and clasped the beads around my neck. In spite of my-self my eyes were starting to moisten. "What you can do is keep making necklaces."

Five minutes later my taste was vindicated. The customer was an older woman who'd looked at every necklace on display with an expression that combined reluctant admiration and disdain. Her pudgy fingers glowed with diamonds as she fingered a nice multi-strand garnet choker. Like so many customers who turn out to be intent on haggling she hadn't given me a glance, but when she looked up her eyes brightened.

"That's a beautiful necklace you're wearing."

I touched it with a proud fingertip. "Thank you. It's a Fibonacci," I said with malice aforethought.

Her eyes widened. "Oh, Italian. You can always tell Italian design. How much is it?"

"I'm sorry," I replied. "This one isn't for sale." Unconsciously my fingers closed over it, as if she might snatch it from my neck.

An indignant reply bubbled on her over-lipsticked lips, but before she could speak Toby was behind me, charming her with a smile.

"That necklace was a special order, but we can have a similar one ready for you in an hour. What colors do you like?"

"Paid in advance, of course," I added. "And the price depends on the beads you choose."

She bought three in different color combinations, and didn't turn a hair when I named a price for each that almost made my own hair curl. Toby promised to have all three ready in an hour and she promised to tell her friends where she had gotten them. I doubted the last part, because she probably wouldn't want to see her necklace on all her friends' necks, but I didn't care.

"Can you manage?" I asked once she was gone. "I need to run to the ladies' room."

Toby looked up from the workbox. "Want me to go with you in case that scary dude is still hanging around?"

He was serious and, to my shame, for a moment I considered it. "No, you've got to finish those necklaces and someone's got to watch the booth. I won't be but a minute." I gave him what I hoped was a lighthearted grin. "If I'm not back in thirty minutes, send out the Texas Rangers."

He didn't smile back. "This is Oklahoma."

I made myself laugh, but all the way to the back of

the building I kept out a weather eye. There were lots of tall, rangy men, most of whom did wear big hats, but my man wasn't there, which oddly enough didn't ease my mind. Where was he?

On the way back I passed Florene's booth and, not content with a nod, she popped out into the aisle like a superannuated Jill-in-the-Box.

"How're things going?"

"Pretty good. Made more sales than I thought. Or rather my nephew did. He's a born salesman."

She grinned suggestively. "He's that and all. And more, is my guess." Her chuckle turned into another cackle as she dashed back into her booth to corner a customer.

Toby was laughing with three young girls when I returned. They appeared to be of high school age, as near as could be estimated through their layers of "glamorous" make-up. Clad in tight jeans and tiny shirts that were just this side of legal, they all giggled and flirted like crazy.

And Toby was enjoying it thoroughly. At least in this way he was a normal boy. I had begun to think he was an aged sage in disguise.

"Aunt Lilias." He jumped as if bitten and instantly the girls shut down into a sullen, silent hostility. I knew teenagers were supposed to be antagonistic toward adults, but their reaction made me feel as if I had stumbled into a foreign and inimical territory.

"Hi," I said as brightly as I could. "Everything okay?"

"Yeah…" Apparently the presence of girls his own age rendered Toby inarticulate.

"Can you manage alone a minute more? I need to talk to…to someone."

It was an inspired lie. Immediately the gloom lifted.

Feeling every bit of my age, to say nothing of being a member of an alien nation, I walked on down the aisle with a light heart. At the moment traffic wasn't too heavy, but even if we missed a sale or two we were already ahead of the game and Toby deserved a moment of youthful indulgence.

I'd give him five minutes.

On the other hand, I hadn't forgotten the tall man in the big hat. I didn't believe for a minute that he was really gone.

He had called me Mrs. Ruiz. The logical half of my mind knew that finding out my name would be child's play. All he would have to do was ask just about any of the regular circuit vendors, or the show office, or even check the license plates on the van. The illogical, emotional half of my mind shuddered at the thought of my name in his mouth. It was too personal, almost a violation.

Carrie Littlewolf had a booth three down from ours. I figured that was far enough away to give Toby space and close enough to keep an eye on things.

"Hey, Lilias. How're you doing?"

"Okay, Carrie. You?"

She shrugged and waved her hands in a middling motion. Carrie sold Indian stuff—painted hides, dreamcatchers, some turquoise jewelry, resin sculptures of eagles and noble warriors, that sort of thing. She even dressed in a fringed buckskin dress and beaded moccasins and wore her hair in two long braids. Carrie was a good-hearted creature and I liked her, though it was no secret to those on the circuit she was a total fake. She had been born to a well-to-do Jewish lawyer and his interior decorator wife in Saddle River, New Jersey. Even her blue-black braids came straight from the tribe of Clairol.

"Not bad, not bad. Tomorrow's going to be a big day, and Saturday will probably be better. Kind of dumb to open on a Thursday, but what the heck? A sale's a sale."

"Yeah, though for a Thursday it's a pretty good crowd. I guess Scott knew what he was doing when he decided to experiment with an early opening. I hadn't planned on coming in until today and setting up tomorrow, but we decided to come in early."

She grinned impishly. "I saw your new partner. Going cougar on me?"

I shook my head. "He's my nephew."

Carrie rolled her eyes. "Whatever works."

I was getting very tired of that attitude.

"Hi, Lilias, Carrie." Red-faced and rotund, Jeff Roemer bounced up to the booth. Jeff never seemed to walk—he always bounced even when he was carrying a load of boxes. A friendly—sometimes *too* friendly—vendor of vintage jewelry and accessories, Jeff was a good enough guy until he had a few drinks too many. Then he became convinced he was another Brad Pitt and was determined to convince everyone else, too. The year before, the facts I was at least a head taller and a generation older had not deterred him from trying to convince me my life was empty without him. Our wrestling match had been short and most unpretty, but he bore me no grudge for the black eye. Since then our relations had been cordial enough, but comfortably distant. "Have ya'll heard about Calvin and Martha?"

"Calvin and Martha? No." A frisson of premonition clog-danced down my spine in icy boots.

"I thought they were going to be here," Carrie said, "but I haven't seen them yet. Are they going to be late?"

"They're more than late," Jeff said, and to his credit he wasn't making a pun. "They're dead."

My insides knotted from the toes up and I wasn't sure my legs would hold me upright. Worse, I didn't know why.

"Dead?" Carrie squeaked.

I said, "But I just saw him in Amarillo a couple of days ago."

Jeff looked at me oddly. "They didn't do the Amarillo show," he said with authority. "Renee was thoroughly pissed with him for canceling out at the last minute. He's one of the popular regulars there."

"But I…" I stopped. Indeed Calvin had come by my booth and demanded Martha's beads back, but I hadn't seen him any other time. Or seen Martha at all.

"What happened?" Carrie asked.

"Apparently an accident. Old Calvin must have had more to drink than usual, because their RV went over the edge of a cliff along some road out in the wilds of Big Bend. It was only by some fluke that the wreck was found when it was. Normally that road is almost never traveled, but some lost tourist saw the fire and reported it."

My stomach roiled and Carrie asked, "Fire?"

"Yep. The rig burst into flames when it hit the bottom. Apparently Calvin's body was thrown out before the fire started, but they can't find Martha. Of course, with a drop that high and that intense a fire there's no telling if there's anything left of her to find."

There wasn't any air. I couldn't get my breath. My lungs refused to function. Big Bend? A huge state park on the far western lip of Texas, Big Bend was rough, beautiful and desolate, being composed mainly of desert, high mountains and scrub. I wasn't even sure if anyone at all lived there. Why would Calvin—drunk, scrappy little Calvin—pass up two of the most lucrative shows on the circuit to head hot-foot out to the wilderness?

Finally I forced enough energy to ask, "But what was Calvin doing out in Big Bend? He was scheduled to do this show and probably Branson, too."

Jeff shrugged. "Dunno. Old Bobby said he'd been acting strangely lately. Drinking more than usual. Guess it finally caught up with him."

Old Bobby was an institution on the art/craft circuit. If there were a fair going on that weekend, any weekend, he was there. Over the years he had sold most everything, from kitchen gadgets to tie-dye clothing, but in the last few years he had hit upon hand-carved bone figurines. Wearing overalls and a tattered shirt, he would sit in a disreputable rocker and carve away, telling stories as he did so. He never charged for his stories, but of course, there was a prominently displayed tip jar at his elbow. Generally he made as much or more for his whopping outrageous tales as he did for his carvings.

If Old Bobby said something about one of the vendors, though, it must be true. There wasn't anything on the circuit worth knowing he didn't know.

"Those poor people," Carrie said, her eyes moistening with the shimmer of easy tears. "When did it happen?"

"Monday. Don't know the time, but it was at night. That's how the lost tourist happened to see the fire."

I felt sorry for Calvin and Martha. I would feel sorry for anyone who died before their time, especially in such a grisly way, but there was something else making my stomach clench and unclench like a nervous fist.

Apparently Calvin had not opened his booth at the Amarillo show, but he'd been there, because he had come to demand that I give back the beads Martha had sold me. Time and miles didn't lie. If they had died Monday, that meant they had gone straight from my booth to Big Bend and died there.

FOURTEEN

"ANNIE? I NEED you to do something for me." I'd walked
to the end of the aisle before digging out my cell phone.
This was near the food court, an open area with scarred
folding tables and chairs, some occupied but most not.
It was unlikely that anyone could overhear me. Better
yet, I could keep a watch out for the tall lanky man in
the big hat.

"This had better be important," she all but snapped.
Apparently she hadn't yet forgiven me for disappearing
up to the cabin. "I was in an important meeting."

I sort of discounted that. All of Annie's meetings were
termed "important" even if they were nothing more than
discussions about redecorating the office.

"I'm sorry," I said with perfunctory courtesy, "but I'm
hoping you'll be able to check on an accident that happened out in the Big Bend area last Monday."

"An accident? Big Bend? Where are you, Lilias? Are
you all right?" Her tone thawed perceptibly. "You don't
sound like yourself."

"It didn't happen to me. Remember those beads I
bought, the ones that were in the back of the van?" I told
her about Calvin and Martha's accident and their horrific
deaths. When I was finished she was silent.

"What were they doing in Big Bend?"

"I don't know. I just know that to get there by then,
they pretty much had to have left right after Calvin came

to my booth and even then they would've had to have really pushed it." I took a deep breath, praying that Annie would see a hole in my argument, that she would rip my scenario to shreds and give me a plausible, comfortable explanation.

She didn't.

"That's weird. Do you know if they had family out there?"

My unease intensified. "I don't think they had much family at all. They married when they were still in the Army. Martha told me once they were both pretty much alone in the world. And with Calvin's disposition they didn't have many close friends, if any. I certainly didn't know of any."

"So they could have disappeared and no one would have been significantly worried about them," Annie murmured. There was a moment of silence, then when she spoke she was normally brisk again. "One always hates to hear of such tragedies. Are you coming home after this show?"

I felt as if I had been slapped. The least Annie could have done was be unnerved with me. "I don't know. Annie—?"

"Look, Lilias, I'm sorry about your friends, but I really do have to get back to my meeting."

"I'm sorry to interrupt your meeting," I replied somewhat snarkily, working mightily to keep my tongue under control, "but I really do need a favor. I want to see that accident report. Can you arrange that?"

"Why?" Annie sounded startled.

"Chalk it up to curiosity. Can you do it?"

"I'll do what I can. Look, Lilias, I really do have to run. Stay in touch…"

She hung up before I could say good-bye. Annie had

never been so short with me, even during the worst of her cases. Maybe she was getting tired of having to look out for my interests, though she'd been more excited about the reconstruction of my house than I had been. Maybe she had just decided it wasn't good to be close friends with someone who found a dead body in her living room.

Maybe she thought I was somehow involved.

No, not Annie. She was my best friend. It had to be something else. It just had to be.

"Aunt Lilias?"

I'm sure that when I reentered the booth I looked like grim death, but it was still startling how Toby immediately jumped to my side.

"What's wrong?"

How much to tell him? "I just found out that two people I knew, two vendors on the circuit, were killed in an accident."

"I'm sorry," he said, then simply stood, waiting. He knew there was more. I could see it in his eyes. And, I decided morosely, he had the right to know. I had allowed him into this mess and he needed to know whatever I knew in order to be able to protect himself. Only thing was, I didn't think I knew much of anything.

"It was Calvin Sullivan. That man who demanded I sell him back the beads his wife sold me. He and his wife died in an accident in Big Bend."

Toby's eyes grew wide, but I could almost see his brain working. "Is there a show out there that he was going to?"

"Not at this time of year. And he was booked both for the Amarillo show and for this one, but he didn't set up in Amarillo. Instead he lit out west after talking to me."

And just after the tall man in the big hat had come along and told him to quit bothering me. My stomach, which had started to relax, clenched rock hard again. That man was here, somewhere in this building.

Toby was thinking. "Your friend was a regular, wasn't he? That means he wouldn't give up these book-ings lightly. Another thing—if that tourist hadn't hap-pened to see the fire, they might have lain there for years without being found. If they ever were. By that time it would have been impossible to discover exactly when they died."

"You watch a lot of television, too, don't you? What is it, a Ruiz family disease?"

Toby stared at me. "I never watch TV. It's stupid and a waste of time."

"But how did you—?"

"Logic." He shrugged. "The beads he wanted back? Are those the ones we looked at last night? After some-one tried to break into the van?"

I nodded miserably. "But they're just beads, and not even very good ones at that. I've looked at them again and again and so have the police. Why would he want them back so badly?"

The wheels in Toby's head were almost audible. "Be-cause either they are something we're not seeing, or because someone thinks there's something in them that isn't there. They think whatever it is has to be there because it wasn't in your house. Remember that note through the window?"

"Remember it? I can't forget it. But I don't have any-thing!"

"Doesn't matter, not if they think you do."

"Wish I'd stayed at the cabin. I wish none of this had ever happened." I couldn't help it. There was a definite sob in my voice. There was only so much one person could stand, and I had just about reached it. I wasn't afraid to stand up for myself and fight if I had to, but now I didn't know what I was fighting. And people were dying.

Toby reached out and hugged me, much as I had hugged him and all his cousins when they were younger and needed comfort. It was extraordinarily pleasant, though at that moment I had irrevocably passed into being one of the "older generation." From one who gave comfort to one who was comforted.

A throat clearing as vicious as a ripsaw sliced through the air. "Are my necklaces finished?" The older woman customer stood there, radiating disapproval from every pore.

Toby patted my shoulder and picked up a folded sack. "Right here," he said.

"My, you're back early," I said, putting on a tight smile. It must have looked ghastly, because she quickly turned her attention to Toby.

"We decided to leave early," she said with an air of disdain, "and I want to cancel my order and get my money back."

"I'm sorry..." I began, ready to tell her that special orders were not refundable and prepared for the scene that would follow, but Toby forestalled me by opening the package and allowing the necklaces to spill over his fingers.

He had done a lovely job. The woman melted almost visibly at the sight of gold and green, two shades of blue, and black and white in three exquisitely crafted necklaces. I did too. Any woman would.

She hemmed and hawed a little, then in the end took her necklaces—but only after trying to haggle for a reduction in the price. Needless to say, Toby saw to it that she didn't get one.

"Whew," Toby said when she had sailed down the aisle with all the aplomb of an ocean liner. "Do you get many like that?"

"She was a cream puff. Unfortunately, a lot of people think artists and craft show vendors are pushovers or that we work just for the recognition. Usually I get one or two like her a show... Not so lucrative, though."

"This is kind of fun," Toby said carefully without looking me in the eye. "I could learn to make lots of things. If I stood down from college and traveled with you for a year, I could probably earn enough—"

"No," I snapped, visions of furious Applegates and Ruizes descending on me. "That is not an option. You are going back to college. You are going back to Minnesota."

"But..."

"No, Tobias Dominic Applegate. I've been glad to have you with me, and we've had a good time together, but it's not permanent. Not only am I accustomed to working alone, it's getting dangerous. Toby, people are dying and I don't know why. I want you out of it." There was more I wanted to say, but couldn't—my lips were shaking too badly.

"Don't you think I want you out of this too?" he asked in a low voice. "You're my favorite aunt, and I love you. I used to wish that you and Uncle Jim were my parents. You never seemed to fight, and you were always good to David no matter what he did. If you were my mother I'd be protecting you."

I couldn't help it. I started to weep, soundlessly but with great oily tears that overflowed my eyes and slid down my cheeks. Apparently conscious that he had told me too much in very few words, Toby turned me so my back was to the aisle and then stepped forward to wait on some customers. I didn't know if they had heard or seen, and didn't really care. Some things were bigger than a minor embarrassment. If David had only been like Toby—

And if wishes were horses, all beggars would ride. I swiped my eyes dry, put on a cheery smile and turned around. Toby was just handing over change. The customers were a young couple and appeared to be very much in love. They smiled and were gone.

"Sold that garnet necklace, the wide one with the hangy-down things in the middle," Toby said proudly.

"It's a bib with interior pendants," I said in a carefully modified version of my old schoolteacher voice. "You need to learn the proper vocabulary."

He was apologetic. "I had to mark it down ten percent."

"Ten percent? That thing's been hanging around for two years. I had it marked down fifty percent a couple of weeks ago and couldn't move it."

Toby began to chuckle and, in a moment, so did I.

"You see, Aunt Lilias, you need me here. I'll make you more than I'll cost you."

"Toby…"

"Let's let it go until the end of the show," he said. "Then let's talk about it."

He had sounded just like his uncle then. Jim had always been the one to talk things through, to find a common ground, to make some sort of a compromise. Of course Toby had to go back to college, and he had to make peace with his parents, but maybe next summer he could come along. Every college kid needed a summer job, didn't they?

Next summer. What would be going on then?

After what had happened so far *this* summer, I almost shuddered at the possibilities.

"Aunt Lilias, if you're okay, I'm going to run to the bathroom."

"Of course. Go right on."

"If that scary dude shows up…"

"I'll scream. Go on. I don't want you having an accident in the booth."

Toby grinned at the memory of his last "accident," which had happened in the back seat of our new-ish car. He had been four. His mother had been hysterical. "I'll be right back."

The afternoon traffic was light, which was to be expected. Tomorrow, Friday, would be big, because that was the traditional opening day, and then Saturday hopefully would be the blockbuster. Sunday would be a toss-up between bargain hunters and packing up. There didn't seem to be anyone much around, so I turned to get out the box with Annie's crystal roses.

I didn't expect to feel a long, hard body pressed against my side, nor have my arm held just tightly enough to control my movements without causing me any real pain.

"Don't make a sound, Mrs. Ruiz," a low, familiar voice whispered in my ear. "I don't want to have to hurt you. Now come along nicely…"

We started to walk. To anyone who cared to look it probably appeared as if the rangy man in the big hat and I were simply strolling arm in arm, almost like lovers. First Toby, now this man—heaven only knew what my reputation would be. If I were still around to have one, that is.

"The booth—" I said somewhat idiotically. "I can't leave it alone—"

"Your booth will be fine. Just don't draw any attention to us."

"Toby… My nephew…"

"He's fine. We're watching out for him. Now come on."

They were watching Toby? He could have said nothing worse. What would they do to him? How could I help him? Could I even help myself?

"You won't hurt him," I said, trying to sound authoritative and not making it.

"No, of course not. We just want to talk to you."

By now we were out of the building and cutting off to the left, away from the open air sales area and heading toward the public parking area. They just wanted to "talk to me." My knees went watery. Everyone knew that was just a euphemism for "extract information"—usually in a rough and painful way—then "get rid of."

My only hope was to get away and get back to rescue Toby before his confederates knew I was loose. Then… well, then I didn't know, but just about anything had to be better than this.

"That RV," he said and steered me toward it. His grip, tight but not painful, hadn't eased a bit.

The RV was parked at the far edge of the lot. Enormous, black and glossy, it looked as big as a house. It was also downright menacing.

Okay, so if I were going to do anything I had to act now.

I twisted quickly, trying not to cry out at the sudden pain in my arm. At the same instant I lashed out with my foot, catching him hard on the ankle. The impact had to be at least as painful for me as for him. Canvas sneakers are no match for the hard leather of expensive cowboy boots. I twisted free and jumped back as he staggered, then quick as a cat regained his balance.

It was only a second or two, but that was enough for me to reach under my shirt, pull the automatic from the small of my back where it had been stuck so uncomfortably all day and aim at him.

When push comes to shove, I have always believed, bad guys are always cowards. This one certainly acted like it. He went pale and motionless, caught in an ungainly crouch that couldn't have been comfortable.

Good.

On the other hand, probably anyone bad or good would react the same way on seeing a 9 mm Beretta, which is not a small gun, aimed at them.

Very slowly he raised his hands slightly in a gesture that was both submissive and calming. "Now, Mrs. Ruiz, don't do anything you're going to be sorry for—"

"Oh, believe me, I won't," I snapped.

"I want to show you something," he said in a low, reasonable tone, the kind one uses to strange dogs of uncertain temperament. "Now I'm going to reach into my pocket…"

"Don't move," I said with more authority than I felt.

What on earth did I do now? I had the drop on him, but without shooting him and alerting everyone in a two-mile radius how could I get away to go get Toby? Things weren't working out the way I'd envisioned them.

"Okay, okay…" he answered, frozen in mid-motion. "Let's not either one of us do anything foolish."

I am a good shot. Jim called me one of the best. On the other hand, there's all the difference in the world in pointing your weapon at a paper target and at a live human being. I had never in my life fired at anything that moved, other than a thrown tin can or bottle. It was distressing to me just how distressing I found pointing the gun at a person. It was also upsetting that I couldn't hold the pistol still. The muzzle seemed to have taken on a life of its own, dipping and swooping back and forth like a trapped bird.

He didn't like it either. He watched it like a cat, scarcely seeming to breathe.

"Mrs. Ruiz, things aren't what you think they are—"

"I don't know what things are," I answered in a kind of howl. "I just know my life is upside down and I don't know why and I don't want any part of it."

"I understand. I'm—"

"All I want is my nephew and me out of this and safe. Now are you going to leave us alone?"

"I can't do that, Mrs. Ruiz." Slowly, so very slowly, he straightened up a little, but didn't move otherwise. "I'm here to help you…"

"Help me? That's why you attacked me in the parking lot in Amarillo?"

"That was the kid who wanted to buy drugs, the one I chased away."

"Drugs? He just wanted to buy some beads. You're lying to me."

Amazingly enough he chuckled and shook his head slightly. "No, ma'am, that I'm not. My partner and I were keeping an eye on you. That punk jumped you, and I knocked him down. He ran away and I went after him."

His partner. I'd forgotten the fresh-faced young man who had been there that first day. Where was he? Sneaking around behind me, ready to jump me and take my gun away? I shook from sheer nerves, sending the gun dancing even more.

"You need to put that down, Mrs. Ruiz," he said with a timbre of authority in his voice.

"I'm an excellent shot," I replied.

"I've been told you are. I'm on your side."

"The hell you are." I seldom swear, but at the moment it seemed apropos.

He chuckled again, but this time it was ruefully. "Patches said you were a strong-minded lady."

"Yes, and you'd better not forget... *Patches?*"

"More generally known as Detective Brian Webber of the Dallas Police Department." Moving a little faster, he stood up to his full height and lowered his hands. "He's been helping us with our investigation."

The ground was starting to dissolve beneath my feet. Suddenly my ears were ringing. The air was getting thick and everything seemed very far away and I was having the most difficult time catching my breath. Almost of its own accord my pistol began to sink, lowering its deadly muzzle toward the earth. The tall rangy man stepped forward with a quick economy of motion and pried it from my rubbery fingers.

"Who are you?"

He reached in his back pocket and held out a black leather folder containing an enormous shiny badge. "Special Agent Thomas O'Connell," he said briskly, "FBI."

FIFTEEN

I WAS DOOMED. Well, I might as well be doomed. Take over, Annie had said. Give orders, Annie had said. I had done both, and look where it had gotten me.

It wasn't bad enough I'd nicknamed a Dallas police detective after a dog, now I'd pointed a gun at a federal officer. Was that a hanging offense? Or just a simple spend-the-rest-of-your-life-in-jail felony?

It didn't make any difference. I was doomed either way.

"Here." Special Agent O'Connell molded my fingers around a mug of coffee from which steam rose in little wisps. "Drink this."

Obediently I took a sip. Not only was it hot enough to blister paint, it was black and almost as thick as tar. I didn't care.

"Now, Mrs. Ruiz…" Special Agent O'Connell leaned back on the edge of the desk. He had shed his hat, revealing a short-cut helmet of dark hair only slightly frosted with silver.

We were inside the big black RV, which from here looked like any office anywhere in the world with desks and computers and faxes and a lethal coffeemaker. The agent had sat me down in an uncomfortable visitor's chair of chrome and black leatherette. Now, perched on the edge of the desk and looming over me, he studied me with steely eyes. Did they make you take a class in how to loom over people at the FBI academy? If so, he must have aced it.

"I didn't mean it. I wouldn't have shot you."

He snorted at that and looked down at his boots. "Well, I hope not. Now, like I said, we need to talk."

"About what?"

"Come now, Mrs. Ruiz. You know what's going on."

"But I don't," I cried desperately. "I don't know how any of this happened. I don't even know what 'this' is. I came home three weeks ago and opened my front door and there was the dead body of a man I had never seen before. Then my house was all but destroyed and you scare me to death by hanging around so—so *sinisterly* and I still don't know what's going on."

He snorted at "sinisterly" but I couldn't tell if he was amused or not.

"This is not the time to play dumb, Mrs. Ruiz."

"I am not playing dumb. I really do not know anything." I put the poisonous coffee back on the desk. Two sips had revived me. It might be dangerous to my health to take any more. "Now I need to get back to my booth and check on my nephew. He'll be worried that I've been gone so long."

"My partner is looking after your nephew," he said and that scared me more than anything.

I might have done something stupid, but the door opened and Toby exploded into the room.

"Aunt Lilias!"

I had never been so glad to see anyone in my entire life. We grabbed each other in a painful embrace and clung. I even cried a little from pure relief.

"Oh, Toby, you're all right. I was so scared."

Toby grinned. I had the feeling that if he were to be accidentally cast into the seventh circle of Hell he would emerge grinning. "I was scared, too, when I couldn't find you, then Agent Harding showed up…"

He gestured to the man who stood behind him and it took a moment for me to recognize the man who had been with Special Agent O'Connell in Amarillo. He looked much more at home in a plain charcoal suit and tie than he ever had in the western gear he had worn before.

"Special Agent Alex Harding, Mrs. Ruiz," he said, nodding most politely.

"You weren't supposed to bring him in until I told you," Special Agent O'Connell said with a frown.

"He tried," Toby said. "He couldn't stop me."

"You said to look after him. You didn't authorize extreme measures." Agent Harding shrugged, but his reasoning was obvious. He was a small man, shorter than I by a couple of inches and lightly built. Compared to Toby he looked like an overdressed child. Since he was an FBI agent there was no doubt he knew any number of methods to restrain an individual much larger than himself, but probably not without harm to whomever was involved.

O'Connell's jaw tightened so much it looked like I could have broken a board against it.

"Are you all right, Aunt Lilias?"

Another time, another place and I might have found Toby's concern annoying. I was an adult and accustomed to looking after myself. At the moment, though, I found it endearing.

"Yes, but I really didn't know Special Agent O'Connell was a policeman when I held the gun on him…"

Special Agent Harding gave an explosive, uncon-

trollable burst of laughter which died instantly under
O'Connell's withering gaze.

If nothing else, Special Agent Harding was a brave
man. In tones somber enough for a funeral he asked,
"She got the drop on you? Tom O'Connell, the FBI's
top quick draw artist?"

"I didn't mean to... I didn't know he was a policeman." Somehow it seemed very important to keep repeating that. Maybe I could get out of prison before I
was a very, very old woman. "Do you know how long
I'll have to stay in jail?"

A dull red flush rose from the knife-edge of
O'Connell's jaw and darkened his face. "Obviously you
thought me a danger to your life, and given the circumstances I can see why. Since I hadn't identified myself
as a law officer I don't see why the incident has to be
mentioned in our report at all."

Special Agent Harding disguised another explosive
snort as a cough, but not very successfully.

Toby looked at me with a mingled expression of disbelief and admiration. "You almost shot a federal agent?"

"I didn't almost shoot him."

"Didn't Uncle Jim teach you never draw a gun—"

"—unless you mean to use it, I know," I answered
with a weak shadow of my old asperity. "I don't need
you to remind me of the basic laws of gun safety."

"Be careful, kid," Special Agent Harding said flip-
pantly. "You might be next."

"Don't be ridiculous. I've had a carry permit for years
and am regarded as an excellent shot." *But*, I added
silently, *only if aiming at an inanimate object*.

"Now that we've had a good laugh," Special Agent
O'Connell said with an edge in his voice that could

scratch steel, "let's get back down to business. How long have you been selling drugs, Mrs. Ruiz?"

I DIDN'T REALLY faint. I never completely lost consciousness or fell down. I just sort of stood there in a few seconds of semi-coma with my mouth hanging open stupidly until I could make the muscles work enough to croak, "What?"

"That's stupid," Toby snapped, and straightened to his full height.

"Sit down," O'Connell snapped back. "We'll get to your part in this later."

"That's ridiculous," I snapped in response to both of them. "Toby hasn't got anything to do with this. We're both innocent."

"You sure haven't been acting like it." O'Connell stood and motioned Toby to sit down in the chair Harding had put behind him. After a moment Toby sat. Then O'Connell took his position of authority behind the desk. It didn't make any difference. He might be farther away and more on a level, but he still loomed.

"What do you mean by that?" Making myself move slowly and deliberately, I seated myself with all the grace and aplomb of a queen regnant, then folded my hands serenely in my lap. It hid their shaking.

"There was a man murdered in your home, for one thing. That doesn't happen to most people."

"It happened to me," I said with an edge in my voice.

"A stranger."

"A stranger."

"Then your house was trashed."

"Yes, and I hold the police department responsible for that. They didn't secure my property."

"Then before the repairs are completed, you're out on the road again."

"I had already paid for the booth space for the rest of the season," I said, trying to sound reasonable and pretty much failing. "I have to sell my beads, and that means I have to keep on the circuit. No one in the government pays me a check, so I have to work for a living."

It was a cheap shot and I was glad he ignored it. Working for the FBI probably wasn't easy. He certainly was working hard now to make me appear guilty.

"And you have no idea who trashed your house."

"None."

"What were they looking for?"

"I don't know."

"It was your house," he said in a deliberately provocative tone.

My serenely folded hands had clenched into a double fist. "Yes, it is my house, but I have no idea what they were looking for. Something the dead man brought in with him, I suppose. You say you've talked to Detective Webber, so you should know about the scheme to use the houses of innocent people for storage."

A smile fleetingly touched his face, transforming it for a few seconds before his features once again froze into a forbidding mask. "Patches? Yes, I've talked with him. Apparently the net is spreading. There've been several more houses uncovered in the scheme."

"You see? I'm not the only one."

"You're the only one who had a man murdered in your house. You're the only one whose house was trashed and broken into. You're the only one who had dealings with and made purchases from a known dealer."

"What?" I whispered, once again unable to get air into my lungs. "Who?"

"Come on, Mrs. Ruiz. Don't play innocent with me. You know very well who I'm talking about."

"But I don't! I don't know any drug dealers." There was a hysterical edge in my voice I didn't like.

"This is stupid," Toby said. "There's no way Aunt Lilias would be involved in anything like that. She's as lame as my folks."

"Be quiet, young man, or I'll have you taken outside."

Toby's jaw tightened pugnaciously. "You and what army?"

"Toby, don't," I said, mother-gene kicking in. "Just because they're being unreasonable is no reason for you to act badly."

"Aunt Lilias, this is serious. Maybe you shouldn't say anything until you get your lawyer friend up here."

Something flickered in Special Agent O'Connell's eyes that made me think he knew about Annie and that he didn't want to tangle with her.

"I can do that," I said slowly, "but I'm innocent, Toby. Innocent people shouldn't need a lawyer. Do I need a lawyer, Special Agent O'Connell? You aren't charging me with anything, are you?"

His eyes narrowed slightly as he leaned back in his chair. "No. Not at the moment. We're just talking."

"Good. I was afraid that with those ridiculous accusations you're throwing around you might be charging me. Since we're just talking, that means I can just walk out of here anytime I want, doesn't it?"

"You're a lawyer, Mrs. Ruiz?" he asked, suspicion dripping from every word.

"No. But on every crime show—"

Harding shook his head and chuckled, earning him a poisonous glance from his superior. "Detective Webber warned us that you liked crime shows."

"Is that how you do your research?"

My own jaw became a trifle pugnacious. "That is enough, Special Agent O'Connell," I replied in edged tones. "Either you start playing fair with me or Toby and I are leaving this moment."

"That wouldn't be wise. You aren't being charged—yet—but you are under suspicion of dealing in drugs, Mrs. Ruiz. That's a very serious situation."

While I had once thought the man good looking in a cheap romance-novel sort of way, I had never liked him. Now I was starting to positively dislike him. "So is false accusation. Who are these drug dealers whom you say I know?"

He stared at me for a moment until I could almost feel icicles forming on my back, then leaned forward, elbows on the desk.

"Calvin and Martha Sullivan."

For a moment the room rocked. Had he said Bugs Bunny I could not have been more surprised. Tipsy, contentious, unpleasant little Calvin? Mousy, tasteless Martha? Drug dealers?

Calvin and Martha were dead in a fiery crash far away from where anyone could have expected them to be.

"Is that why they died?"

It was a simple question, but it had an electric effect on the two agents. Harding, who had been leaning comfortably against an empty desk, started to his feet. O'Connell, his mask momentarily shattered, leaned forward sharply.

"How did you know that?"

I blinked. "Jeff Roemer told me. Right after lunch, when I was visiting with Carrie Littlewolf."

The two agents exchanged a glance that seemed to

communicate a lot. Exactly what, I didn't know, but it didn't make them happy.

"How did he know?" Harding asked.

"I don't know," O'Connell answered tightly, "but you're going to go find out. Now."

I could have told them that Old Bobby had told Jeff, but that wouldn't help them any. They'd just want to know how Old Bobby knew, and I had no idea. Besides, I was feeling far from helpful at the moment.

Harding stood reluctantly. "This place is like a carny. Close-mouthed and clannish. It's going to blow our cover."

O'Connell thought a moment. From his expression it wasn't pleasant. "So be it. We need to know how he knew."

"Everyone's already suspicious," Toby said and I could swear the little wretch was being smug. Sorry, the young wretch. There was no way he could be considered the little anything. "When you swooped down and had your men start packing up everything in our booth I could see everyone looking."

I gulped. Until that moment I had forgotten the booth, my stock, my purse, everything. "Oh, Toby, we could have been stolen blind! Did you notice…?"

He patted my hands. "It's all right, Aunt Lilias. They were already packing it up when I got back."

"Who?"

"We had agents on either side of you, Mrs. Ruiz, and an observation station across the aisle."

"Those two men were agents? The one with the T-shirts and the…other one?" I babbled, unable to remember what he had been selling. On TV they said that good undercover agents didn't stand out in crowds. That man must be a wonderful agent, because he was next to invisible. "And a camera across the aisle? In the hunting lodge booth? Why?"

"Don't be disingenuous, Mrs. Ruiz. We wanted to keep you under surveillance." O'Connell had a feral little smile. "We also wanted a record of who visited your booth and what you did."

"Well," I said with outraged asperity, "I hope it was a good show."

"Middling."

"How did you arrange it? This fair has been sold out for months."

"As soon as we were sure you were coming here we spoke to Mr. McCallum about requisitioning the booths. He was most cooperative."

I groaned. That would explain Scott's coolness toward me when I had checked in this morning. I had found his attitude baffling, as we'd always had a cordial relationship.

"My God, he'll probably ban me forever. I hope you're enjoying ruining my life for nothing."

"I don't regard drug dealing as nothing."

Toby would have spoken, but I squeezed his hand in a demand for silence and for once he obeyed me, though his expression was mutinous.

"I tell you again, Special Agent O'Connell—" his name sounded like a profanity in my mouth, "—that I have nothing to do with drugs. Period. What have you done with my things?"

"We've loaded everything in your van," he replied easily, "including your personal items, both from the booth and the motel. We did this to keep a control over them. I'm hoping you will give us permission to do a thorough search as it will save time, but it won't take long to get a warrant."

"I have nothing to hide," I said sturdily.

"Aunt Lilias, don't you think you should talk to your lawyer before you do something like that?"

"Why? I'm innocent. Everything in that van has been gone through several times by me, you, the detectives in Dallas. You know there's nothing in there but my stock. Assuming," I added in bitter tones to Special Agent O'Connell, "that I still have a career left after they get through with me."

"As you said, innocent people have nothing to fear."

"I'm learning very quickly *that* is a load of horse-puckey," I snapped.

"You're contradicting yourself, Mrs. Ruiz."

"I don't care. I'm innocent and I'm scared to death. You've already seriously damaged my reputation here and heaven only knows where else. And you seem more intent on finding evidence to convict me of something than you are of looking for the real crooks."

"Speaking of the real crooks, how did you know the Sullivans were dead?"

"I told you. Jeff Roemer told me."

"How did he know?"

"How am I supposed to know?" I all but spat the words. "Why are you harping on that? Calvin was a drunk. I suppose it was inevitable he would crash that huge old RV someday. It's tragic, but it's just a traffic accident."

"Sullivan's body was thrown free of the vehicle about halfway down the canyon. If he'd stayed in the vehicle the crash and the fire might have destroyed his body. As it is, he's pretty badly broken up, but—"

"Please," I said, biting my lips against a sudden wave of nausea. "I didn't like him or Martha very much, and

I can't believe they were drug dealers, but they're dead. You don't have to be so graphic about the accident."

"It wasn't the accident that killed Calvin Sullivan," O'Connell said in measured tones. "An RV accident doesn't leave its victim with a bullet hole through the skull."

SIXTEEN

"You did what?"

"I gave them permission to search my van. Please don't yell at me, Annie. I couldn't have stopped them."

"I could have," she said and the knife edge of her voice almost sliced through the speaker of my cell phone. "At least for a while. Oh God, Lilias, what have you gotten yourself into?"

I wondered that myself. We'd been transported to a large empty warehouse, presumably in Tulsa, since we hadn't driven but a few minutes. Toby and I had been ordered to stay in the RV while O'Connell and Harding and a couple of other anonymous agents removed everything from my van. When I say everything, I mean everything. They had not only unloaded every box, bag and suitcase—including the stuff we had left in our hotel rooms—but had taken out the seats and the dash with the speed and skill of car-strippers.

We'd been offered drinks and snacks and free run of the RV kitchenette, but it was scant comfort. I wouldn't have been surprised had they locked the door. Neither my purse nor my computer had been returned. Luckily my cell phone had been in my pocket. I'd wanted to call Annie before they realized and took it away too.

"I have gotten myself into nothing," I snapped. "Things are just happening, and I don't know why, but I intend to find out."

"Go careful, Lilias. These are powerful people," she said. There was a ghost of trepidation in her voice I had never heard before.

"I can't believe you of all people are saying that."

"Look, Lilias, the dead man in your house and the Sullivans and all of this are just a small part of a big case. Patches said the FBI has been involved from the beginning."

"Thanks for telling me."

"I couldn't. I was under direct orders not to. I think they've even got a mole here in our office. In any case, I'm an officer of the court. I can't endanger an ongoing investigation."

"Gee, thanks. What about your client?"

"You weren't in any danger. At least, you weren't until you gave them permission to search your van. I can't believe you did something so stupid."

They had everything out of the van now, set in neat rows across the concrete floor, including the seats and the dash and even the doorpanels. I sure hoped they knew how to put a car back together as well as they did to take it apart.

"And why shouldn't I? Annie, I'm innocent. I don't know what's going on. I've been through everything in that van. So have you and Detective Webber and Detective Costigan and Toby and heaven knows who else. There's nothing there to find."

"I hope so. Who's the field agent in charge up there?"

"Special Agent O'Connell."

"Thomas O'Connell?" Annie's voice dropped almost an octave and I could hear her gasping for breath. "Oh, cripes, Lilias, you are in some deep trouble. I had no idea he was working that end of it."

Somewhere near where my stomach used to be a great knot of ice formed. "Tell me."

"He's a driven man. Hard as hell to work with and meaner than a snake. One of the highest case closure records with the Bureau, but a maverick. He's been suspended a time or two, come close to going rogue a time or two. Makes his own rules. The only reason he gets away with it is that he's been very lucky so far. He's dangerous, Lilias. Both to the bad guys and to anyone who gets in his way."

"How do you know so much about him?"

"We have a history," she said shortly. "It was a long time ago, but he was still an…uncomfortable man then. Look, I had better come up there. I can get Charlie to take over the Chiswick depositions…"

"No, don't. Go ahead and do what you're doing. If I need you I can call and you can come up then."

"Lilias…"

"No, think about it. I'm innocent, Annie. I am. And if I suddenly drag my lawyer up here when there's nothing to be found, it's going to look bad. I don't have anything to fear because I have done nothing."

"You are either a saint or a fool, Lilias Ruiz. You have no idea of what's going on."

"No, because no one will tell me anything."

"Aunt Lilias, someone's coming," Toby said. He had stationed himself as lookout at the window. In another situation the spectacle of him trying to be inconspicuous would have been funny.

Annie'd heard too. "Lilias, I'm—"

I never did hear what she said, for I snapped the phone shut and slid it into my pocket only seconds before Special Agent Harding opened the door.

"Mrs. Ruiz? Toby? Will you come with me, please?"

The warehouse was bigger than it had appeared from inside the RV. It was also hot and oddly stuffy. Once out of the air conditioned comfort of the RV the heat wrapped around us like a thick moist blanket. The shadowy emptiness of the huge building seemed to go on forever, bleak concrete and small dusty windows set high in the walls and dismal fluorescent lights, only half of which worked. It was a good fifty feet to the wreckage of my van and as I approached its violated hulk I couldn't restrain a tear.

"Aunt Lilias?"

"That was Jim's van," I said in a choked voice.

"We'll put it back in working order, Mrs. Ruiz," Special Agent Harding said.

"You damn well better!" Angrily I swiped away the damning tear. I couldn't afford to be weak or sentimental now. "This is an outrage."

"Protesting again?" Special Agent O'Connell asked. His mouth twisted as if he'd just tasted something bitter.

"Again and always. You have no right to harass decent people like this."

"I have every right to do my best to find and arrest criminals." His voice was cold.

"Then why don't you do it, and leave me alone?"

His mouth worked as if he wanted to say something, but he didn't. After a moment he waved his arm toward my belongings with an almost courtly gesture. "Could you please tell us about these things?"

I stared. Nothing like this had ever happened on any of my crime shows. Well, I thought somewhat heatedly, if he wanted a tour of my possessions, I would most certainly give him one.

Whether by accident or design our bags were first. I opened mine and showed them everything—including,

I'm afraid, my dirty laundry—giving a running commentary on where I had bought each item, if it were comfortable and any interesting anecdotes attached to it, like the time I spilled coffee on my checked blouse just before having to give a demonstration on making beaded flowers.

Jim used to say I was prickly when annoyed and downright contentious when angry.

I was angry.

Very angry.

At first Special Agent O'Connell's eyes sparkled with repressed anger, but as I worked my way through a suddenly very large suitcase of totally commonplace belongings the anger seemed to fade and a kind of sardonic amusement took its place. At least I think it did. Reading any emotion on his stony face was sort of like trying to figure out the true inner feelings of the figures on Mt. Rushmore. Special Agent Harding was less in control of his features, for he repeatedly tried to stifle a smile. The other agents, assuming they were agents, seemed to have faded into the shadows.

Toby was less dramatic. When my bags were finished, he took his backpack and gave a somewhat shamefaced inventory. "Underwear, walking shorts, two shirts, some socks, tooth and shaving stuff." Then he held up three of the biggest books I had ever seen. "And my books. *Foundations of Differentiable Manifolds,* and *Lie Groups, Matrices, and Vector Spaces,* and *Mathematical Modeling of Finite Elements.*"

"Going in for light reading?" Special Agent O'Connell asked sarcastically as he flipped through each volume.

Toby waited until he had the books back in his hands before shrugging, then answering with an insulting casualness. "Just keeping refreshed on the elemental stuff."

Putting the books down carefully, he turned the back-pack inside out to show it was truly empty, save for a heroic accumulation of lint and dust. And crumbs. Lots of crumbs.

I was still angry when we moved on to the beads. We went through every box. I showed them the ex-hippie necklaces and Toby's new Fibonacci design. I showed them the bib, waterfall and multi-strand necklaces and explained—at length—the differences between them and the construction problems inherent in each design. I showed them the earrings and bracelets, though there really wasn't much to say about most of them.

Then we went on to the flowers. I was talking about an arrangement of three calla lilies when one of the other agents, a nice enough looking but unremarkable man in his thirties, brought Toby and me Cokes. I almost said I preferred Dr Pepper and it had to be diet, but decided not to push my luck. Whatever it was, the soda was cold and wet and good on my parched throat. Somehow the temperature in the warehouse seemed to have soared, but that wasn't the only reason a film of sweat covered my body.

We finished the small collection of beaded arrangements and went on to the single roses. I explained about the white/crystal roses, saying only they were a gift for a friend and not for sale, then opened a box of red/green Lover's Roses.

"But you're familiar with the Lover's Roses, aren't you, Special Agent O'Connell?" I asked sweetly. "My offer of a bulk discount still stands, if you're interested."

He made an indistinguishable sound deep in his throat. Out of the corner of my eye I could see Special Agent Harding had lost control and was grinning widely.

"And here we have the loose beads." I held up the big

glass jar. "I keep these on the counter more as a deco-
ration than anything. I don't really sell beads per se,
though sometimes people think I do."

Special Agent O'Connell poured the jar's contents
onto a piece of cardboard that seemed to materialize
from nowhere and poked through the beads carefully,
examining a few at random, but it was Special Agent
Harding who put the beads back into the jar. Then we
worked our way through the loose beads, which was a
misnomer as they were all carefully confined into zip-
pered sandwich baggies, plastic refrigerator containers
or small boxes—sometimes all three. Although I was
tiring and my anger fading into a chill apprehension, I
refused to let the agents' silence intimidate me and continued lecturing, giving origins, designs and potential
uses for each kind of bead.

Somehow I was surprised that although everything
had been obviously packed very quickly (the tablecloths
were wadded into a great wrinkled ball) some care had
been taken and nothing was damaged. Sure, there was
a bent leaf here and there on some of the flowers, but
nothing more than I would do and had done before.

Finally there was nothing left but Martha's boxes,
which had been put at the tail end of the parade. It was
easy for anyone to see that they were different. While
my supplies and stock were either in white plastic tubs
or the plain brown cardboard boxes in which they had
been shipped, Martha's liquor boxes were dirty, scarred
and mashed in several places, held together with myr-
iad layers of masking tape. I knelt beside them with
a certain reluctance, apologizing in my heart for the
uncharitable thoughts I'd had about the Sullivans. *De
mortuis* and all that...

"These are the boxes I got from Martha."

"Did you often buy from Martha Sullivan?"

"No, I didn't. This was the first thing I ever bought from her, and I had second thoughts about that."

"Why?" Special Agent O'Connell's eyes were like lasers.

"Because in general she had crappy stuff. I'm an artist. I make some cheap jewelry because it helps pay the bills, but most of my creations are art. Martha's weren't."

"So why did you buy from her this time?"

It was something I was beginning to wonder myself. The truth was the truth, however, and I had nothing to be ashamed of.

"Economics. We were at the big arts and crafts festival in Beaumont last month. I was just heading back to my booth from the ladies' room when Martha stepped out of her booth and stopped me. She told me she was selling off all her beads and wondered if I would like to buy them."

"Was that unexpected?"

I shrugged. "Kind of, because she'd done it for so long, but people are always changing what they sell. Look at Bernie and Carole Freeman—it seems they have a different product every show. But they aren't artists, they're salespeople. Of course, Martha wasn't an artist, either. She just strung beads. Maybe she'd found something she liked better and wanted to get rid of her stock. I don't know and I didn't ask."

"But you bought it even though you didn't want it."

"Yes. She didn't have much good stuff—or much taste, either," I added, feeling bad at talking so of the dead, even if it was the truth.

"You say she was insistent."

"Yes. She even brought some examples over to show me. These—" I dug in one of the boxes, "—and these.

These are glass spinners, probably made close to World
War I. Definitely pre-WWII. These teardrops and these
glass ones are nice too. There's a couple of other fairly
good things in here, but not many. There were a few
reasonably decent tools—a couple of clamps and pliers
and the like—and a few findings, but the rest is pretty
much cheap junk. Lots of big wooden beads, like they
put in old-fashioned macramé, and some plastic. And
then there's the curtain." The curtain had been dumped
unceremoniously into the last box, leaving it in a ghastly
tangle. It would take quite a while to get it straightened
out again, even if I wanted to.

Special Agent O'Connell didn't say a word, but he
was listening louder than anyone I've ever seen.

"What about the curtain, Mrs. Ruiz?" Special Agent
Harding asked blandly.

"What about it? Martha always had it hanging behind her in their booth. It's a great big mish-mash of all
kinds of beads strung in no kind of pattern that I can
make out."

"But you bought it."

"Not knowingly."

Special Agent O'Connell's eyebrows rose.

"I didn't know I was buying it. Martha and I agreed
on a price for these beads—the teardrops and the rhinestones and the spinners and the rest of the good ones.
The ones I could use."

"How much?"

"Forty dollars. It's low, I think, but it's fair. Anyway,
Martha suggested it. I had to get back to my booth, so
she said she'd bring everything down to me later." I
stopped, remembering that afternoon. Everyone had
been busy. It was the last afternoon of the show and the
bargain hunters had been rapacious, wanting everything

for nothing. I had just gotten rid of a particularly insistent specimen by telling her if she said one more word I was going to call Security on her for harassment when Martha had trundled up the aisle, towing the three battered liquor boxes on a dolly.

"Yes, Mrs. Ruiz?" O'Connell prompted.

"I was just thinking. Martha seemed almost frightened that afternoon. I put it down to it being closing time and we were all in a rush to get loaded up and get out of there, but in retrospect it seems like more than that."

"Did she say anything unusual?"

"For Martha to say anything was unusual. She was a very quiet person, and about all she ever said was 'hello' or 'good-bye.' Calvin was a talker, though. About anything. He thought he knew everything about everything."
Like most men, I almost said, then shook my head and went on. "Anyway, when I saw those three boxes I knew there was more in there than I had thought I was buying. I thought she might be trying to pull a fast one on me."

"Was she?"

"I don't think so. At least she wouldn't take any more money. When I pointed out that the beads I had bought would barely fill one box, she just said that she found some others and she wanted them all out of there. She was so insistent she even dropped the price to thirty-five dollars."

"And so you bought all three boxes."

"Yes."

"Sight unseen."

"Yes," I answered testily. "At that price, wouldn't you?"

"About the curtain," Special Agent Harding said smoothly. "Why did you hang it?"

I shrugged. "Why not? I do sell beads. It's not very

pretty, though there are a few good beads in there—
some amber and some semi-precious stones. I'll probably
take it apart and salvage them." If I were free to do so.

"You weren't trying to attract Martha Sullivan's clientele?"

"You don't know much about the art fair circuit, do
you, Special Agent O'Connell? With the kind of things
Martha sold she wouldn't have had a clientele. She sold
cheap, pick-up, impulse jewelry. Now I have several repeat customers in every venue and I'm getting a name
for quality beadwork, but poor Martha…"

I was surprised to find my eyes moistening. Poor
Martha indeed. She hadn't been much and hadn't had
much, but she'd deserved a better death.

"There's one more box," Special Agent O'Connell
said.

Strange—I wouldn't have thought of him as a glut-
ton for punishment, but if he wanted it, I was going to
give it to him. I squatted by the box and started pulling out plastic bags. These were bigger, either quart or
gallon sizes.

"This is all the stuff I don't want. You can see it's
nothing like my stuff. Here's some yummy 1980s plastic in absolutely nauseating colors. Here's two bags of
odd wooden shapes. I don't know what they are, but they
aren't beads. They look," I added, my nose wrinkled as if
I smelled something spoiled, "like scraps from someone
cutting designs out of plywood. Here are some wooden
beads that haven't even been drilled yet… Oh."

"Yes, Mrs. Ruiz?"

There was a small sifting of powder in the bottom
of the bag. "It looks like some sort of bug has gotten in
there and been eating. Oh well, I was going to get rid
of them anyway."

I was going to toss the bag away, but with the quickness of a striking snake O'Connell snatched it from me and opened it. As I watched in amazement he took out one of the beads, scratched it with his fingernail, sniffed it, then rolled it in his fingers before dropping it back into the bag and pressing the zipper shut with a hissing sound. He had an unholy look on his face.

"It will have to be tested, of course, but I'll bet that your undrilled wooden beads are compacted cocaine worth about half a million on the street once it's powdered and cut."

I fainted.

SEVENTEEN

I CAME OUT of my faint almost before I hit the concrete floor. Toby had leaped to break my fall, as had, surprisingly, Special Agent O'Connell. O'Connell had been quicker, and it was no special pleasure to open my eyes to the sight of his saturnine face hovering above mine. They took me back to the RV, installed me in a reasonably comfortable chair and plied me with more iced Coke. I seldom drank non-diet sodas and found it almost unbearably thick and even sweeter than the one I'd had before. If this kept up pretty soon I wouldn't be able to fit into my jeans.

If I could still wear jeans, and not be restricted to prison... Well, whatever it was they wore in prison.

"Are you sure you shouldn't be lying down, Aunt Lilias?"

I shook my head. Somehow that would seem to be an admission of weakness and I had to be strong.

"Didn't think you'd get found out, did you?"

"I suppose it's futile to tell you I had no idea what that stuff was." I shot a poisonous glance at Special Agent O'Connell, who was again behind his desk, leaning back in his chair, fingertips tented in front of him. He was halfway smiling as if contemplating something delightful, like tossing me into a dungeon and throwing away the key.

"Yep."

He did it. He actually said "yep" in the best tradition of the old movie cowboy. Smug son of a so-and-so. Probably practiced saying it in front of a mirror.

"I really thought they were wooden beads. I never even opened the package." And why oh why oh *why* hadn't I just tossed them in the trash when I first saw them?

"Come on, Mrs. Ruiz! After all that's gone on, why keep harping on that old story? Why don't you make it easier on yourself and give us the names of your suppliers?"

"Because the only suppliers I have are the ones who sell beads," I snapped. "Plain old beads that are nothing but beads, and I'll be happy to give you their names. I don't have anything to do with dope, I have never had anything to do with dope, and I don't like your thinking that I do."

"Sure. That's why you're carrying a shipment of illegal drugs worth half a million dollars."

"Quit harassing my Aunt Lilias," Toby said stoutly. "She's a good person."

O'Connell directed his attention toward Toby with an intensity that came close to a physical slap. Leaning forward, he pointed a finger almost as intimidating as a weapon.

"You be quiet, young man, or I'll have you sent back to your parents, and believe me, after talking to them I think you're a lot better off here."

"You talked to my parents?" Toby said in a sinking voice while I cringed. Chrissy and Hank—not to mention the rest of the Ruiz tribe—would have my head for getting Toby involved in this, however innocently. Toby's voice slid up a notch. "Are they really angry?"

Special Agent O'Connell's lips turned up in an ugly

little smile. "If I decide to hold you for charges it might be considered protective custody."

"You wouldn't dare," I roared, mother-gene kicking in. "Toby has nothing to do with this."

"With what?"

He'd set his trap and I had fallen into it. Here was where I was supposed to have a rush of conscience and confess everything. Usually this happened about forty-five or fifty minutes into the program, leaving just enough time for a humorous wrap-up scene and the final commercials.

Except this was not a television program and I was not guilty of anything.

"With whatever fantasy you have cooked up in your pointy little head and seem determined to hang on me."

"Aunt Lilias—"

"So not even the threat of having your nephew charged as an accessory will make you tell the truth?"

"I have been telling the truth. I have told the truth ever since this began. Why won't anyone believe me?" Anger and tears warred both in my soul and my voice. I didn't mind it in the privacy of my soul, but I loathed giving this superior so-and-so even the tiniest bit of satisfaction by letting him see how scared I was.

"Why should I?" he asked in suddenly quite reasonable tones. "Look at it from my perspective. You have a dead man in your house—"

"About whom I knew nothing."

He made shushing motions with one hand. "Just hear me out. Then you can yell all you like. You have a dead man in your house, one who is known to be trafficking in drugs. Then your house is trashed by someone or several someones obviously looking for something.

We find your house has been used as a drug drop and storage place by someone who knows the alarm code."

I opened my mouth to protest that I knew nothing about that, but a glare from Special Agent O'Connell kept me quiet. I couldn't help what he believed, and to be practical, as long as he was talking, he wasn't arresting me.

I hoped.

"Then you don't even wait for your house to be repaired, but go back out on the road to the Amarillo show, taking with you the…merchandise—"

"Beads," I snapped, unable to contain myself. "Beads, beads, beads!"

"Very well, beads." Special Agent O'Connell's voice stayed low and reasonable and infuriating as he showed off his superiority. "You took with you the beads you bought from Martha Sullivan, a known drug dealer. You were under surveillance, of course. You set up your booth and hung up the bead curtain though you have repeatedly told any number of people you think it is ugly. A bead curtain, I might add, that several of our informants have told us is a sign that drugs are available in that booth."

I felt physically sick. That would explain some of the customers who had come to the booth looking for loose beads, perhaps even some of the ones who had gotten into involved discussions about "other kinds of merchandise." I should have seen immediately that something was strange about them. How could I possibly have been so ignorant?

"Then," he continued without a break, "after the show was over, you disappeared from the radar for over three days, finally showing up in Tulsa with a confederate in tow. Now tell me, Mrs. Ruiz, are those the actions of an innocent woman?"

This time only the pressure of Toby's hand on mine kept me from acting most unwisely. Special Agent O'Connell sat there, leaning back in his chair as if he didn't have a care in the world, that dratted superior little smile on his face. I wondered if this was how a mouse felt when cornered by a cat.

Well, I wasn't a mouse and at the moment, Agent O'Connell appeared to be more rat than cat. Taking a deep breath, I counted to ten in my mind, then did it again just to be sure. When I did speak, it was with a voice that was both composed and steady. The rest of me might have been a wreck, but my voice sounded great.

"I am always amazed at how different people can see the same incident in such different ways," I said with gracious aplomb. "Colored with their own prejudices, of course. As an innocent person I see everything I've done as perfectly logical. I return from a trip and find a dead body in my house. Of course I am upset, but that doesn't mean I know anything about it. I believe Detective Webber explained to you about the way the alarm company was used by those crooks?"

O'Connell nodded, but his expression didn't change.

"Then my house was destroyed, and so was I. If I were involved in something illegal, why would I use my own home and put my own things at risk? Some of the things destroyed were irreplaceable. Oh, they had little or no intrinsic value, but they were irreplaceable to me." In spite of all my good intentions my voice quavered and I took a moment to compose myself. "No one wants to see the things they love broken, Mr. O'Connell."

"That's Special Agent O'Connell," he said quietly.

"Considering how I'm feeling at the moment," I said

silkily, "you should be satisfied with 'mister.' Anyway, you wondered why I would leave before the repairs were finished. The answer is simple. I have to work for a living, and right now my living comes from the road. Spaces in these shows, good spaces especially, are neither cheap nor easy to come by. I couldn't just let them go. Annie and Don are both in Dallas and both are looking out for my house, which I appreciate more than you could ever understand."

The agent's expression darkened. "That's Annie Monroe and Don Garnett."

"Yes."

"How do you know them?"

"I gave you the courtesy of listening without interrupting," I said with a poisonously superior gentility. "Is it too much to hope for the same from you? Annie is my best friend. She lives across the street. Don is a retired developer who lives down the street around the bend."

"Is he your best friend, too?"

"No. I hardly know him. I think he's bored with retirement. May I continue?" I asked, getting a curt nod as an answer. "I want you to know that I knew nothing about either the curtain or the drugs. I bought them as beads and had no idea they were anything but beads. I even showed them and the curtain to both the detectives back in Dallas when they wanted to search my van. They thought they were nothing but beads too."

Special Agent O'Connell's expression went a shade darker.

"As for going off the radar for three days, I wanted to relax and think about things, which was, the last time I heard, not illegal. The Amarillo show had been upsetting. There was an element in those who came to my booth I'd never had before, probably because they knew the message you say was in that beaded curtain when I didn't. Then you and your partner kept popping up like Jack-in-the-boxes and saying the most extraordinary things. For a while I thought you might be running a protection racket. I was attacked leaving the show that night—but of course you know that. I recognized you."

"I explained that. I chased away that druggie kid."

"So you say," I said remorselessly and had the satisfaction of seeing his eyes narrow. "But you can't prove it, can you? Like I said, it's strange how different things can look to different people."

"Your point is made, Mrs. Ruiz." His voice was a thin wire of sound that could have sliced bone.

"I wanted to go think, so I went to a cabin in the Ouachitas that belongs to my late husband's family. It's very isolated. When I got there I found Toby."

"Who is on the run from college."

"And my parents," Toby admitted, giving his goofy grin. "You see, I hate basketball."

"So I gathered from your parents. You're a fool, boy." He gave Toby one dismissive glance then turned his attention back to me.

Toby's hands clenched convulsively around mine, but he merely straightened and said with an adult dignity, "I am not a fool, and I am not a boy."

O'Connell's face might have been carved of stone.

"Obviously I could not leave him there—"

"I hate chili, too," Toby added.

"—so I brought him with me. On the way here I learned my house had been broken into. Again."

That interested Special Agent O'Connell! "And?"

"I'm sure Detective Webber would be glad to give you the details. As I was not there anything I might say would only be hearsay evidence, and I'm sure that doesn't interest you."

He frowned. "Don't get too cocky, Mrs. Ruiz. You haven't said one thing yet that proves your innocence."

"And you can't prove my guilt because I am innocent. Those men you had on either side of me and that camera across the aisle will show that I didn't do anything illegal."

"Other than carry around a half million dollars' worth of drugs."

"I thought they were beads."

"Yes. You've said that repeatedly. However, repetition is not proof."

"How do you prove a negative?" I snapped.

"And under the law," Toby added stoutly, "a citizen is innocent until proven guilty. In my history class…"

"But your aunt is guilty of possession if nothing else."

My stomach dropped away to somewhere far beneath me. That was true and ignorance of the law was no excuse. They might even confiscate the van and then how could I manage? I couldn't afford a new vehicle.

Assuming, of course, that I would be free to need one. In spite of what we like to believe, innocent people are sometimes convicted.

A thought struck me and pulled me back from an abyss of despair. It turned my desperation into a cocky fearlessness. "Detective Webber didn't think so, and he handled that same bag. Of course, we only have your word for it that those beads are drugs, don't we?"

Special Agent O'Connell's face tightened with rage.

"For that matter, we only have your word that you're a real FBI agent. You could just as easily be part of the drug ring or whatever they're calling it these days."

"Aunt Lilias!"

"I showed you my badge and ID, if you recall."
O'Connell's taut mouth made the words into tiny,
poison-dart slivers and sent them flying across the room.

"I recall that you showed me an ID and a badge. I
barely glanced at them, if you recall, which is probably
what most people do when faced with the threat of a
powerful authority. Not that it guarantees anything. You
can make an ID card on just about any computer today,
and badges of all kinds are available all over the place—
gun shows, probably even here if you look hard enough."

"Would you like to see it again?" More slivers of
poison dart.

"No. Like most people I wouldn't know a real one
from a fake. Or maybe it is real and you're just a bad
cop. What better way to interact with the drug dealers
than by being an agent? You could do whatever you liked
with impunity, deal with those you want to, eradicate
the ones you don't, all in the name of law."

By now O'Connell's eyes had narrowed to slits. Inwardly I was quaking and I could hear Toby gulping
heavily. Had I gone too far? Probably, but if I were going
to be hanged, it might as well be for a sheep as a lamb.
I pulled out my cell phone.

"Instead of taking you at face value, perhaps I should
call Washington and see if you really are legit."

I really had expected him to laugh nastily and then
tell me to go ahead. I didn't expect the wave of pure hatred that went over his chiseled features, nor the quick
way he jumped up from behind the desk.

"Give me that phone."

"Why?"

"Because I say so. You are under interrogation and
being restrained under suspicion of drug trafficking and
possession." His voice had taken on a deep, thunderous

tone that could have been the voice of an ancient god. A very angry ancient god. "Now if you want I can make the arrest formal, and I can take your phone away, but I think you'd rather just give it to me now."

Wordlessly I extended it. He snatched it up and put it in his pocket. For a moment his face was so dark, his look so hard, I thought he might hit me. Then Special Agent Harding stuck his head in the side door (when had he left?) and said, "O'Connell, come out here. There's something you need to know."

Without a word O'Connell turned on his heel and stalked to the door. "You two stay here. Don't try to come out and don't touch anything," he snapped, then slammed the door behind him.

We sat in silence for a minute before Toby finally pried his white, squashed fingers out of my iron grip.

"Wow, you were certainly going there." His voice was full of awe. "Accusing him of being a fake agent or a dirty agent and a dope dealer on top of that."

Wordlessly I groaned and buried my head in my hands. What had I done? Why had I done it? Jim had always said my temper would get me into trouble one day.

"It doesn't make any difference," I said wearily. "I've already pulled a gun on him and no matter what he said a man like him would never forget it. He believes I'm guilty, Toby, he really believes I'm guilty, and he's going to do his best to convict me no matter if there's any evidence or not."

"But you aren't guilty," Toby said.

"I know that, and you know that, but that isn't going to make any difference. I'm just sorry I got you mixed up in this."

"I'm not," Toby said with the idiotic teenaged security of being invincible. "This is real life. This is exciting. This has nothing to do with basketball."

"If you get arrested, that'll probably be the end of your scholarship. I know, you'll probably think that's a good thing, but think about it. I know you don't like basketball, but it's only four years."

"Two. I'll be a junior next year."

"That's even better. Just two years of doing something you don't like in order to have a degree and a career in something you do like that will last you the rest of your life. It's not a bad bargain."

"That's what Mom and Dad say." He sounded sulky, as if an ally had suddenly become a turncoat.

"And you know they're right, don't you?"

He looked away. "But…"

I sighed. A lifetime of being subject to other people's rules, most especially your parents', got harder and harder to bear the older you got. It was paradoxical, but by the time the end was in sight it often became unbearable and something to be escaped at all costs. It had been true in my case and catching up after rebellion had been difficult. How tragic that now, just as Toby was realizing this, all of it might be snatched away because of me.

And I had done nothing, doggonnit. Well, yes, I had pretty much cussed out an FBI agent, but that by itself wasn't a jailable offense so far as I knew, and Special Agent Harding would probably help me about holding a gun on O'Connell. One thing I did know was that I had never had anything to do with drugs.

Proving it, though, was going to be another matter.

I don't know how long we sat there, but it felt like at least a century or two. None of the agents entered the RV and we didn't dare poke our heads out. After a while Toby got a soft drink and a handful of string cheese sticks from the little refrigerator and nothing happened, no bells or sirens or men entering with drawn guns, but still we sat. Toby asked if I wanted a drink or anything to eat, but I shook my head. Even the mention of food made me slightly nauseous. I wished I had told Annie to come up immediately.

When the door did open, it sounded almost loud enough to wake the dead. Special Agent O'Connell stalked into the RV. His face looked as hard as it ever had, his eyes like stones, but he was smiling broadly. The effect was horrible.

"Well, Mrs. Ruiz, you played your part well and you might have gotten away with it, but it's all over now. We just arrested your partner."

EIGHTEEN

"My PARTNER?" I squeaked as soon as I could talk again. "What partner? I don't have a partner."

"Give it up, Mrs. Ruiz. It's all over."

"But I tell you I don't have a partner. I've never had a partner. I've never done anything where I had to have a partner."

Somehow O'Connell managed to keep his ghastly smile and look contemptuous at the same time. "Protesting to the end, huh? Well, it's not going to do you any good."

"I don't know what you're talking about. I've never had a partner." I pounded my clenched fists on the chair arms to punctuate every word. By now I suppose I was starting to sound a little hysterical, as if that mattered. "I don't know what kind of charade you've dreamed up hoping to make me confess to something I didn't do, but it won't work."

"You're good, Mrs. Ruiz. Very good. Now…"

Before he could finish his thought the door to the RV flew open. I wondered who and/or what they might bring in to claim as my partner, but it was only Special Agent Harding who looked in.

"Tom, you—"

Suddenly he vanished, jerked backward, a look of intense surprise on his face. Visions of movie horrors stirred uneasily in my mind. I mean, what else had we missed?

What stepped through the door was much more frightening than any special effects creature Hollywood could ever dream up.

Stretched erect to her full five-foot-nothing, with steam practically blasting out of her ears, Annie Monroe—no, A. R. Monroe, Esq.—stepped into the RV in a worse temper than I had ever seen. Fury radiated from her like heat from a stove.

"O'Connell…"

Special Agent O'Connell was very good. There had only been the slightest flicker in his eyes that betrayed this was not a normal, everyday event. Now that flicker was gone and his craggy face immobile.

"Annie," he replied in a carefully neutral tone.

"Lilias?" she asked without removing her gaze from O'Connell. "Are you all right?"

"Yes, we're fine. How did you get here so soon?"

"I told you one of my partners has a plane. He flew me up."

"You know I haven't used a rubber hose on anyone in years," O'Connell said absolutely deadpan.

"Get out of here, Lilias."

"Now wait a minute—"

"Shut up, Tom," Annie snapped. "Lilias, get out. This is private."

I didn't wait to be told again, though I would have given a great deal to be able to hear what was coming. Grabbing Toby's hand, I dragged him to the door and out into the warehouse. Neither of them noticed that we were gone, as they were staring at each other with an intensity only seen in fighting animals.

"How did you find us?" O'Connell asked.

"I called Koenig. He'll be here as soon as he can get

a flight, and I hope to God you can make him understand, because I don't."

"This could be the biggest drug bust in this century," O'Connell said. His voice was low, but with enough energy behind it to have been shouting. "We can take down the entire Battarde cartel if we can just get this woman to talk."

"This woman has nothing to do with it." Annie's voice was like a razor. "You've gotten to where everyone is guilty of drug trafficking to you whether they are or not. You're obsessed."

"You're damn well right I am, and who has better reason?" O'Connell asked. He said more, but we didn't hear it because he reached out and slammed the door shut. Oh, we could hear voices, angry and bitter, but short of putting an ear to the window there was no way to distinguish any words. I might have tried it, though, if it hadn't been at least a foot above my head.

And if Special Agent Harding hadn't been watching.

He had picked himself up from the concrete floor and was moaning slightly as he stretched.

"Got you, didn't she?" Toby asked.

The officer looked almost as embarrassed as angry. "She caught me off guard. Doesn't she know it's a federal offense to attack a federal agent?"

"Since she's one of Dallas's top criminal attorneys, I would guess she does," I said with relish at his expression of surprise. "And, unless you want to look like a fool, you'd best forget it ever happened. Do you want the world to know that you, an FBI agent, were overpowered by a woman who has to stretch to be five feet tall?"

Another flush of anger went over his face, then

he stopped. "It was just that when she grabbed me I overbalanced…"

Toby snorted his laughter into his hand. "Anything that gets you through."

That remark earned him a hard look from Harding and it sobered me. While I was almost giddy with relief at Annie's appearance we weren't out of the woods by a long chalk.

Something new had been added. Between us and the wreckage of my van and possessions sat an anonymous black SUV, its tinted windows opaque in the dull light of the warehouse. Although it was almost as large as the van it reminded me of a crouching beast.

Inside had to be whoever they claimed was my partner.

Special Agent Harding grabbed my arm. "Stay here."

I hadn't realized I'd moved toward the SUV. "I have a right to know who is in there."

"Not now, you don't."

Why had I ever thought this man young and soft? Probably only by comparison to his boss. His grip, his face and his voice were all inflexible.

"I have a right to see my accuser. It's in the Constitution or someplace."

"In court, ma'am."

"But I don't have a partner. Whoever that is in there is lying."

"That's for the courts to decide." Inexorably he guided me toward a half-dozen or so prosaic lawn chairs set up at the back of the RV where a wholly inadequate fan pushed the air around. "Why don't you two just sit down and wait here?"

The sound of voices from inside the RV escalated. Annie and O'Connell had to be shouting at each other, but maddeningly I still couldn't understand a word they were saying. Perhaps the RV had been outfitted with some sort of special soundproofing.

Toby and I sat. The fan helped a little, but not much. I felt gritty and dusty and sweaty and I wanted a bath. A nice long bath, followed by a nice long sleep in a clean bed. Then maybe when I woke up all this would be nothing but a nightmare.

"You!" Still radiating anger like a corona, Annie leaned out of the RV's open door and pointed to Special Agent Harding. "Bring them in. All of them, including whoever you have out in that SUV."

"Ma'am, I've been told—"

"Do it." Special Agent O'Connell's voice rumbled from inside the RV.

"And quickly," Annie added. "Lilias, come in here."

Somehow it seemed odd that the interior of the RV was unchanged. After such a titanic battle, whose strong emotions still jangled in the air, it seemed it should have shown damage like burn marks and bomb holes and scars. Grateful to be back in the air conditioning, I sat where Annie indicated. Special Agent O'Connell leaned against the edge of a desk, his face a thundercloud.

Under other circumstances it might have been funny when Annie truly saw Toby for the first time. The top of her head barely came to where his tie tack would be, if Toby had ever worn a tie in his life. She looked up with much the same expression of awe and disbelief on her face as people have when they first see the giant sequoias or the Pyramids.

"My God," she murmured.

Toby looked like he was going to make some silly remark but the entire atmosphere of the room suddenly changed. The door opened and the man who'd had the

T-shirt booth next to mine stepped in, pushing a small, dumpy, gray-haired older woman in front of him. She wore a polyester pantsuit of an unfortunate shade of green and a coordinated print blouse. The outfit had probably been one of Wal-Mart's best sellers some twenty years ago. She was handcuffed and terrified eyes bulged out of her pale, sweaty face.

"Well, Mrs. Ruiz," Special Agent O'Connell said in an unbearably smug voice. "Do you know who this is?"

In spite of everything I felt a rush of pity. The woman looked as if she might die of sheer fright.

"Of course I do. She's Martha Sullivan."

"I'M SORRY, LILIAS," Martha said, then burst into tears, keening and sniffling at the same time. "I'm so very sorry. So sorry. So sorry."

If O'Connell got any more puffed up he'd turn into a pumpkin.

The man from the next booth was still wearing his T-shirt, a black one stamped with a revolting design of bones, knives and roses dancing around a demonically laughing skull. He was gentle with Martha, though, taking off her handcuffs and helping her into a chair. Now she was weeping with abandon, burying her face in her hands. Special Agent Harding handed her a box of tissues.

"So what is this little bit of grandstanding about, O'Connell?" Annie asked bluntly. "I thought she was supposed to be dead in the bottom of a canyon in Big Bend."

"So did I," O'Connell answered. "But instead here she is in Tulsa, walking the aisles of the Chestnut Plaza Art Fair looking for Mrs. Ruiz. Care to enlighten us, Mrs. Ruiz?"

I shook my head, the sound of jail doors clanging shut echoing in my ears. "I don't know what's going on."

Martha raised a tear-ravaged face. "Calvin's dead, isn't he?"

"Yes. Shot through the head," O'Connell said with cold, joyous deliberation.

"You don't have to be so vicious about it," I snapped. I'd lost a husband too, and though Calvin Sullivan and Jim Ruiz were poles apart, there was still that marital bond that when broken, sundered not only a couple but a mindset. In an instant one went irrevocably from being a wife to being a widow, becoming only half of what used to be a whole.

Recovering her composure almost sniff by sniff, Martha at last blew her nose, then sighed. "It's over, then."

"What's over, Mrs. Sullivan?" Now O'Connell was standing by her chair, deliberately looming. I don't know if she even saw him or not.

"Everything. I told Calvin that if he kept skimming off the shipments he'd get into trouble. Those were mean people and they wouldn't forgive anything. Of course Calvin didn't believe me. Calvin thought he was smarter than they were. Calvin said we were taking the risks and not getting enough money for it. Calvin said they had more money than they knew what to do with and they wouldn't notice if a little bit was missing. And they didn't, not at first." Her fingers picked the damp tissue to shreds that fell over her lap like the first tentative snowflakes of winter.

"Who are 'they,' Mrs. Sullivan?" For all that he was standing fully erect O'Connell was now a cat at a mousehole, tense and ready to pounce. "Who were your bosses?"

Martha ignored him. The words spilled out of her as

if a boil had been lanced. "Then when that young man Patrick came—"

"Patrick Goodman," O'Connell said hungrily. "The man who was killed in Mrs. Ruiz's house." He might have been speaking to Martha, but he was looking at me. The clang of jail doors slamming shut got a little bit louder.

"Oh, is he dead too?" Martha asked blankly and began to shred a new tissue. "He said he was starting a new organization and would Calvin help him? Calvin got greedy and said he would. Calvin was always greedy. He always thought he should have more than anyone else. I told him it was foolish, but he wouldn't listen. Said it was our chance at the big time. I said our boss wouldn't like it."

"Who, Mrs. Sullivan? Who was your boss?" The urgency in O'Connell's voice was almost visible.

"Then we started stealing from the shipments," she went on as if she hadn't heard him. Her eyes were fixed on a distant point only she could see. "We split the stuff, keeping half for ourselves. Then we'd double cut the stuff we sold for the boss and give both batches to Patrick. He'd figured out a way to store our stuff where it would never be found. He said no one would ever think to look where it was supposed to be. We had planned to hold on to it for a while, then start out with a big supply. Calvin said we'd never get caught, but I didn't believe him."

O'Connell opened his mouth to speak, but apparently even he realized that her spate of words could not be stopped, that she probably wouldn't even hear him. She was saying what she had wanted to for so long. The look of frustration on his face was priceless.

"Then Calvin got even greedier and started keeping

out a little bit from Patrick. Not much at first—just a couple of grams. Then he took a little more. And then a little more, until he was doing to Patrick what they had done to the boss. He made it into big tablet-like chunks with one of his old machines and stored them in my beads. I didn't like it, I didn't want to have anything to do with it, but Calvin said we had to look out for ourselves." As if reminded of her loss, she began to weep again, sniffling into a tissue. "I never wanted any part of it. Calvin just thought he was owed so much out of life…"

For a moment there was no sound in the RV except for the drone of the air conditioner and Martha's weeping. O'Connell looked as if he were going to move in for the kill, but she began speaking again suddenly, loudly, as if the words were exploding from her mouth.

"He shouldn't have put us at risk like that. When he got a phone call from the boss he started sweating and I knew it was all over. He asked me to go with him, but I'd had enough. I wouldn't go, and now Calvin's dead. If I'd have gone, I'd be dead too."

She almost howled the last words, then began to wail in earnest.

His patience at an end, Special Agent O'Connell put a hand on her shoulder. His voice became soft and sincere. "And when did Mrs. Ruiz start working with Calvin?"

Startled, Martha looked at him, her eyes wide. "Lilias? Lilias has nothing to do with any of this."

It's probably a sign of my small soul that I thoroughly enjoyed the shocked look of dismay on O'Connell's face. He looked, I thought with uncharitable glee, like someone had just kicked him where it would hurt the most. Or maybe that was just wishful thinking on my part.

"But you sold her your beads for next to nothing. The

drug beads," he added so there would be no misunder-
standing. "Why did you do that?"

"I wanted to throw the drugs away," she said with
a lovely simplicity. "But Calvin and I were always too
close. I couldn't do anything without him checking up
on me. That, plus he kept checking on them to make
sure they were there. He said they were the last shipment from the boss we'd ever have and we were going to
keep them for ourselves. Then one day they were gone,
and I thought Calvin had hidden them someplace new.
That's when I sold the beads to Lilias. I wanted them out
of there so Calvin couldn't hide behind me any more. I
didn't know they were back in that box, I really didn't.
I'm sorry, Lilias, I'm so sorry. I just wanted to get rid
of everything." Her voice once again rose to a keening
wail and she buried her face in a fresh tissue.

Special Agent O'Connell's expression was a study of
dark emotion. I was only glad he wasn't directing his
attention to me. By comparison, our conversations had
been little more than tea-table chit-chat.

"So your husband put them back sometime."

"Yes. While I was in the ladies' room, I guess, after
Lilias agreed to buy them and before I took them down
to her. Calvin was so angry. He kept saying I'd killed us
both. I told him about our insurance policy, but he just
wouldn't listen…"

It seemed that ears went up all over the room and suddenly there was a thrum of attention in the air.

"What insurance policy?" snapped O'Connell. "What
are you talking about?"

"Why, the…" Martha began, but Annie stepped in
and physically clapped her hand over Martha's too-
ready mouth.

"Don't say another word, Mrs. Sullivan. Just give me a dollar."

Both O'Connell and I knew instantly what Annie was doing, but Martha didn't. Her soft, lined face was quizzical as she moved Annie's hand from her mouth.

"I can't. They took my purse…"

"Wait." I scrabbled in my pocket and pulled out a bill. Without even looking at what it was I handed it to Martha. "I am giving you this, so it's your money. Now hand it to Annie."

Wordlessly, a bemused and white-faced Martha took the bill and extended it to Annie, who snatched it with a sourly triumphant smile. She waved it in the air in front of O'Connell's nose, much as she had at Patches, and tucked it in her bra.

"What the hell do you think you're doing, Monroe?" O'Connell growled.

"You know exactly what I'm doing. This is a retainer, Special Agent O'Connell, and as Mrs. Sullivan is now my client I am advising her not to say another word until we can discuss things in private."

"She's a lawyer?" Martha asked.

"Yes," I said, "and you couldn't have a better one."

"Don't meddle in this, Annie."

"It's obvious that my client has been most shamefully used by her husband and any information she has should be used to negotiate her rights." It was impossible for Annie to stand nose to nose with O'Connell, but she still glared at him.

"This is Oklahoma, not Texas."

Annie's smile was small but frightening. "No problem. Our office has a reciprocal agreement with several Oklahoma firms. I'll call in one of their attorneys right this minute if you like, but Mrs. Sullivan's not saying a word until we've talked." Her smile, not pretty to begin with, tightened into something almost fearsome. "I learned my lesson well, O'Connell."

"I just hope this time you know which side you're fighting on," he snapped.

"I would like to confer with my client," Annie said with great dignity. "Alone."

"But I want them to know," Martha said, tugging at Annie's sleeve. "I was afraid… That's why I insisted on insurance…"

I don't really know exactly what happened next, because everything seemed to happen at the same time.

O'Connell started yelling something—I don't remember what.

Annie yelled something back.

Toby tapped my arm for attention and asked if I thought it was all right for him to get something from the refrigerator because he was starving.

Special Agent Harding began to pick up the cloud of shredded tissue that surrounded Martha's chair like a nimbus.

Eyes bulging, Martha grabbed her chest and gasped for breath, then slowly toppled forward into the arms of a very startled Special Agent Harding.

Annie screamed, "She's having a heart attack."

"Damn it all," O'Connell roared.

NINETEEN

"Come on, Toby, Annie," I said, all but grabbing my purse and cell phone and Beretta from a very disgruntled Special Agent O'Connell. "Let's get out of here."

Once things had started happening, they happened very quickly. Accompanied by a tight-faced Special Agent Harding, Martha was taken to the hospital in an ambulance with siren and lights going.

Even before the ambulance arrived, Annie was demanding that I be released with a fierceness that made Toby's eyes pop. He'd practically moved into the refrigerator and was eating his way methodically through its contents, probably as much from nervousness as hunger. Finally, after Annie brought up yet again the fact that Martha had exonerated me and several mentions of the name Koenig—whoever he was—O'Connell reluctantly informed me that I was no longer a person of interest and I could go. The technicians or agents or whoever they were reassembled the van with as much speed and precision as they had used dismantling it. They even repacked all my boxes and put them inside, as if anxious to see me gone.

Annie shook her head. "I've got to stay and protect Martha Sullivan," she said in crisp tones that were not directed at me.

"Are you sure?"

"Go on, Lilias, and get out of here. You're going home?"

"Yes." My reply was definite. The idea of going back to the show and manning my booth as if nothing had happened was repugnant. There was no way I'd get my space rent back for the rest of the Fair, and after today Scott might never let me come again, but at the moment I didn't care. I just wanted to get home and lock the doors and windows and try to forget all this. "Now. How will you get back?"

"I'll fly home commercial. Oh, and your new code is 7913."

As Annie was terrible with remembering numbers I'm sure there was some arcane reason for that particular sequence, but at the moment nothing mattered less. I was going back to Dallas. I was free!

The sun was just setting when we left Tulsa. It was going to be an all-night drive, but neither Toby nor I had any objection to that. We stopped to eat something at an anonymous truck stop somewhere. It was all bright fluorescent lights and cheap souvenirs, and I found it terribly depressing. Toby was uncharacteristically quiet and, after polishing off only three hamburgers and two large orders of fries, went to sleep. He snored, which somehow surprised me.

He didn't even stir when the telephone chirruped. It was irritating, but the chirp had been the least annoying choice of ringtones. I had been promising myself to download something better for almost a year now.

"Martha's dead, Lilias," Annie said without any preliminary greeting. She sounded utterly exhausted.

"What?" Once again the world seemed to rock around me. "She made it to the hospital all right, didn't she?"

"Yes, and they got her stabilized. Then sometime in the night she woke up. I guess she got addled and started looking for her purse, probably looking for her nitro pills. She had ripped off her EKG feed when she got up and that's what alerted the nurse, who found her on the floor. She was still alive, but the doctors couldn't save her. She didn't last but a few minutes. Do you know if she had any children? Any family?"

The pit of my stomach was a knot of ice at the sheer horror of it. Poor Martha. This was hardly any better than being in a burned-out wreck in the bottom of a Big Bend canyon.

"I don't think either she or Calvin had anyone. I think she was raised in an orphanage, and went into the Army right after high school," I said slowly.

"The nurse said she was very agitated—kept talking about someone named Kurt. Kept saying the name over and over until she died a few minutes later. Whoever he is, he must be important to her. Do you know him?"

"I don't have any idea who it could be. I don't think I ever heard her mention a Kurt, though I'll admit we never did talk much."

"Well, we're going to have to try and find him. Maybe he can straighten out some of this mess."

"You say Martha had nitro pills? So she knew she had a heart condition."

"Apparently she'd had one for some time, but it was pretty much under control. That's why she carried the pills in her purse. The purse that they took away from her." Annie's bitter voice left no doubt as to who "they" were.

"Would she have lived if she'd been able to get them?" Another horror to haunt me.

"The doctors are ambivalent about that. They don't want to commit themselves when the FBI is involved. After all, what's one old lady more or less?"

The fury and the pain in Annie's voice were sharp

as obsidian blades. I couldn't decide if she was more upset with the simple injustice of it all or if this were just something added to her mysterious history with O'Connell. It really didn't matter. The whole thing was ugly.

"Any news on who killed Calvin?"

"I thought Calvin died in an accident."

"O'Connell told me there was a bullet hole in his skull."

Annie swore, using words that were both colorful and fluent. "He didn't say anything about that to me."

"I wonder if it's true. He was trying to get me to confess involvement. Would he use a scare tactic like that?"

"He'd do anything to anybody to close a case," Annie said in tones of acid. "He can't even spell ethics."

"You two have a history, you said." I was shamelessly fishing.

"Yeah." The word was short and crisp. I waited for more, but when Annie spoke again everything was different. "Look, you and Toby better stay at my house for the next day or two. I'm going to be up here and your place is finished, but there's not any furniture in there."

I hadn't thought of that. "Thanks, Annie."

"You owe me dinner. Several dinners. Still got your key?"

"Yes." I owed her a lot more than a couple of dinners. A dozen crystal roses would not cover what she had done today, even without lodging included. Somewhere I would find the money and pay her. "Are you going to be all right, Annie?"

"I'm always all right," Annie said with a tarnished brightness. "And I'll be better when I see that bastard get caught."

She hung up before I could ask what she meant, and I'm not really sure I wanted to know.

IT WAS IN the not-so-wee hours before dawn when I finally pulled into my driveway and pummeled Toby partially awake. He arose from sleep ponderously, thickly, as if fighting his way up from some uncharted depth.

"Are we here?"

"Yeah. I want to take a quick look at my house."

"You said you'd let me help drive." He sounded almost wounded, yawning until it seemed the top of his head would flop over backward.

"You were asleep. I don't let zombies drive my van. Come on." I jumped out of the van, all too conscious of the stiffness of muscles, the cracking of joints. For a moment I wondered if I could stand without leaning on the door. Getting older was not much fun.

Even Preston Road, that twenty-four-hour artery of an enormous city, was almost quiet. There was a slight rustle of breeze in the leaves and somewhere far away a siren wailed, but it was unbelievably quiet for the heart of a metropolis the size of Dallas.

That was until Toby slammed his door shut. It sounded like a cannon in the soft, once-silent night.

"Quiet," I snapped in a hoarse whisper. "People are trying to sleep."

"Sorry." He followed me across the lawn, looking ludicrous as he tried to tiptoe.

The new code worked like a charm and if I had had any trepidation about entering the living room where I'd found the dead body, Toby's comforting if somewhat sleep-sodden presence dissolved it.

Nothing was the same.

It was almost like going into a brand-new house

where no one had lived before. The living room was bereft of furniture, as blank as a white canvas. No, not white. The walls had been painted my favorite blue, but in a very pastel version, so pale it was not easy to see the contrast with the white woodwork. The dining table, which had sustained a broken leg in the vandalism, had been fixed. It and the chairs sat in lonely splendor in the dining room. This room too had been painted blue, but a slightly darker version, which made the white wood-work pop out.

I wandered through the house, turning on lights and marveling at what Don had done. The place was perfect, apart from the pervasive smell of paint—acrid and yet somehow clean. There were no traces of destruction, except in my own memories. Toby followed, still more asleep than awake, but interested in my interest.

"So this is what they tore up, huh?"

"Yes. This is so fantastic… You can't believe what a mess it was."

The kitchen shone like a new penny. The stove and refrigerator and dishwasher had survived the onslaught and looked almost like old friends—but in what a set-ting! Before, the kitchen had been an uninspired pale yellow. Now it was papered in black and white stripes with a frieze of stylized chickens around the top. The countertops were a pale gray granite and all the wood-work a cool white.

Even the stairs were different. Before, they had been carpeted with a dark indoor/outdoor stuff made more to prevent slips than for beauty. It had been one of those things I had been going to change "someday." Now they were more or less the same wood as the floor, but with a granular surface for safety. It would be difficult for someone to sneak upstairs, for the wood resonated beneath our feet.

Upstairs there had been less structural damage and consequently fewer changes. All the rooms had been painted in shades of blue with white woodwork. The nightmare visions of the destruction and the dead body began to fade.

This was going to be home again.

"You don't have any furniture," Toby said.

He was right. Almost everything was gone except the dining suite and the two barstools in the kitchen. My bed was nothing but a frame and some slats. In the office the desk had been built in. The worktable was there, too, a great slab of wood set on square wood legs and immobile as a mountain. The guest room was an empty shell.

"Everything but what you see was destroyed," I said, a catch of memory in my voice. "I'm going to get all new stuff."

Toby draped a bracing arm around my shoulders. "I didn't guess it was that bad. I'm sorry."

"I'm just glad it's all over. Come on. We can catch a few hours' sleep."

"Where? You don't have any furniture," he repeated.

"We're spending the night at Annie's."

We walked into her home as if we owned it. Annie's industrial-chic décor impressed Toby, but not in a good way. He made some remark about sleeping in a warehouse before I trundled him into the suffocatingly sweet guest room. His comments on *that* were colloquial, fluent and would have shocked his mother to death.

I claimed Annie's room, not even bothering to change the sheets and barely stumbling into my pajamas. I was looking forward to a good sleep for the first time in what seemed like years. Everything was over. No more intruders, no more accusations of being a criminal, no more sinister men hanging around. Now life could return to normal. Tomorrow I could go furniture shopping and begin my regular life again...

I was asleep almost the moment my head touched the pillow.

One hour and seventeen minutes later by the bedside clock someone broke into the van.

IT WAS DÉJÀ vu all over again. The van shrieking. Me on the driveway in my ratty old pajamas. Eventually the garish lights of the cop car nightmarishly illuminating the scene as it parked in front of the house. The puzzled looks of neighbors staring, some in their pajamas standing in their front yards, some slowing their cars to a crawl as they began their early commute to work. The intensity of the stares increased as Toby, barefooted and wearing nothing but a pair of jeans, prowled around trying to be helpful. I could almost hear the gossip and speculation running around the neighborhood like an evil wind.

This time they (*who?*) had actually gotten into the van. Two or three boxes had been tossed out onto the lawn, but unopened. Obviously the alarm and the lights going on in Annie's house had scared the intruders away. The patrolman, an earnest young man apparently not long out of the academy, seemed determined to do everything by the book.

I was giving him the long and convoluted history when another car pulled up. The young officer appeared skeptical as I told him of what had been going on the last several weeks. I didn't blame him. I would have been, too, had I not been at its center.

"Mrs. Ruiz?"

"Detective Webber." Inwardly I groaned. Maybe if I kept it formal, he would forget "Patches." "What are you doing here?"

"I had just gotten up when I heard the call." He shrugged. "Thought I'd come on over and see what was up."

He must have come directly from his home. Unshaved, wearing jeans and a polo shirt and loafers, he looked more like any number of unsavory things than a police detective.

"Excuse me, sir." The young officer turned his attention to the newcomer. "And you are...?"

Detective Webber pulled out his badge and flashed it authoritatively. "Detective Brian Webber. My partner and I were the original investigators when the house was broken into."

The young officer gulped. "Yes, sir. According to the complaint—"

"Just stand there for the moment. What happened, Mrs. Ruiz?"

"Someone broke into the van. Again. But it's all gone. Whoever it was started throwing the—"

"I know," he said, his hand flapping in the "shut up" signal. "Annie called me. Did they take anything?"

Annie?

He called her Annie? What had happened to *Ms.* Monroe?

And she had called him about the drugs? Hardly "official channels." I filed that little nugget of information away for future consideration.

"I don't know. I don't think so. I'm going to put a sign on the lawn saying that everything's gone and there's no reason to break in," I said bitterly.

"Why don't we take everything into your house and you can look through it. See if anything is missing."

The stuff had to go into the house eventually, so I nodded. At least the house had been spared this time. The lock and the alarm were both as I had left them. Patches nodded enigmatically as he watched me unlock and turn off.

"We went through the house last night," I said. "It's completely redone and nothing was out of place."

"Let's hope it stays that way." The detective nodded toward the young patrolman and Toby, saying, "Okay, let's get this stuff inside," but when I reached to pick up a box, he stopped me and shook his head. "We'll do it," he said. "You've been through enough."

So I stood and watched as the three made short work of carrying everything in the van into the house. By now the sky had turned a pinkish color and dawn was well underway, the nightshadows fading. The neighbors weren't, though. Some had brought out cups of coffee to sustain themselves while they watched the show. I could smell it on the air even over the faint metallic taste of early rush hour and it made my mouth water. My pride wouldn't let me go beg for a cup, though, no matter how hard my veins pleaded for caffeine. If they didn't offer it, I didn't want it. Before I left for Amarillo some of these people, people I had regarded as friends ever since I moved in, had snubbed me, as if by ignoring me they could keep whatever was happening to me from happening to them. So be it.

"Hey, what's going on? You okay?"

At least there was one friendly soul left in the neighborhood. I smiled at Don Garnett and received one in return. Apparently he'd been out for an early morning run, for he wore a cotton T-shirt, gaudy shorts and athletic shoes, all soaked.

"Someone broke into my van a little while ago."

"You're kidding. I didn't even know you were home."

"Got back in the wee hours. Hadn't been here more than a couple of hours before this happened. Woke us up."

"Woke you...? Surely you aren't sleeping here? There's nothing—"

"Nothing in the house, I know. We're staying at Annie's. She's away on a case and said we could sleep there until I can get some furniture."

He wiped sweat from his face with the back of his hand. "Well, I'm glad your house is okay. I'd hate to have to do it all over again."

"You did a wonderful job. I'm sorry—I should have said that right off. It's beautiful, Don, it really is. You outdid yourself."

He shook his head in self-deprecation. "It wasn't so much. I kind of enjoyed doing it. Slinging a hammer again was sort of fun."

"Well, I can only say thank you. And that I hope you have a lot more fun, but not here."

At that he laughed. "Agreed."

"If you'll give me your bill," I said, taking a deep breath. I knew it wasn't going to be small. "I'll pay it."

"I'll get it to you. No rush. How do you like your pergola?"

I shook my head. "Haven't seen it. Didn't go out back when we got here, but I know it will be spectacular."

"Mrs. Ruiz?" Detective Webber called from the door. "Are you ready?"

"I need to go in, Don. The police want to look through

the van contents again. I can't seem to convince them there's nothing there but beads."

"That was a policeman?" He looked up and down the street. The gallery of nosy neighbors had thinned, but there were still enough around to make me uncomfortable. "I guess I'd better get on before Bettina thinks I've fallen in the creek."

"Thank you for everything, Don."

"Enjoy your new place." He gave me a grin and was gone, jogging slowly down the street.

I walked into the house. All the boxes had been set on the kitchen counters. They looked more grubby than usual against all that pristine newness.

"Um, Aunt Lilias?" Toby asked with some hesitancy. "Maybe we should get dressed?"

Blame it on insufficient sleep and a deficit of caffeine, but I had completely forgotten that I was wearing nothing but a pair of ratty pajamas. My hair wasn't even combed nor my face washed. I had been out in the street talking to policemen and a male neighbor I didn't know at all well, and all in my pajamas. No wonder the neighbors stared. I wouldn't have a shred of reputation left.

Jim would have laughed his head off.

"I think we should. Detective…?"

"I'll guard all this faithfully." His tone was serious, but his eyes were twinkling. "You two go along. May I dig?"

"Of course," I replied through unsteady lips. "I'll even bring you some coffee."

"And a treat?" Now his eyes were sparkling wickedly. "I'd like a Milk…"

I ran from the house.

TWENTY

FIRST, COFFEE. I set the pot to working before going up-stairs. Dressing didn't take long—jeans and a T-shirt and sneakers. A sundress would have been a lot more comfortable on this hot and sticky summer day, but all my city clothes—those that had survived the vandal-ism—were packed away in garbage bags in the garage. Not much was left, though. I'd have to go shopping for clothes as well as furniture.

I'd have to shop for a whole new life.

I would, that is, as soon as the irritating remnants of all this *whateveritwas* were gone. Who could have broken into my van and what did they think they would find? Could they possibly believe that the drugs were still there? After the van had been taken hostage and stripped by the authorities?

But what if they didn't know the FBI had been over the van and found the drugs?

And who in the name of heaven were *they?*

I groaned and went back to the kitchen, where Toby was methodically munching his way through Annie's refrigerator. Of course, it had been at least a couple of hours since he had eaten, so he had to be on the brink of starvation. I tried desperately to remember if there was an all you can eat buffet anywhere in the neighbor-hood, then remembered I had no transport. After De-tective Webber left I'd have to call my long-suffering insurance agent, look up the number of Annie's automotive wizard and see about finding a rental car for the duration. If nothing else, I'd need it to take Toby to the airport for his trip back to Minnesota.

"Your friend doesn't keep much food around," he said from the depths of the refrigerator.

"She eats out a lot." I couldn't resist. "There's probably some chili in the pantry."

His only response to that was a low growl and the sound of determined chewing.

I put the coffee carafe and all the necessary accessories into one of Annie's ugly but very practical wire baskets, added a handful of individually wrapped Danish pastries that Toby hadn't yet found and set out across the street.

The patrolman and his car were gone. Detective Webber had opened a few of the boxes, but apparently that was all he had done. At the moment he was sitting on the barstool, smiling at something someone on the other end of his cell phone was saying. I put the coffee down and, manners be switched, poured myself a cup. The hot liquid going down my throat was like ambrosia. I could almost feel that heavenly caffeine twitching down the veins and capillaries of my poor sleep-deprived body.

"She's here now. Talk to her," the detective said and shoved his cell phone at my face.

"Hello?"

"What do you mean your van was broken into again?"

"Annie?"

"Of course." She sounded grumpy, as if she'd had as little sleep as I. "Who did you think it was?"

"I didn't know. Detective Webber just—"

"Your van," she said with elaborate patience. "Who do you think it was who broke into your van?"

"I don't know. We had just gotten to sleep when the alarm went off and there was nobody there when I got downstairs. I don't think anything's missing, though this time they really did a job on the side door."

"Damn. Either they don't know the drugs are gone or there's something else in there we haven't found yet."

Neither prospect filled me with elation. "There can't be. Remember, the FBI took everything off of it but the paint. And we've taken everything out of there. Again. Everything. Now it's here in the house. Detective Webber and I are going to go through it. Again."

"Is Patches looking after you okay?"

"I wish you'd stop using that…"

"Okay, okay. Has he told you yet that we think we've found that Kurt fellow?"

I looked over at the detective, who was happily tearing his way into a raspberry danish. "No. Who is he?"

"One of Goodman's goons was named Curtis Donaldson. We don't know of any direct contact between him and the Sullivans, but it's the best lead we've got."

"How did you find out about him so fast?"

"The FBI has resources," Annie said shortly, then yawned so prodigiously that even a couple of hundred miles away my jaws ached sympathetically. It was all I could do not to yawn right back.

"O'Connell told you about him?"

"Not voluntarily. Now all we have to do is find him."

"I hope you do it soon. I want this to be over."

"It will be," Annie promised with fervor. "We're going to end this."

"When are you coming home?"

"Tomorrow, probably. Maybe the day after. There are some things up here I want to settle." There was something in her voice that made me very glad I was not one of those "things." Somehow I had the feeling she was gunning for Special Agent O'Connell's scalp, or perhaps other, more vulnerable body parts.

"Do you want to speak to Detective Webber again?" I enunciated his name very carefully, eliciting a tired chuckle from Annie.

"No, just tell Patches I'll talk to him later," she said, then hung up.

I handed the telephone back to Detective Webber. "She said she'd talk to you later."

Nodding and chewing, he closed the phone and put it back in his pocket. "Mmm," he mumbled around a mouthful of crumbs, "I do like raspberry. Could'a been a Milk-Bone, though."

I could feel a flush run from my toes to the top of my head. "Detective, I do wish Annie hadn't told you about that—that moment of silliness of mine. I certainly didn't mean…"

He was ignoring me. "You know, I had a terrier when I was a kid. Little mixed breed called Scrappy. Best friend I ever had. I think your Patches was a good dog, right?"

"The best. We never had one again after him."

He nodded, then smiled. "There's a lot worse things than being called after a good terrier."

"So you aren't angry?"

"I tell you, Mrs. Ruiz, after some of the things I see in my job, it's kind of nice. Now, why don't we go through these boxes?"

And we did, box by box. I even gave him the short tour guide version, but one in much better spirit than I had for Special Agent O'Connell. Patches was enchanted by the Lover's Roses and especially about the colorless version I was making for Annie. Perhaps it showed my prejudices about "dumb cops," but I was surprised at how impressed he was by some of the jewelry. Of course, he had seen it before, the first time we had gone through the van's contents in Annie's garage, but then that had been just a fast look-see. He hadn't paid such attention to each piece.

It went faster when we got to the loose beads and my workbox. Then there were the floral bouquets, all of which he had seen before too, and that dratted ugly curtain. We didn't even try to unsnarl it. Quite frankly, I was thoroughly sick of all of them and thinking of what else I might do to earn a living.

At last we closed the final box and rinsed our hands in the sink, using a corner of one of the tablecloths for a towel.

"I can't see that there's anything there that anyone would want to steal," he said, running clawed fingers through his hair in frustration. "You've got some nice stuff, but hardly valuable enough to break into a van for."

"I know, but we both missed the…the other stuff. The only thing is, I bought everything that's in there. I made most of the jewelry, and it's all just what it seems to be. Beads!" I poured us both another cup of coffee.

"That means whoever broke in doesn't know that the…the other stuff is gone."

"Great. How do we convince them it is? I don't want to live the rest of my life with people breaking in looking for what I haven't got."

"So we'll just have to catch them."

"And how do you plan to do that?"

"Dunno. Probably good police work, like always. Now I've got to go back home and dress and get downtown. Anything you need before I go?"

I shook my head. "No, I've got to get busy on the

phone and call my insurance agent. Then I've got to go buy some furniture. Annie said she'd be home tomorrow or the next day and we can't stay there forever."

It was small, and quickly smothered, but a surprisingly sweet smile touched Patches's face. Interesting. "Okay. At least let me help you put up this stuff. Where do you want it?"

"Oh, I'll just put it in the garage with the rest of the boxes, but don't worry about it. Toby will…" I stopped. I hadn't seen Toby since leaving Annie's house. Where was he?

"Your nephew?"

I hadn't introduced them this morning. Apparently that was another thing Annie had told Patches.

"He must still be over at Annie's. I'll go get him."

Toby, now fully clad, stepped into the kitchen. "I've been in the living room. I didn't want to interrupt."

Patches looked up, his face a study. "Good God. I thought this morning was some sort of hallucination. Just how tall are you?"

"Seven foot three," Toby replied patiently. "And I've grown half an inch in the last year."

"Whatever you're feeding him, you'd better stop it," Patches said with a grin. "He'll eat you out of house and home."

Toby grinned back, though I was sure he'd heard that feeble witticism a million times before. "Aunt Lilias says I already do that."

"Is there anything left over at Annie's?"

Toby shook his head. "Nothing good. Wow—pastry." He stripped off the cellophane wrapper in nothing flat and wolfed down the last cream cheese one, the one I had been saving for myself. "I'm going to need some more money."

"For what? Where have you been?"

"To pay your friend Annie. I used her telephone."

"Well, I'm sure she wouldn't mind you making a call…"

"It was long distance. And it was a long one."

"Who did you call?"

"My folks." Lounging back against the counter, he unwrapped the next to last Danish. It was cinnamon, which I hate, but apparently Toby liked it. It disappeared fast enough. "I told them I would go back to college for the fall semester and use the basketball scholarship to finish my undergraduate degree."

"Oh, Toby, that's very wise. I'm proud of you."

He held up a hand for silence. "But only if I could spend the rest of the summer working with you."

"What?" My shrill squeak echoed eerily in the nearly empty house. In spite of heroic efforts to control his expression, Patches couldn't quite contain a gurgle of laughter.

"I'll earn my keep. I can sell, and help you move things, and make stock. You won't have to pay me any salary."

"Toby, I can't—"

"Wait a minute, Mrs. Ruiz. It sounds like a good idea to me."

"What?"

The policeman shrugged. "Until we get these guys, it might be a good thing for you to have some company."

"I will not have Toby put in danger."

"Aunt Lilias—"

"No!" I all but shouted. Somehow I had to take control of my life again. "You can't tell me your parents agreed to this."

"They said they knew you'd take good care of me." Toby's face was a model of sweet reason.

"You didn't tell them anything about what's been going on, did you?"

"No…not really. Special Agent O'Connell had told them some, but not everything. I didn't tell them anything except that everything was okay and we were back in Dallas." His expression was mendaciously seraphic. "I didn't see any reason to worry them."

Detective Webber snorted with laughter, but I was on the edge of an apoplexy. This was shaping up to be one of the unwinnable arguments we'd had so many times with David. Perhaps I had done my son a disservice. Perhaps all Ruizes—or perhaps all boys—were so unmanageably devious.

"You will let me, won't you, Aunt Lilias?"

"What if I don't want you?"

"But you do. You know how helpful I've been."

He was right, there, darn it. But I didn't have the right to put him into danger. And I didn't want a nineteen-year-old dictating to me.

"Besides," Toby went on, "I like the beadwork. I've got some designs in mind based on other mathematical series. I'd like to see how they work."

"What did you tell your parents you'd do if they didn't agree?"

"Go traveling for a year or two," the young wretch replied unrepentantly. "I told them I'd call them every couple of months."

"That's a horrible thing to say to your parents," I sputtered, mother-gene in full spate. "You know doing such a thing would worry them to death. I should spank you."

This time Patches couldn't restrain a shout of laughter. "Now that I'd pay money to see."

"And you're not helping matters."

He was instantly sober. "I'm sorry, Mrs. Ruiz, but it seems the young man has made up his mind."

"Thank you, Detective," Toby said with due gravity.

"And like I said, it'd be a good idea for you to have someone around."

"We're right, Aunt Lilias. Uncle Jim would never forgive me if I didn't look after you."

It was trite manipulation of the worst kind, but it brought a spring of tears to my eyes. Toby knew that the memory of Jim was my weak spot, which meant that he knew using it would make me capitulate. In spite of the fact he knew I was a capable adult, Jim would have wanted someone to look after me. I tried not to think of our son, or I would have started bawling in earnest.

"All right," I said with shaky hauteur. "If you're determined to work for me, you can start by carrying all those boxes into the garage. I'm going back to Annie's to do some telephoning."

Patches handed me his card. "I don't know if you still have the first one I gave you or not, but hang onto this one. It's got the department number, my cell number and my home number on it. Call me for anything anytime."

"Thank you…Patches."

His grin was infectious. "Arf," he said and then was gone.

MY INSURANCE AGENT was not glad to hear from me, but when I gave him the number of the police report he grudgingly agreed to set things in motion. Annie's wizard of a mechanic had the van picked up mid-morning, only some thirty minutes after the rental car people delivered our temporary wheels.

It was very seldom that I had to rent a car, but when it happened I always got the smallest, cheapest available.

I hadn't thought of what the mixture of a very small car and my very tall nephew would be like.

The van had barely left on its flatbed before we decided to head for the nearest grocery store. The sight of Toby trying to fold himself into the front seat, even with the seat pushed all the way back, was something unforgettable. I bit my lips to keep from laughing.

"Maybe you should stay here," I said with a determinedly straight face. "I'll go to the store and get supplies."

"I want to help…" Toby groaned as he tried to extract his foot from a twining embrace around the floor-mounted gearshift.

"I'm sorry. I should have gotten a bigger car."

"It's not the size," he grunted. "One of my friends has a car smaller than this, but it's somehow made differently…" His foot and the gearshift parted company with an almost audible pop that sent him falling nearly all the way out the door. "I can get in and out of it without trouble."

"Well, you can't get out of this one. You go back in the house for now and I'll make a quick run to the store."

He looked relieved. "You'll be sure to get potato chips, won't you? The lime-flavored ones?"

"And regular Dr Pepper and some candy bars. I'll even get frozen waffles."

Toby's grin spread from ear to ear. "Great! And some blueberry syrup? I love blueberry syrup."

Another Ruiz family trait, but one that couldn't be genetic. I'd always had a partiality for blueberry syrup myself. Jim had preferred maple. I'd get two bottles, maybe three, just to be on the safe side.

After spending a small fortune at the grocery store to stock my kitchen and replenish Annie's, I almost wished I'd gotten a bigger car. The trunk was full. The back seat bulged. Even the front seat was stacked. My wallet, however, was almost completely empty.

When I pulled into the driveway at home, I fully expected Toby to come rushing out to inspect the food, if not devour some on the front lawn to get the strength to take the rest into the house. The fact that he didn't was mildly alarming. Surely he hadn't gone off and left the house unlocked. He didn't have a key, but being a kid he might think that because the house was empty it didn't need to be locked. There was no television or radio in there and my computer was locked up in Annie's house.

I gathered a couple of the lighter bags, leaving the heavy stuff. If he wanted to earn his way the next few weeks, he could start by hoisting groceries.

My alarm increased when the door swung open at a touch. He didn't have a key, but it didn't take a key to turn the lock on the doorknob.

"Toby?" I stepped into the house, then screamed at the sight of a body sprawled prone on the staircase with another figure crouching above it.

TWENTY-ONE

THE CROUCHING FIGURE raised its head. "Hi, Aunt Lilias."

"Morning again, Mrs. Ruiz," the body said, which belonged to an obviously live and healthy Don Garnett. He was clad in cargo shorts and a polo shirt instead of running gear, but he still looked fit and athletic.

My heart started to beat again.

"Here, let me get these for you." Toby bounded down the stairs and snatched at the grocery bags. "Wow! You got lime chips and salt and vinegar ones too. Thanks, Aunt Lilias. Wait until you see what Don did to your stairs. It's too cool."

I extricated my fingers from the grocery bags' strangling plastic handles. "Put these in the kitchen, please, then bring in the rest from the car. And don't start eating everything in sight."

"But it's past lunchtime."

"You'll survive. Now go on." I turned my attention to Don, still spread out on my stairs, while Toby slumped off to the kitchen. "I didn't expect to see you back so soon. Brought my bill?"

He sat up and dusted off his knees. "No, I just remembered something I wanted to tell you and thought I'd drop by. You weren't here, but your nephew was. He asked me to stay and we got to talking. That's one smart boy you've got."

"I hope he didn't bore you to tears with mathematical formulas." What I really hoped was that Don Garnett didn't start "dropping by" with any thoughts of a further relationship. He was charming and good looking, two things I liked, but he was also quite married. I hadn't even been out to dinner with a man since Jim had died and I wasn't interested in exploring a relationship now, especially with a married man. But, being so out of practice, I wasn't sure how to read the signals.

"Actually, I kind of like math, but he's light years beyond me." Don shook his head. "What he really wanted to do was call me to account for some sloppy workmanship, except it really isn't and he spoiled my surprise for you."

Toby trotted through the living room on the way to the car. "It's really neat, Aunt Lilias. Let him show you."

Was this one of the "little extras" Annie had mentioned? I had already found several—the expensive wallpaper in the kitchen and baths, the granite countertops, the non-slip treatment on the stairs and heaven only knows what else I hadn't noticed. I could see the small profit I had hoped to realize with the insurance settlement evaporating.

"What are we talking about?"

Don walked over to the staircase. "See there?" he asked, pointing. "The fourth tread down?"

I couldn't see anything but the tread and the riser and said so.

"Well, that's the way it's supposed to look. I didn't expect to have a young giant in the house."

Somehow his comment about Toby grated on me, but I knew we could expect more of the same, if not worse, from the world at large, so I merely asked, "The way what's supposed to look?"

Toby, his arms loaded with an impossible number of

plastic bags, headed toward the kitchen again. "Show her how it works."

Don grinned. "Can't keep any secrets with him around. Come on up."

Obediently I followed Don up the stairs and lay down where he said, my arm hanging off the edge of the steps. The balusters were of iron and were of the "flying" variety, which meant they didn't go through the flat part of the step itself but rather curved out and up from the wall to support the banister rail. The step itself was flush with the wall and had only the slightest of projections over the riser. There was one baluster per step, but the effect was still modern and airy.

After I was arranged to his satisfaction, Don crouched on the stairs beside me. Seen from this angle, his legs were exceedingly hairy, a fact I hadn't noticed before.

"Now what do you see?"

My nose was practically flat against the rise of the fourth tread from the top, but that was all I could see.

"Your nephew has better eyes than you." Don chuckled. "He called me to account for leaving the bottom of that lip rough next to the wall."

Now, of course, I could see a small irregularity, like a small split separating from the main part. It would be invisible from above, practically invisible as one was climbing the stairs and hidden behind the angle of the stairs themselves from the hall or living room. To anyone except someone of Toby's height, of course.

"Well, it looks a little rough, but who's going to see it?" I asked in pacific tones, hoping that Toby's complaint wouldn't affect my bill.

Don chuckled again. "Push it toward the wall."

I did, slipping my thumb into the surprisingly large

chink, and was surprised by a metallic click. Don lifted the step, exposing a hollow space beneath.

"A hidden compartment," I exclaimed. "Shades of Nancy Drew."

"I think everyone should have a little hidey-hole where they can stash stuff," Don said with a grin. "Do you like it?"

"I love it. What a clever idea. Thank you." Like a child with a new toy I pushed the step back into place, then punched the latch again and heard the metallic click of release. "As Toby says, it's cool even though I probably won't be needing it."

"You won't…? You aren't moving, are you?" Don sounded shaken, which made me a little uncomfortable. He'd hardly noticed me before. Or did he worry that I would skip without paying his bill?

I snapped the step down again just for the pure pleasure of pushing the hidden button one more time. In my youth I had devoured dozens of the "teenaged girl detective" mysteries, in which a hidden compartment had almost been a requirement and had thought how cool they were. Now I had one of my own.

"No. I thought about it, but I'm going to stay. I am going to change alarm companies, though."

"Surely you don't have to do that. It'll cost a lot of money."

I shrugged, which, considering my position, doubtless looked grotesque. "Probably will, but I don't care. I won't feel secure until I do."

From the kitchen came an ominous crash and a subdued "damn it" from Toby. It had to be groceries. There wasn't anything else in there to fall. I only hoped it wasn't something messy.

Don snapped the step shut, then stepped down and grabbed my arm to help me rise.

"What the hell is going on here?"

I froze, glancing down to see the one thing I'd never expected in my tiny hallway. In front of the wide-open front door, his face dark with anger and his hand reaching toward his hip, stood Special Agent Thomas O'Connell.

I SHOULD HAVE been more understanding, since I'd had much the same reaction on seeing Toby and Don in a similar position. I should have been more respectful to an officer of the law. I should have been a stronger person and simply ordered him off my property.

Unfortunately, all I did was pull myself into a standing position and look down at him with what I most sincerely hoped was an expression of distasteful hauteur.

"We were examining the steps. What are you doing here, Special Agent O'Connell?"

Don looked sublimely uncomfortable. "Special Agent?"

"Of the FBI. He's very fond of telling people that. I don't remember inviting you inside, Special Agent O'Connell."

"You didn't." He straightened and his suit jacket slid back into place, but not before I could see that his hip, where he had reached with such an apparently instinctive reaction, was bare of firearm or holster. "I was coming up the walk to knock, but the door was open. Then there was a crash, and I came in to see if anything was wrong, and there you were on the stairs…" He stopped, then grinned. It transformed his face back into the image of a drugstore romance-novel hero. "It was an interesting situation."

"Aunt Lilias?" A sullen Toby stood in the kitchen

doorway, one pants leg dark with liquid, and a faint air of sweet brine wafting out. "What's he doing here?"

"I came to talk to your aunt. The door was open."

"I'm unloading the car," Toby said, his eyes sending me mute apology. "I…"

"And you apparently broke the pickles." I had reached the bottom of the stairs and the smell was unmistakable. Messy, but it could have been worse. "Clean up the mess before you try to do anything else, and make sure you get up all the glass shards. Is there anything in the car that needs to come in right now?"

"There's only a couple of cartons of soft drinks left. I put all the milk and fruit and stuff in the refrigerator."

"If you're okay, I guess I'll be going, Mrs. Ruiz," Don said, easing around me. He was eyeing O'Connell as if he were a snake.

"I'm fine. Mr. O'Connell won't be staying long," I said with delicate emphasis.

"Don't you want me to stay in here with you, Aunt Lilias? You might need a witness." Toby looked as belligerently heroic as anyone could when they're nineteen years old and covered in pickle juice.

"Go clean the kitchen, Toby. I'll call you if I need you."

O'Connell didn't move until Don was gone, the front door closed behind him, and Toby back in the kitchen. Only when the front door latch snicked shut and there was the unmistakable sound of running water did he move, walking into the center of the living room. He looked around as if preparing to make an offer to buy.

"Nice place, Mrs. Ruiz. You might have gone a little overboard on the minimalist décor, though."

"As you know, my things were destroyed. I haven't had a chance to go shopping yet."

"Surely you aren't staying here, not with it like this?"

Surely it was none of his business where I was staying, but the specter of jail bars and a normally law-abiding nature made me say, "No, we're staying at Annie's. You know, across the street."

He gave me an amused glance. "No, I didn't know."

"She told me you had a history together."

The amusement spread to his lips. I was glad he didn't smile often, because it made him very handsome. "You should be working for the Bureau, Mrs. Ruiz. You have the touch to make a good interrogator."

"Thank you, no. I don't like intimidating or threatening or frightening people."

"Why, you seem to have a very prejudicial view of what we do. I don't know how that happened. But, to answer your unasked question, I've never seen Annie's house and didn't know exactly where it was until now. She didn't buy it until after we divorced."

I couldn't get my breath. Divorced? That meant Annie and this man had been married once upon a time. Annie had never even mentioned being married, let alone to someone like this!

"It was a long time ago."

"Why did you divorce?" I wanted to know, but I hadn't intended to ask. The words just popped out all by themselves.

"Why does any couple divorce? Different viewpoints. She likes the law. I like justice."

"Aren't they to the same end?"

He shrugged. "Apparently it depends on who's looking at it."

"What are you doing here, Mr. O'Connell?"

He didn't correct me. "I could just say that I wanted to tell you I'm happy you were exonerated."

"You came a long way from Tulsa just to tell me that."

"No. I came a long way from Tulsa to tell you that I don't think this thing is over. Neither Calvin nor Martha Sullivan had the brains to run an operation like this. Goodman is dead and we still don't know who the big boss is. We don't even know who sent you that threatening note. Whoever the boss is, he's still out there, and he might not believe you as innocent as I."

"I thought they worked under Goodman, whatever his first name was." For one horrific moment the pristine, deserted living room appeared as it once had, full of my old furniture and the darkened, distorted body sprawled over the Mexican rug.

"They worked under him," O'Connell said patiently, "and they stole with him hoping to set up their own organization and then they stole from him, but he wasn't the brains—just the go-between."

My heart started to thud irregularly. "And you think this brain believes I still have the drugs?"

"It's a possibility. Apparently someone still thinks you have something, or your van wouldn't have been broken into."

"We've got to get away," I said softly, sinking down into a cross-legged position on the floor. My legs simply would not hold me upright any longer. This was not the way it happened on TV. They either caught the bad guy or the bad guy died, and the innocent bystander went on to live a peaceful life. "I've got to get Toby out of this."

"I'm in a position to offer you protection."

"For how long? This isn't going to go away in a few

hours or a few days. For that kind of money they'll keep after me for years. I can't give them what I don't have."

"Are you quite sure you don't have something, Mrs. Ruiz?"

I stared at him in astonishment. "You've seen everything I have. Want to search the house? Go ahead—everyone else has."

"Is everything all right, Aunt Lilias?" Toby stomped out of the kitchen, looking very fierce and protective. "I heard you shouting."

"I'm angry, that's all. Here." I tossed him the key to Annie's front door. "Go over to Annie's right now and be sure you lock the door behind you. And stay there. Don't open the door to anyone but me."

"Aunt Lilias, if there's something wrong—"

"Do it!"

Even Jim hadn't dared stand up to me when I used that tone of voice. Toby had never been exposed to it before. Obediently he took the key and trotted off across the street, leaving the water running in the kitchen.

"I've got to get him back to Minnesota," I murmured, ignoring O'Connell's politely outstretched hand and scrambling to my feet. "I've got to make sure he's safe."

"You need to make sure you're safe too. These are dangerous people."

O'Connell's comment had been made in a deliberately neutral tone, but for some reason it made chills dance up my spine. This wasn't an intellectual exercise. There were people out there who would kill me without a second thought. By this time tomorrow I might well be dead. Suddenly the idea of life—my life—seemed very precious.

"What can we do?" My mouth was dry and it felt abraded, as if the words had been wrapped in sandpaper.

"Well, this afternoon there's going to be a very careful leak to the press about a half-million-dollar haul of uncut cocaine seized by the FBI in Tulsa. It'll be put out just in time to make the six o'clock news, so there'll be the maximum publicity with the minimum of journalistic meddling. Your name won't be mentioned—they'll just say it was taken from an innocent party who was transporting it without knowledge. The right people will know it's you, so we're hoping it will put you in the clear."

"And if it doesn't?"

Wonder of wonders, my legs still worked, albeit stiffly. I lurched into the kitchen and turned off the water. Toby had done a good job of cleaning. The wood floor (Wood? Vinyl? How strange I didn't know.) was still wet but I couldn't see any glass shards there or on the counter. The tangy smell of sweet pickles was pungent in the air and a wet, lumpy plastic bag lay in the sink.

"They'll keep trying to catch them, of course."

"*Trying* being the operative word."

O'Connell didn't answer. Instead he simply looked with approval at the new paper and countertops, then boldly opened the back door as if he owned the place.

I hadn't been out here since returning home. The minuscule lawn was more weeds than grass, both mainly turned to brown under the relentless summer sun. The lawn went from fence to fence and was broken only by the spindly lavender tree outside the dining room, which seemed determined to retain its original shrub state no matter how often I trimmed it. I'd put in no flower beds, no landscaping, and hadn't wanted any, but suddenly, seeing it through his eyes, my little back yard looked bleak and pathetic.

At least the pergola was in. A timber framework, it covered the patio completely. The roof was latticework, allowing a dappling of sun to dance over the concrete. There was even a ceiling fan hanging in the center. No, I definitely wasn't going to make any profit off the insurance settlement, but I didn't really care. Except for the broiling days of deep summer, this would be a wonderful place. Mentally I added a patio set to my shopping list of furnishings.

"You're not a gardener, I see," he said neutrally.

"No. I'm on the road too much."

He waited until I stepped back into the kitchen, then closed the door behind us. I had seen that trick on TV. Someone, usually the bad guy, closes the door but doesn't lock it so they can come back in later. Ostentatiously I made sure the lock was engaged.

It was.

O'Connell must have watched the same shows as I, for he only smiled in an amused way, then opened the door to the garage.

Oh, heavens, I hadn't even peeked out there. It was just as Annie had said—all Jim's boxes had been rearranged, but it didn't look as if any had been opened. The stuff from the van huddled close by the door, as if they felt like intruders unsure of their welcome.

"Your late husband's things?"

"Yes. I keep meaning to go through them."

"It's never good to be in a rush to close off a portion of your life." O'Connell smiled that devastating smile again. "Don't worry, Mrs. Ruiz. You're going to be all right."

"You sound bloody sure of that."

"I am. If you aren't, how could I ask you out to dinner once this is all over?"

TWENTY-TWO

"WHAT?" MY MOUTH didn't quite fall open, but it might as well have. I couldn't have been more shocked had he struck me.

"You. Me. Dinner."

What kind of ploy was this? The threatening caveman hadn't worked, so now he was trying the romantic route? Good cop and bad cop all in one?

"I thought there was some regulation against officers seeing suspects socially."

He shrugged. "There probably is. You, however, are no longer a suspect, and I'm not sure if I'm still an officer or not."

Memory finally kicked in. "You aren't wearing your gun."

"So you saw that, huh? Good eyes. Another reason to find you interesting. They relieved me of my badge and my gun. Temporarily, they said."

"So why aren't you an officer any more?"

"I'm on administrative leave, pending a hearing about the way I've handled this case." His face tightened for a moment—just a moment—but it became so hard it was unnerving. "It appears our friend Annie has finally gotten her revenge."

Curiouser and curiouser. "Revenge for what?"

"I'll let her tell you that. Right now we need to be concerned about you."

"You said you could get me protection. How can you do that if you're off the case?"

"Here I am, a trained federal agent, ready to protect you." His smile widened, making him even more handsome. It scared me to death.

"And who's going to protect me from you? No, Mr. O'Connell, thanks but no thanks."

The uncomfortable flippancy vanished from his face, leaving behind the more familiar saturnine expression. "You don't have to like me personally, Mrs. Ruiz. I just want to stop you from getting killed."

"You know, until I met you I thought the FBI was a bunch of good guys out to get the crooks. Then you tried to hang this drug thing on me any way you could. You browbeat me trying to make me confess. And I was innocent. I am innocent."

"I believe you."

"Now you do. What would you feel like if Martha Sullivan hadn't cleared me before she died?"

"We have to go where the evidence points, even if we don't like it." He leaned up against the wall and wiped his face as if it were sweaty, as if he were trying to wipe away ugly thoughts. "We can't afford the luxury of personal feelings. What matters is preserving the law."

"I thought you believed in justice."

"Only when the law doesn't provide it."

I didn't want to go there, and he must have realized it, for the odd moments of almost-intimacy were over. He straightened, stiffened, and once again became Special Agent O'Connell, whether he had a badge and gun at the moment or not.

"Do you know what drugs cost our country? Not just in money, but in grief and danger and lives lost? There are times the law actually protects the scum that is poisoning our people, just because they know how to use it. We're constrained to play by the rules while they can do anything they want."

"If we don't play by the rules we'll sink to their level."

"If we do play by the rules, they win and we'll be below their level. We'll be their property."

I didn't agree with him, but couldn't think of an argument to prove him wrong. Instead I walked into the living room. "Goodbye, Mr. O'Connell."

He followed me, but stopped at the door. "We have to stop it, Mrs. Ruiz. We have to stop where it starts. The problem isn't the stupid fools who use dope or even the dumb middlemen like the Sullivans. The problem is the big guys, the ones who make millions out of crime and human misery and will do anything to make more money. We have to stop them. *That's* where it starts."

I almost agreed with him, but didn't want to start another dialogue. He might be very interesting to talk with, and under different circumstances—much different circumstances—I might have enjoyed it. Instead, I silently opened the front door. Outside at the curb was a plain white Buick. There was no black, tinted-windows SUV in sight. More than anything else that convinced me he was, temporarily at least, no longer a Special Agent.

For a moment it seemed he would say something, but I stood immobile by the open door, my body language all but shouting at him to leave. Finally he walked out without saying a word, and I closed and locked the door behind him.

By COMPARISON, THE rest of the afternoon was downright boring. I chose the groceries that went to Annie's and carried them over, leaving Toby to put them away while I returned to my place to make us a gargantuan sandwich lunch. Even though it was stripped and bare, it was my house again, and I enjoyed being in it.

Toby and I sat at the dining table and ate, while my mind wrestled with redecoration. I wasn't going to buy all new furniture at once. I'd just get the basics—a bed for me, a sofa bed or futon for the office, a television, some everyday dishes. Then I'd get the other pieces one by one as I found things that spoke to me. This was the first time in my life I could do exactly what I wanted, and it would probably be the last time I'd buy a significant amount of furniture. I wanted to do it right.

One thing I did have to do right now was curtains. I'd always made my own to get what I wanted, but I didn't have time for that luxury. If I didn't find anything that I loved I'd just buy some cheap white ones, something to cover the windows. I didn't want to give the neighbors anything more to gossip about.

Toby downed his third sandwich and scraped up the last of the lime potato chips out of the bag. "Now what?"

"Wash the dishes," I said, balling up the paper towels we'd used and tossing them into an empty grocery bag. "So easy. I might start doing this all the time."

"At least you can't serve chili that way." Toby was dead serious, but I laughed.

"So what's for dinner?"

"You just ate."

"I know. I just wanted to start planning."

"Hamburger cheese casserole. It was one of your Uncle Jim's favorites." It was one of mine too, because it was so easy and quick to fix, but I didn't think he needed to know that.

"With onions? And peppers? Like you used to bring to the cabin when we'd meet there for Labor Day?"

A wash of sweet nostalgia for what was past and beyond reach swept over me. *Jim*... What a pity one could never go back.

"Yes. And in almost the same proportions."

Toby laughed and stood, carrying the jars of pickles and mayonnaise and mustard back to the kitchen. I followed with the few remaining scraps of lunch meat and bread.

"Now," I said as threateningly as I could, "to work."

We spent the afternoon measuring. We measured rooms, windows, distance between doors, every single thing I could think of so that when I did go shopping there need be no hesitation about whether something fit or not. I'd never been so prepared in my life.

As we got closer to finishing, Toby grew restive and at last I sent him back to Annie's for a snack and some television. I also sent along a roll of wire and some crystal beads. He could prepare a couple of starter strings while he watched cartoons.

After he was gone I locked the door and turned the alarm onto its "Stay" function. Perhaps I was being a little paranoid, but so what? Too much had been happening lately and too much didn't seem to add up. On the other hand, I was tired of being driven out of my home. I wanted it to be a home again, a real home, safe and secure.

There was no way I could really begin to set the house aright until I had bought some furniture and drapes, but at least I could "play house" a little by doing what I could.

I went to the garage and simply stood in the doorway, looking. There were Jim's boxes, of course, which I would have to force myself to go through someday. They held some things that belonged to the Ruiz family. If something happened to me I had no illusions that David wouldn't sell the entire mess as a job lot.

A smaller, but no less daunting, pile was the stuff I'd saved from the wreckage of the vandalism. A few dishes, a few pictures, some linens and personal things—a lot of which had been saved for sentiment and should probably be discarded. Not much to show for a lifetime, not that we'd ever had that much anyway. Don had moved all the salvageable furniture into the house, except for a small coffee table and a chair from my bedroom, both hideously scratched. I'd probably donate them to the Salvation Army.

Right by the door, as menacing as a heavy conscience, were the boxes from the van. At the moment I didn't care if I ever saw any of them again.

I grabbed one of the plastic garbage bags in which the clothes that had survived the vandalism had been stored and lugged it up to the bedroom. Since the painting was done I could at least put my clothes in the closet. Until it was time to go feed Toby, that is. He'd be perishing for food around six or six-thirty, which meant I had to go over about five or so to get the casserole in the oven.

One thing was for certain. I needed some new clothes. As the garments came out of the plastic sack and went into the closet, about a third of them ended up in a pile on the floor. Tired, limp, boring… All were years old. How could I have allowed myself to become such a frump?

A few nice, new outfits, I thought. Some things that were fresh and bright and stylish. Even though Dallas bulged with high-level outlets and discount stores, it had been years since I'd bought anything at all. After all this I deserved some new things, new things for a new life. The house wasn't the only thing altered by this situation. I too was undergoing a metamorphosis.

I also realized that now was not the time to be deciding what to keep or not. My judgment was sorely compromised. I pushed everything, bag, donations, everything, into the closet and closed the door.

What to do now? I didn't want to go join Toby. Maybe it was silly, but I wanted to be in my house by myself, and reestablish a pattern of normalcy.

Something twiggled uncomfortably at the back of my mind. What was there about a pattern…? Was it something Toby had said? About the pattern of his necklaces? No…

I couldn't remember.

Luxuriating in the silence, I lay on the floor and looked around at the space and new paint. The place hadn't looked this good even when I moved in. It could have used a good painting then, but I was a new widow, scoured by grief and concerned about finances and worried almost to death by my son's unreasonable demands. The place had been clean, decent and affordable, and had given me a little left over from what selling the big house in Garland had brought.

This time I was going to do it right—a new beginning. This entire dead-body-and-drug mess had, for better or worse, changed my life forever.

There was another twiggle in the back of my mind. Most unwelcomely, I could hear Special Agent O'Connell in my mind's ear.

"Where did it begin, Mrs. Ruiz? Where did it begin?"

Drat—the man was annoying even when he wasn't here.

But that wasn't what bothered me. Ever since I had come home to the body in the living room, I'd been overwrought and driven by fear, by circumstance, lurching from one situation to another. In an attempt to recapture normalcy, whatever that was, I'd deliberately avoided thinking about what was behind all this. A turtle, that's what I had been, or an ostrich with its head in the ground. Somehow, some way I was involved in this, and I had to figure out why.

The first question was, why me?

Because my house was empty for fairly lengthy stretches of time, of course. But who would know that? The Sullivans? Possibly, but we didn't always do the same shows. How would they know when I was gone? There was the man working at the alarm company, but he would have no way of knowing when I was gone for any length of time other than the fact I didn't show up—a fairly risky proposition for the storage of high-dollar drug shipments. Once alerted by the Sullivans to the possibility of using my house the bad guys could have kept watch, but that seemed a rather haphazard and labor-intensive proposition.

It had to be someone who knew my comings and goings.

Annie was the only one who always knew where and when I was, and I would just as soon believe Toby was a drug dealer as she.

I shook my head in frustration. For every answer there was a "but" with an opposite answer, and none of it got me any further forward. I didn't even know all the questions.

Okay, I'd go to it with another tack. It was hard to believe that Calvin and Martha Sullivan had been drug dealers, even in the face of unassailable proof. Aside from Calvin's perpetually dissatisfied expression, they looked like the image of archetypical loveable grandparents straight off the cover of *The Saturday Evening Post*.

Another proof I was getting older, as if one were

needed. Who today remembered *The Saturday Evening Post* and its relentlessly wholesome covers?

Who would ever have thought such a pair would be something so loathsome as drug dealers?

Something clicked in my brain. How did people know to go to them for drugs? My knowledge of that world was almost non-existent, but the Sullivans hadn't sold drug paraphernalia or the wild counter-culture stuff that seemed to indicate a dealer. Calvin had sold ratty and overpriced old junk he called antiques. Martha had sold bead jewelry, for which she had no artistic gift at all.

Of course, there was the factor of repeat business, but where did it begin? How did someone know to come to them for drugs the first time? I was sure there was some sort of underground information network (*go to the bead booth for the good stuff...*) but that wouldn't reach everyone who wanted…

I sat up with a start. Of course! How could I have been so stupid, so blind, so absolutely idiotic? O'Connell had even told me.

I dug my phone and Patches's card out of my pocket. He had to know this immediately.

He didn't answer any of his numbers, drat the man.

I left a message on every line. "This is Lilias Ruiz. Patches, it's the curtain. The bead curtain. O'Connell said that's how the buyers knew they had drugs available, but there has to be more to it than that. There has to be some sort of message in it. The curtain. Please call me immediately."

I hauled my suddenly stiff bones off the floor and started down to the garage. I wanted a better look at that curtain.

Why hadn't I seen it before? When that unwashed creep in Amarillo had been so insistent about buying a certain type of bead in the curtain I should have realized something was strange. It was a sign, an advertising sign. Drugs for sale. No wonder Calvin had wanted it back so badly. Each bead must have a meaning, or a pattern…

A meaning.

Beads with meaning.

Patterns.

My head was swirling with ideas, so much so that I almost felt dizzy. I sat down on the stairs and put my head in my hands. The afternoon sun lanced through the naked windows, filling the room with a golden dazzle that hurt the eyes.

A pattern.

Beads in patterns.

Messages in beads.

Martha'd had her heart attack talking about her insurance policy. She had died calling for a Kurt, but Kurt wasn't a person. She had been trying to say "curtain." The curtain was her insurance.

Patterns…

Messages in beads.

A tiny bubble of memory surfaced. Once Martha had told me that she and Calvin had met when they were both young and in the Army. I'd been politely skeptical, but she had insisted—Calvin had been in the Quartermaster Corps and she had been in Communications, and in those days Communications meant radio. Of course she would have known Morse code.

Messages in beads.

Another, uglier thought intruded. Special Agent O'Connell had seen the curtain. Special Agent O'Connell had been there that night in Amarillo when I had been assaulted. I had only his word he'd been trying to protect me. From my viewpoint it could have been either way.

Special Agent O'Connell had ordered Martha's purse taken away, the purse that contained the potentially life-saving nitroglycerine. Had he known she had a heart condition that might give way under stress?

Was now ex-Special Agent O'Connell one of the bad guys?

He would fit equally well into either role, and while thankfully rare it was not unknown for lawmen to take advantage of their position to indulge in criminal activities.

My hands began to shake. Where was Patches? Why didn't he call me back?

I wanted to take another look at that curtain. Dragging it from the garage, I spread it out on the floor. Against the pristine newness of my redecorated living room it appeared shabbier than ever, but now I was examining the individual details more than the artistic entirety.

On each side there were strings of clunky wooden beads, interspersed with the small, ugly metal spacers. Sitting on the floor I examined a couple of them, just to make sure they were wood and not more of that compressed dope. As far as I could tell, without actually cutting into them, they were just wooden beads.

Holding one of the ugly spacers between my fingers, I gave it a rub with the ball of my thumb. It was definitely metal. There was a bluish gleam through the black. I rubbed harder, then used my shirttail over my thumb. The bluish gleam turned whitish and there was a black streak of tarnish on my shirt.

These ugly metal spacers were either silver or silver-plate—I would bet money on it. There had to be at least a hundred of them scattered through the curtain, probably closer to two hundred. Even if just silverplate they would be worth a tidy sum. If they were sterling, it might be a small fortune. Nothing near the value of even one of the drug beads, of course, but still a lot.

A big enough fortune to kill for? Could this be what everyone was looking for?

It could. I had no illusions about how greed could drive people. Every day people were killed for the most trivial sums.

What else was in this curtain?

Patterns.

Messages in beads.

I looked at it, trying to see only patterns of beads, not the beads themselves. If I only knew Morse code. Toby might, but I didn't want him to know about this yet, not until I'd told the police.

Under closer scrutiny, the bottom foot of the curtain looked different. It and the top part had different kinds of beads. The ones on the bottom were smaller and finer and much more uniform, as if the whole lower part had been added at a later time. The stringing was different too, being much more regular. Every other string was either plain or a simple strand of alternating colors, but the in-between strings were a mish-mash of colors in asymmetrical patterns.

Letters? Were they letters?

I needed to write them down. My purse was up in the workshop. I'd stuffed the pad and pen from our measurings in it. I would copy these patterns down and then email them to Patches. He'd be able find out if they meant anything.

I was halfway up the steps when my phone rang.

"Patches?"

"Most certainly not!" snapped a frigid and unfortunately familiar voice. "This is Mrs. Ronald Parkhurst, Mrs. Ruiz, and I am calling to demand my money back."

My fingers ached reminiscently at the sound of her voice and the memory of thousands of tiny beads made into white roses for a bride's crown. What had gone wrong? I had nightmare flashes of roses falling off as the bride went down the aisle, or of the crown somehow coming apart in a rain of tiny beads.

"Why? Was there something wrong with the crown?" I managed to keep my voice steady, even as I sank to sit on the steps. Annie had handled this woman with ease. Surely after all I had been through I could manage. "Why do you think you should get your money back?"

"I know I should get my money back. I bought a headpiece for a wedding, and there was no wedding. My foolish daughter decided to elope with her piano teacher two days before the wedding." She caught her breath in a gasp of pure fury. "As there was no wedding there is no need for a bridal headpiece, so I deserve my money back."

Inwardly I gave a little cheer for Emily, who was perhaps not as downtrodden and obedient as I thought. Outwardly I bit my lips and gripped the edge of the stair in an effort to keep my unruly tongue from telling Mrs. Ronald Parkhurst the third exactly what I thought of her.

There was a familiar metallic click beneath my fingers. Good grief, I had activated the latch on the hidey-hole stair. What were the chances of that?

Except I hadn't. The hidey-hole stair was the fourth from the top. I was sitting on the—I turned to count—eighth step from the top.

There were two hidden compartments. My brain

began to swim, swirling thoughts into heretofore un-anticipated patterns.

Patterns that fell together with fearsome clarity.

Had Don been going to show me this, and O'Connell's dramatic entrance interrupted him?

I stood and without my weight the stair lifted, reveal-ing an empty space identical to the one above. Were there more? I crept down a few steps and felt close to the wall for the latch. There wasn't one on that step, but there was on the one below. The latch worked smoothly to reveal another empty hidey-hole.

"Mrs. Ruiz! You had better listen to me, Mrs. Ruiz." Mrs. Parkhurst's voice had reached a new degree of shrillness.

"I'm sorry," I murmured absently. "There's some-thing going on here—"

"I do not care about your personal problems, Mrs. Ruiz, I just want my money back."

"Our contract was fulfilled," I said slowly, my mind filling with a new and dreadful notion. "There was noth-ing in there about the wedding actually taking place."

"I don't care. I bought the thing specifically to use in a wedding and there was no wedding, so I should get my money back. Anyone with any sense will agree with me."

She said more, but I didn't hear her. All that I could hear was the sound of the front door opening then clos-ing, and the little electronic tune that played when the alarm system turned off.

"Call the police, Mrs. Parkhurst," I hissed urgently into the phone. "Call the police now and send them to my house."

"I most certainly will call the police. This is out and out theft…"

   She was still complaining when I snapped the phone shut. I didn't care, because the person I had been so tragically late in realizing was the mastermind stepped into my living room and pointed a gun at me.

TWENTY-THREE

"HELLO, LILIAS. I was afraid you'd figure it out."

"Hello, Don," I replied in a voice that sounded surprisingly normal. "I hadn't really, until just now."

"I'm surprised. I thought you had it a long time ago."

I thought of the old quote, *The guilty flee where no one pursues*, but said nothing. Somehow being flippant in front of a man pointing a gun at you didn't seem to be a wise idea.

"It was all you, wasn't it? You're the mastermind behind all this."

He chuckled. It was not a reassuring sound. "Don't try to flatter me. I'm just a businessman, with suppliers and customers. Nothing more."

"You knew when I was gone. You thought about getting around the alarms. You killed that man here."

"Guilty to all. You and all the others weren't using your houses. Why shouldn't we? It wasn't like we stole or broke things. No one got hurt."

"My house was destroyed, and that man got killed."

"Patrick was stealing from me. He and those idiot Sullivans thought they could branch out on their own. No employer would put up with an employee who steals."

"But why did you trash my house? Break my things?"

"Because I wasn't sure you weren't a part of it. It was the Sullivans who told me about you, you know. Yours was the first house we used. After I found out Patrick had a boyfriend who worked for the security company it seemed destined. When a significant part of my product started disappearing, I found out Patrick and the Sullivans were stealing, and deduced they were hiding their stash here, along with my merchandise." He shrugged. "I had to find if it was here."

I couldn't stand it any longer. As a teacher I'd seen what horrors drug abuse could cause. "Product? Merchandise? You're selling drugs, Don, illegal drugs! You're a rich man. Why are you doing something so awful?"

Improbably, he laughed. "Awful? I'm merely a retailer, supplying a need. If those dopers didn't get their junk from me, they'd be getting it from someone else. As for being rich, nobody could be rich enough to keep up with a wife who spends money like mine. And I don't have to work near as hard as I did as a builder. Did you know I can earn as much in an hour as I used to in two weeks when I had my own company? And I was making what I called good money back then."

I opened my mouth, then closed it again. There was no way, no use even to try, to reach someone whose moral sense was so unmistakably dead. Right now my problem had nothing to do with justice or ethics. Right now my main concern was staying alive.

"You were in the Navy. You knew Morse code. That's why you were so shocked when you first saw the curtain. That's why you pretended to have that asthma attack, so we wouldn't look at it, and then you tried to buy it from me."

"But you wouldn't sell. Martha had told me she had an insurance policy, the stupid bitch, a policy that named me. Thought she could dictate to me!" Something very angry and ugly flared in his eyes. "She should have died with her husband. Who would have guessed that after a hundred years together they would split up."

"So you—"

"Shut up." He waggled the gun in my direction and my heart jumped. "Come on and let's get this over with. Bettina's got us scheduled at the club for some fancy do or another tonight and she'll be pissed if I'm late."

I had the awful feeling that by "this" he meant my life. My brain seemed frozen. I had to do something, but what?

Apparently stress brings out the worst in me, for I snapped, "Well, don't let me interfere with your social life. Go on and go."

"You're a gutsy woman, Lilias. We could have worked well together."

"Never." The idea that I had once thought this man attractive made me ill. "You're disgusting."

"Don't worry—you won't have long to think about it." He raised his gun and squinted down the sights.

What could I do? And, as I've never believed in the cavalry arriving at the last minute, whatever happened was going to be up to me. He was between me and both the outer doors, so that only left up the stairs—a bad tactical choice, I knew, but the only one available. On the other hand, there were two, maybe three step hidey-holes behind me all open and gaping. Getting over them would be a trial even if someone weren't shooting at me.

"Don—"

The knob on the front door twisted, but apparently Don had relocked it. Whoever it was knocked, first lightly, then with a couple of heavy thuds.

The cavalry? Did the cavalry knock?

"Aunt Lilias?"

It was as good as it was going to get. Don's head

snapped around to the door. I screamed, "Run, Toby, run!" and threw my cell phone right at Don's head.

I've never been an athlete. I was a disgrace to my high school softball team. On the other hand, I am considered a very good shot and, let's face it, it's hard to miss someone who is less than ten feet away from you. The phone made a very satisfying "thwacking" sound against Don's face and he cried out—either in anger or pain or both.

I didn't stay around to find out which. I went up the stairs on all fours like a monkey, flying over the open hidey-holes as if they weren't even there. I didn't even slow down when a wild shot went barely inches to one side of me but flung myself toward the landing. Then, simply because it was the closest, I dashed into the workroom and hid behind the ajar door, holding my breath so my bellowing panting wouldn't betray my position.

Not that it was going to do much good. The landing was minuscule and there were only three doors off of it. I could hear Don coming up the stairs, cursing fluently under his breath.

"That was a damn fool thing to do, Lilias. You can't get away. Now come on out here and let's get this over with."

I stayed still. Despite a lack of oxygen—I was still holding my breath—a plan was forming. Carefully, so very carefully, I reached behind me toward the big worktable, on which sat an assortment of beads in various plastic boxes. If I could throw a handful of beads in Don's face and startle him, I could maybe knock him out...or lock him up...or something where I could get away.

Okay, as plans go it was pretty dumb, but at the moment it was the best I could do.

There was a crashing sound from below and a bellow of "Lilias!"

Don swore, fired a shot what sounded like down the stairwell and, gun extended, stepped into the workroom.

Almost into the workroom. As soon as I saw his extended hand I threw my full weight against the door and tried not to listen as the bones of his arm snapped like small branches. He screamed, but I didn't release the pressure, at least not until I had his gun safely in my own hands. My own trembling hands.

Don Garnett didn't go down easily. His right arm hanging in an angle never intended for a human appendage, he was still coming toward me, his eyes alight with a hatred that could only be called mad. His left hand, fingers menacingly crooked, reached for my throat.

And caught me. The workroom is not that big a chamber, and though I had moved to the other side of it, pointing his gun at him, he lunged across and grabbed my throat in a death grip. I suppose he realized that everything was over, but that he could at least punish the instrument, however unwitting, of his destruction.

"Lilias!" There was a thunder of feet on the stairs. It sounded like an army. I would never not believe in the cavalry riding to the rescue again.

Don's hand was very strong. The pain in my throat was incredible. Small black dots danced in front of my eyes like floating beads.

I pulled the trigger only once, but there were two shots, hardly a second apart.

His look of furious hatred melting into an expression of intense surprise and then into a blankness of nothing at all, Don's fingers slipped from my throat and he slid to the floor where he lay in a spreading red pool.

Tom O'Connell exploded into the room, with Toby

right on his heels. Both stepped over Don's body as if it were nothing but a pile of unimportant rubbish. One pulled Don's gun from my shaking hands and the other embraced me. At the moment I was gasping too hard for precious air and too close to blacking out to tell which was which.

What's more, I didn't really care.

WHEN THE THREE of us staggered out of the house it was to face an arriving phalanx of police cars, their sirens and lights on full blast, and a growing audience of neighbors, come to see what the newest scandal at my house was. O'Connell's white Buick was parked half on my driveway, half on my lawn.

"How…?" I asked, the single word a piece of jagged glass in my throat.

"I don't know," O'Connell said, attempting to support me on one side. "Toby?"

"I didn't call them," my nephew answered, attempting to support me on the other.

Remembering O'Connell's reaction to Don's assistance on the stairs, I quit my admittedly feeble struggle to free myself. I didn't need to be supported… I didn't think. Maybe this wasn't a good time to find out.

There were only three cars. Sturdy, muscled uniformed officers spilled out and dashed across the lawn.

O'Connell nodded curtly to them. "Special Agent O'Connell, FBI. This is the householder and her nephew. The bad guy is upstairs dead and the house is empty." His words were terse and stung like flung pebbles.

Two policemen stayed with us while the others went upstairs. The older officer dug out a pad and pen.

"You'd better roll an MICU," O'Connell said sharply.

"This lady was nearly killed a few minutes ago. I want her checked out."

I wondered when the officer—Harrington, according to his name tag—would ask O'Connell for his ID, what would happen then and what would I do about it. Should I be prepared to faint or would a simple bout of hysterics cover things?

And why did I care?

Before Officer Harrington could open his mouth there was a scream of brakes and a nondescript sedan, a flashing red bubble light stuck askew on its roof, jumped the curb and came to a screeching stop in the middle of my lawn. In the middle of what had been my lawn. Now it looked more like a parking lot. Before the car finished sliding, the passenger door opened and Annie flung herself out. Patches at least waited until he had killed the engine before following her.

Both O'Connell and Toby stepped back instinctively, leaving me on my own. No, I didn't need support, but that didn't matter, because in half a moment Annie was twined around me, alternating thanking God that I was all right and berating me for getting myself into such a spot.

Then and only then I began to cry.

MUCH TO THE disappointment of the hovering neighbors that was about it for the moment. Detective Webber—Patches—spoke to the uniformed officers and then we were all over at Annie's house. We were all separated, of course, and there were what seemed like a great number of people talking to us. Somewhere in there the paramedics showed up, and though they wanted to take me to the hospital I wouldn't let them. Finally they left.

It was harder to get rid of the various detectives and

officers and FBI agents, but eventually they too de-
parted, at last leaving us alone. At some time someone had brought fresh clothes and allowed me to take a
shower to cleanse myself of an unholy amount of Don
Garnett's blood. Although our debriefing (O'Connell's
word) seemed to go on forever, in retrospect it was quite
a short one, considering the magnitude of the occasion.
Perhaps it was O'Connell's and Patches's influence. I
didn't care. There would be much more questioning later,
and still later probably testimony, but at the moment all I
wanted was to sit with my friends and enjoy being alive.

After the last policeman left, we all gathered in Annie's living room, glasses of various libations in our
hands and all talking at once. I had no idea what time
it was, only that it was dark outside and probably quite
late. I was both tired to death and jazzed with the pure
sensation of being alive.

The story was fairly simple, once we got it pieced together and straightened out. Annie had flown in from
Tulsa. Patches had picked her up at the plane and taken
her out to eat and, wanting to concentrate on her, turned
off his phone. O'Connell raised his eyebrows at that, but
said nothing. When they finished and he finally got my
message, he could see the danger even if he didn't know
exactly who the bad guy was.

"For a while," he admitted somewhat hesitantly,
then took a deep drink of his beer before continuing, "I
thought it might be you, O'Connell."

All eyes looked toward O'Connell, who took a sip of
his own beer. "I don't know if that's a compliment or
an insult, Webber."

"Just an observation," Patches said mildly, but Annie
was made of sterner stuff.

"I kind of wondered it myself, O'Connell." She was

perched on the sofa arm, right beside Patches even though they weren't touching. "You would make such a wonderful villain."

I still couldn't believe that she and this tall, saturnine man had ever been married. She had certainly never mentioned once being married and I knew I could never talk about it, not until she brought the subject up.

"You always thought I was," O'Connell retorted, but he was smiling.

"Some things I don't understand," I said slowly and carefully. Words were no longer like broken glass in my throat, but they were still far from comfortable. The brandy everyone had insisted I drink helped though, even if it did blur the edges of everything and not just the pain. "How did all the police get here so fast?"

"As soon as I got your message I knew you had to be in danger," Patches said. "I called for a unit to be sent to your house immediately and we started over. Whoever it was had been waltzing in and out of your house for months. We couldn't take the chance that the alarm code being changed would keep him out. For the dynamite that the curtain contained, they'd have blown a hole in the wall."

"But he had the code. He's the one who changed it for me," Annie said bitterly. "I deal with crooks every day. Why didn't I see that Don was a criminal?"

Patches patted her hand tenderly. It was a startling statement that he did so openly. Even more surprising was that Annie accepted and seemed comforted by his touch.

"You can't suspect everyone," he said simply. "You can go crazy doing that."

"Besides," O'Connell added, "most people don't like

to think that people they know are dishonest. Unless it's you thinking of me."

"Don't push me," Annie said in even tones. "I know too much about you, O'Connell."

"Then," Patches said just a little bit too quickly, "one of the neighbors called and told 911 that they had heard gunshots coming from your house. That combined with my call made your house a priority. Luckily there were a couple of patrol cars on Preston and they could get here in a hurry."

"Thank you," I said, then took another swig of brandy as much for courage as to soothe my throat. "Special Agent O'Connell, what made you show up right then? I threw you out."

O'Connell smiled that bazillion-watt smile at me and my head started to spin. It was at least as potent as Annie's very special old brandy.

"Yes, you did, didn't you? Good thing I didn't listen to you."

"But..."

"I knew that someone thought you had something important. You did, as it turned out, but we didn't know what. I also would have bet my reputation—which I value," he tossed as a pointed aside to Annie, "—that someone was going to try and break in and find whatever it was. It's my failing that I didn't think it would happen in the middle of the afternoon."

"You're admitting to a failing?" Annie said softly, and her voice was only slightly snide.

O'Connell ignored her. "I went to get a bite to eat. Then I was going to come back and keep watch and catch the villain red-handed. Did a beautiful job of that, didn't I?"

I would've said something then, but my treacherous

throat wouldn't comply and by the time I could make it work once more he was talking again.

"I intended to cruise the neighborhood, then park outside—probably down in that little shopping center lot—and come back. I was going to sit in your back yard all night waiting for whoever it was to show up." He smiled again, but now it was only an ugly, harsh twisting of his lips.

"Did you know it was Don Garnett?" Annie asked before I could.

"No, though he acted funny this afternoon, but a lot of perfectly innocent people do when they come face to face with a federal agent." He smiled again, and this time it was marginally less ugly. "I didn't have to wait, as it turned out. I was just turning the corner on my reconnaissance run when I saw Toby knocking on the door, then heard you scream at him to run, and heard the shots. The rest you know." He shrugged.

An accident in timing. That was what had saved my life. Had he been a couple of minutes earlier or later I might be dead, and perhaps Toby too. No—I couldn't think that way, for that way lay madness.

Disciplining my features to a bland sanity, I turned to Toby, who sat collapsed on the floor surrounded by drifts of empty potato chip and cookie bags. He was decimating a box of crackers and held a can of something he was making very sure I couldn't see. For a moment my mother-gene started to kick in, but I ruthlessly stifled any questions. Toby was mature enough to make his own choices now. In the last few days he'd earned that right. "And you? How did you know? What made you try to distract Don?"

He looked up and his face was sad and set and unmistakably adult. That trusting childlike look was gone, replaced with a darkness no nineteen-year-old should ever have. I could only pray it wouldn't be there forever.

"I didn't know anything," he said, and then in a twinkle his goofy grin was back, "except that I was hungry and it was time for you to start cooking dinner. Can we eat now? I'm starving."

WHAT HAPPENED LATER

THEY WERE NEVER able to tell which bullet actually killed Don. Mine had hit his chest, while the one from O'Connell's throwaway gun had ventilated his head. Of course there was an investigation, but no charges were brought. For a while there I thought they might give us a medal, as Don's death severely damaged one of the largest drug distribution rings in the Southwest. Martha's cleverly coded curtain not only gave Don's name, but several of his high-ranking lieutenants as well.

Apparently the curtain had started out as something to show that this booth sold beads. Later, as the Sullivans had started to deal drugs, it became a beacon to those wishing to buy. Still later, when she started to become fearful, Martha drew upon her knowledge of Morse code and added the bottom foot or so onto the curtain, but being sure that it was low and would be hidden from view by the boxes and stuff they always had in their booth. Pity she hadn't told me about the hidden message. Secrets always cause problems.

Mrs. Parkhurst did not call the police, but she did go to small claims court. Annie, being perhaps the first attorney from Corgill, Watson and Monroe ever to appear in that venue, made mincemeat of her. The judge even awarded me compensation for some reason or another, and once I received it I sent it on to Mrs. Parkhurst's daughter Emily and her new husband, figuring they might need all the help they could get.

After everything was over it was amazing how the money flowed in. A mortified Bettina Garnett vanished almost immediately and I never could find anyone to pay for my remodeling. Although he'd paid the suppliers on a regular basis, Don had never presented me with a bill and, as Bettina was gone, Annie advised me to keep the money. I put it into a separate fund, where it could grow and yet be safe. My unacknowledged fears about the future were quieted.

There was also a very nice reward for breaking up the drug distribution ring. Annie advised me to keep it as well, but instead I kept only half. The other half was divided among an orphanage for abandoned animals (in memory of Patches, no less), a fund for the families of fallen police officers and an anti-drug organization. I also put a decent headstone on the Sullivans' grave for poor Martha's sake.

Also against Annie's advice, I sent David several thousand. His only reply was to complain that it was not enough to get his new deal underway and could I send him more? This was a sure thing and he could positively double his money in just two weeks if he had adequate capital.

I didn't.

I bought new furniture—slowly, a piece at a time— and took the rest of the summer off. Somewhat to my surprise Toby refused my offer to help pay for the rest of his education. He had, he told me, decided that being a basketball star would look good on his resume when he was ready for grad school, and that he was going to work at it. He did not, however, turn down my offer of a small monthly allowance for as long as he was in school. I figured with his appetite he could use a little extra money.

O'Connell was reinstated as a full agent within days. Perhaps my impassioned testimony on his behalf to his superior helped, but I don't know for sure. He promised that in the future he would be less overtly aggressive toward suspects, but I didn't believe him. O'Connell, as I was discovering, was simply O'Connell. As far as I could tell that meant he was sort of like a force of nature, whether he was sporting a badge and official gun on his hip or not.

It was a long time before I could go into the workroom without a qualm, but I made myself, and not just because of what O'Connell said to me after we left the house that climactic afternoon. I went because when we do something, anything, there are always consequences—sometimes good, sometimes bad, but whichever, consequences must be faced. That afternoon I hadn't known who was coming up the stairs. It might have been just Toby, and to let him walk into danger was unthinkable. Conversely, it could have been an ally of Don's.

For that matter, I had been so close to losing consciousness I might not have lived long enough to find out who was coming. I could have done nothing, and as a consequence died. I could have defended myself, and as a consequence lived.

I chose life.

And I would do the same thing again.

* * * * *

REQUEST YOUR FREE BOOKS!

2 FREE NOVELS
PLUS 2 FREE GIFTS!

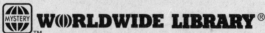

MYSTERY **W@RLDWIDE LIBRARY**®
TM
Your Partner in Crime

YES! Please send me 2 FREE novels from the Worldwide Library® series and my 2 FREE gifts (gifts are worth about $10). After receiving them, if I don't wish to receive any more books, I can return the shipping statement marked "cancel." If I don't cancel, I will receive 4 brand-new novels every month and be billed just $5.49 per book in the U.S. or $6.24 per book in Canada. That's a savings of at least 31% off the cover price. It's quite a bargain! Shipping and handling is just 50¢ per book in the U.S. and 75¢ per book in Canada.* I understand that accepting the 2 free books and gifts places me under no obligation to buy anything. I can always return a shipment and cancel at any time. Even if I never buy another book, the two free books and gifts are mine to keep forever.

414/424 WDN F4WY

Name	(PLEASE PRINT)	
Address		Apt. #
City	State/Prov.	Zip/Postal Code

Signature (if under 18, a parent or guardian must sign)

Mail to the **Harlequin® Reader Service:**
IN U.S.A.: P.O. Box 1867, Buffalo, NY 14240-1867
IN CANADA: P.O. Box 609, Fort Erie, Ontario L2A 5X3

Want to try two free books from another line?
Call 1-800-873-8635 or visit www.ReaderService.com.

* Terms and prices subject to change without notice. Prices do not include applicable taxes. Sales tax applicable in N.Y. Canadian residents will be charged applicable taxes. Offer not valid in Quebec. This offer is limited to one order per household. Not valid for current subscribers to the Worldwide Library series. All orders subject to credit approval. Credit or debit balances in a customer's account(s) may be offset by any other outstanding balance owed by or to the customer. Please allow 4 to 6 weeks for delivery. Offer available while quantities last.

Your Privacy—The Harlequin® Reader Service is committed to protecting your privacy. Our Privacy Policy is available online at www.ReaderService.com or upon request from the Harlequin Reader Service.

We make a portion of our mailing list available to reputable third parties that offer products we believe may interest you. If you prefer that we not exchange your name with third parties, or if you wish to clarify or modify your communication preferences, please visit us at www.ReaderService.com/consumerschoice or write to us at Harlequin Reader Service Preference Service, P.O. Box 9062, Buffalo, NY 14269. Include your complete name and address.

WWLI3R

Reader Service.com

Manage your account online!

- Review your order history
- Manage your payments
- Update your address

> *We've designed
> the Harlequin® Reader Service
> website just for you.*

Enjoy all the features!

- Reader excerpts from any series
- Respond to mailings and
  special monthly offers
- Discover new series available to you
- Browse the Bonus Bucks catalog
- Share your feedback

Visit us at:
ReaderService.com